No Broomsticks Allowed

HEATHER HARRISON

This is a work of fiction. Names, characters, places, and incidents are products of the author's imagination or are used fictitiously and are not to be construed as real. Any resemblance to actual events, locations, organizations, or persons, living or dead, is entirely coincidental.

World Castle Publishing, LLC
Pensacola, Florida
Copyright © Heather Harrison 2022
Hardback ISBN: 9798804796229
Paperback ISBN: 9781956788877
eBook ISBN: 9781956788884
First Edition World Castle Publishing, LLC, May 2, 2022
http://www.worldcastlepublishing.com
Licensing Notes
Cover: Karen Fuller
Editor: Maxine Bringenberg

Dedication

For the love of my life, whose always been my support and showed patience through those times I wanted to give up, I love you. To my children, who are a never-ending source of creativity, I will never find my heart empty. As for the rest of my family and friends, I wouldn't have this wild of imagination without you. I love all you crazy people.

In Memory of Chris Miller 1979 – 2022

I never thought I would see the end of your journey in this world. I believe in my heart your story will continue. May you run with the wolves and save the damsel in distress.

"Go then, there are other worlds than these." Jake Chambers. (Stephen King, *The Dark Tower series*)

P.S. Give Akira my love.

Chapter 1

Azrael darted past the landlord's office, the monstrosity in her duffel bag lurching back and forth.

"Knock it off." She whispered the words, thrusting her elbow against the bag. It stopped twitching, but the steady sound of typing coming from the landlord's office came to an abrupt stop.

Dammit.

Azrael hastened across the lobby. The stairs were so close. Just another foot. She laid a finger on the worn banister.

"Miss Larken!"

"Crap," she mumbled, skidding to an abrupt stop. Clutching the bag tightly behind her back, she turned to face Lance. He stood in the middle of the dim lobby, arms crossed over his chest, eyebrows raised. Although he was only a few years older than her, the stern way he pursed his lips made her feel like a child. The bag twitched again.

"Hey, Lan—Mr. Jacobs, I mean. Sorry, but I can't stay and talk. I've got, um, an emergency to deal with."

He pressed his lips into a thin line and ran a hand through his unruly black locks. Her eyes followed the movement, followed his arm as he lowered it, zeroed in on his chest, the way his black T-shirt stretched over it. She cast her eyes to the ground, mouth dry. *Why the powers above wasted so much sex appeal on a douche bag, I'll never know.*

"Do you know what day today is?"

She cleared her throat. "Um…Tuesday?"

"It's the eighth. Rent was due on the first." He tapped his foot on the ground. "And you, once again, are late."

A low-tuned whistling noise came from her bag, like air releasing from a balloon, followed by a stench that sent her stomach reeling. "Look, I have this work emergency—"

"So do I. It's called my tenants won't pay their rent," he said, rubbing his hands over his dark stubble. "I don't care what your type does, what emergencies you have, as long as my rent gets paid."

"My type?" She glared at him. "Oh, you mean the witch thing?"

"That's not…," he started, shoulders slumping as he raked a hand through his hair again, "what I meant."

She should go. Make a big scene of storming up the steps while she had the chance. It'd be the smart move. What she wouldn't give to be the type of person who made smart decisions. "Then, by all means, what does 'my type' mean? Please explain."

"Look…." He inhaled a deep breath and let it out slowly. "By all rights, I could've kicked you and your roommate out several times by now, but I haven't. That doesn't mean I will let you get away with not paying rent." He locked gazes with Azrael, those piercing blue eyes making her stomach clench. "You are a pain in my ass, that's true, but the comment about your type was rude, and I apologize."

She bit her bottom lip. Not once had he apologized to

her during one of his "lectures," as she called them. Any other day, Azrael would have used her advantage. Made him squirm. Today was not the day, though. "Apology accepted."

His lips twitched into a rare grin, one which accented his distinct cheekbones and dark brow.

Whoa, she thought, her lips parting as she stared at him. The bag twitched again, nudging her back to reality. "Well... anyway...I gotta go."

She pivoted and fled up the steps, heels clicking against battered linoleum.

From below, he bellowed, "What about the rent?"

"I'll get back to you on that," she yelled back. *Of all the places to live, we just had to pick this one.*

Lance had been on Azrael's ass since day one. Within seconds of her eyes landing on him, he'd inspired enough sexual fantasies to fill a penthouse novel. Then he spoke, ruining it all. It was clear he had a festering issue with witches. It didn't help that she'd wheeled in her unconscious roommate, who, even in his drugged state, was still moaning and screaming. By law, Lance couldn't refuse to rent to her because of those things. Although he could kick her out for the creature, which was tossing itself back and forth inside her gym bag.

"What the hell am I going to do?" she mumbled under her breath. "Caleb's going to freak."

Her roommate wasn't known for his patience with pets, especially not one like this. That, on top of the other news.... Well, he would be miserable to be around for months.

"No sense in putting it off," she mouthed, sliding the key into the lock and opening the door.

The result was instantaneous. She barely registered the peeling paint and threadbare furniture before all six-foot-one inches of Caleb came barreling around the hallway, baseball bat in hand.

"Whoa, Caleb, chill." Azrael dropped the bag on the floor and threw her hands in front of her. He wasn't a big guy, but he had one hell of a batting arm.

"Jeez, Azrael! What the hell are you doing home this early? You damn near gave me a heart attack," he said, lowering the bat and shoving his sandy hair out of his eyes.

"And when did it become illegal to take half a day off work?"

"You always call first," Caleb accused, frowning as he leaned against the wall, hand resting on the top of the bat. "You're the most predictable person I know. Which leads me to believe you being home is a bad thing."

Azrael finished shutting the door, taking her time to latch the top lock so she could use her foot to nudge the bag under the small entry table.

"Well, it's nice to see you, too," she said, stepping past him to the kitchen—or rather, the small alcove with a semi-cold fridge and a stove with two broken burners. Pea green wallpaper adorned the walls, the floral pattern etched on it wilted after years of bubbling and peeling. Azrael focused on re-attaching a loose strip.

"I didn't say it wasn't nice to see you, baby girl, but I know you, and right now, I'm sensing trouble brewing." He slid onto the barstool on the other side of the counter, locking her in an unrelenting stare.

Azrael grabbed two dusty glasses from the top cabinet and wiped them off on her shirt. "I could be sick, you know. Ever think of that?"

"Are you sick?"

"No," she replied, turning her back to him to grab a half-full bottle of cheap whiskey out of the freezer. She filled both glasses and handed Caleb one. "Cheers."

"Azrael…."

"Drink first, then we can talk."

She tilted the glass to her lips. The whiskey burned her throat, but with the day she'd had, she welcomed the burn. Caleb respected her request, allowing her to finish the entire glass before starting his questioning again. She loved him for that.

"How bad is it?" He set his empty glass on the counter, one hand absently rubbing his chin like he did every time he was worried.

"I got laid off."

"Crap, Azrael," he said, his eyes wide. "What the hell for? I mean, are they laying off a lot of witches?"

"No. Just me."

Azrael poured another glass, tears stinging the corners of her eyes. She hated crying. Hated how weak it made her feel. She'd be damned if she was going to break down now. Not when she needed to be strong for Caleb.

There was a moment of silence. Without looking, she knew he was studying her, but she couldn't control her trembling hands or flushed face.

"You know what? Screw that place," Caleb said, throwing up his hands. "Those bastards don't recognize talent when they see it. Witches Corp is all about the politics, not about the people. The question is, are you okay?"

"Not really." She pressed her fingers against her temples.

"Come on." Caleb grabbed her hand and the bottle of whiskey. "Let's go sit, and you can tell me all about it."

She followed him to the couch, taking a seat on one of

the threadbare cushions. Caleb set the bottle on the coffee table, causing it to wobble on its gimp leg. A tiny TV sat in the corner blaring some talk show. The caption on the screen said, *Wife claims demons have been abducting and impregnating her.*

Caleb grabbed the remote and switched it off.

Azrael sighed. Telling him would be tough. Caleb was in full console-your-best-friend-mode for the time being, but that would change when he realized why she was laid off. She threw a casual glance toward the door. Her bag was still there, shoved partially under the table, but it was gaping open.

Oh crap.

"Look, baby girl," he said, interrupting her thoughts. "I know this is tough, and yeah, it sucks, but we've been through worse."

He took a swig out of her glass and passed it to her. She drank deeply, her eyes taking in the dirty walls and matted carpet. Spider webs nested in every corner. No matter how many times they cleaned the apartment, the stain of poverty remained.

If this is all we can afford now, what happens when the money runs dry?

Caleb depended on her, and she'd failed him. Yeah, they'd been through worse, but when the hell was it ever going to get better?

"Ugh…what is that smell?" Caleb asked, causing her to choke on the whiskey. While she tried to clear her throat, he rummaged around the couch, picking up pillows and sniffing them.

"Caleb, I'm not sure this is something we can get through," she said when her throat was clear.

"Of course it is. We'll just have to buckle down. Weren't you telling me the bakery down the road was hiring a waitress, and you were thinking of taking a second job? I'm sure they're still needing someone. You can work there while you're laid off. I'll work day and night if I have to, try to get more customers to my website." Caleb slid off the couch, peering beneath it.

"Can you please sit back down? I really need to explain."

His head popped up over the corner of the couch. "You can't smell that?"

"I can, but this is more important. Please sit."

He pulled himself off the floor and sat, tossing his arm over the back of the couch, nose crinkled. Azrael sniffed, struggling not to gag. Honestly, the smell wasn't that bad now that she was getting used to it.

Taking a deep breath, she said, "I won't be able to get a job at the bakery, or anywhere else for that matter. I got laid off because I messed up a summoning spell. I was supposed to have summoned a pink demon as a surprise for a client's daughter for her birthday, but I accidentally summoned—"

Azrael's explanation was cut short by the small, pinkish-red creature that jumped onto her lap. Caleb sprang off the couch, sprinting to the other side of the apartment. He turned, pointing his finger at her. "You summoned a stink demon! How the hell did you make that mistake?"

"I don't know," Azrael said, pushing the demon off her lap and standing. She paced, hands pressed against her temples. "Look, I was distracted. It was a two-step spell, the summoning, then the attachment...."

"Oh, god, Azrael." Caleb covered his mouth, gagging as the creature rolled over, scratching its back on the couch. "Please don't tell me this thing is attached to you."

"Only for a few months. The client didn't pay for the full attachment, thank goodness."

"A few months?" Caleb asked, shaking his head. "Azrael, no one will hire you with a stink demon attached. And god, what if the landlord finds out? How can he not? We will get kicked out."

Azrael fought the tears that threatened to spill. Secretly she'd hoped Caleb would have a plan, some words of wisdom. They barely had a place to live and food to eat, but at least they weren't starving on the streets. Now she'd ruined the few things they had to hold on to.

"I'm sorry," she whispered, tears falling down her cheeks. "I really am."

"Oh, Az," Caleb said softly, coming over to pull her into a hug. "It's not your fault. I'm the one who's holding us back. You've taken care of me all these years, and if I wasn't so messed up, I could go out and get a real job to tide us over. Please don't cry."

Azrael held on to him and let the tears flow, too choked up to respond. She didn't want Caleb to think he was a burden on her. So what if he couldn't venture outdoors or get a job? He was the best support system she'd ever had. No matter what, she wouldn't let this tear them apart.

"I might have a plan," she said, pulling back and wiping her nose. "First though, I want you to promise me you know you are not a burden. Life would be awful without you."

"I guess I can't be much worse than a stink demon," he replied, a glint of humor in his eyes.

She gave him a shove. "Maybe it is time I find myself a new best friend."

"Looks like you already have one." He nodded at the monstrosity curled up on their couch. Azrael sighed and stared at the demon. It wasn't ugly, necessarily, at least not compared to some things she'd seen. It was scaly, with pointy ears and a razor-sharp tail, but its eyes were large and bulbous, making it look innocent. She'd have to work on the biting thing. Those teeth, although small, were sharp as razors. Of course, the smell was the biggest problem. It reeked of putrid trash and dead animals. Nothing could cover up the smell of a stink demon.

Thank God I don't have a love life. At least the demon can't take that from me, she thought.

"So, you said you had a plan?"

Yes, she had a plan, one she had come up with on the fly. It wasn't a good one, it wasn't something she wanted to do, but it was all she had. "You know that notice I told you was hanging in the lobby for help wanted a few months ago?"

"The one for the maid?"

"Yes. Well, it's still up. If I got the job, I would be close to the apartment. I could check on the stink demon between cleaning rooms. That should keep him from breaking out and following me. No one would ever know."

"Yeah, but Lance hates you."

"Oh, he reminded me of that today when he caught up with me in the lobby about the rent."

"So, how are you going to convince him to hire you then?" Caleb asked.

Azrael didn't have an answer for him.

Chapter 2

"Can't you use your magic to do something about him?" Caleb nodded toward the stink demon who was currently snoring in her lap. With its ears flattened against its head, the thing reminded her of a teddy bear. *A stinky, scaly teddy bear.* An empty bottle of whisky sat on the table — beside it, a half-empty jar of street-grade moonshine. Candles dotted every bare surface, their flames making the shadows on the walls dance, but not even the scents of lavender, sandalwood, and cloves combined could smoother the odor of the creature, or "Smellicious," as Caleb had named him.

"You know as well as I do that I can only summon."

"Then summon something up to eat that thing. Problem solved."

"Caleb!" She kicked him. "You are a heartless bastard. Plus, it's against the law. He was registered the moment I summoned him; therefore, he is now considered a civil resident with the same rights as you or I. Trust me, I looked into it."

"And you call me heartless."

"No, I call you my gay bestie. The fact you're a heartless bastard is an observation."

Caleb clutched a hand over his heart. "How dare you call me gay. That does not do me justice. I am deeply hurt."

"Is there another term for I'll sleep with anything that breathes, as long as it's not female?"

"Yes, it's all-male-sexual. And at least I don't sleep with shapeshifters, unlike someone I know. At least *I* know what type of demon I'm really sleeping with." He grabbed a pillow and threw it at her. She dodged it, waking Smellicious in the process. The demon jumped off her lap and attacked the pillow, clenching it between its wide jaws.

"That was five years ago," she said, cringing. "You're never going to let me live that down, are you?"

"Not as long as I still have the memory of waking up to a Gigorian beetle in my kitchen, making a cup of coffee with one of its six arms."

Azrael grimaced and poured them both another glass. Good thing she didn't have to work in the morning because she was sure to have the hangover from hell. Still, a best friend drinking night was exactly what she needed.

"Here." She handed him his glass. "Speaking of exes, I saw Garrin today."

Caleb narrowed his eyes. "Jesus, baby girl, you have had a bad day. What was that sick bastard doing? Did he talk to you? He better not have."

"He came by the office, big bosomed redhead hanging on his shoulder, asking people for interviews. Of course, he didn't ask me but stopped to snap a pic right as I was trying to summon the demon. He's the reason I messed up the spell. Fricking bastard is always ruining my life," she said, her voice slurred.

"He took a picture of you? He did that crap just to rub it in. I'll kick his damn ass."

"He's not worth it. I'm over it. Everyone in the world has seen me naked by now, so what's the point?"

Azrael shrugged and cast her eyes down. She knew Caleb meant it. When the magazine had come out with her naked picture on the centerfold, Caleb did everything he could to leave the apartment, fully intending to kill Garrin. When she'd found him in the hallway, crying and clutching the walls, she begged him to stop and told him that seeing him suffer was worse than anything Garrin could have done.

Caleb leaned forward and squeezed her hand. "If it's any consolation, you look sexy as hell in that picture. That dark red hair spilling over your perfect porcelain skin damn near made me wish I liked women."

Azrael wrinkled her nose. "Don't be gross. I just wish we could have afforded a lawyer. Promise me that when your online matchmaking company takes off, we're gonna sue the hell out of that bastard and win this time."

"Damn right we are."

She sat her empty glass on the table and stood. The room spun, causing her to lose her balance. Caleb chuckled, and she gave him a dirty look before walking away.

She was halfway to the bathroom when a knock came from the front door. Azrael ran back into the living room, looked at Caleb, then down at the stink demon, who was strewing cotton from the shredded pillow all over the room. At the same time, they both raced toward Smellicious, who, sensing he was the center of unwanted attention, bolted across the room.

Azrael managed to grab his legs, but he squirmed out of her grasp, climbing onto the top of the couch. She ran to one end, blocking him, while Caleb snuck up from behind. The stink demon tried to jump over the back of the couch, but Caleb dived, wrapping his arms around the wiggling creature.

The knock came again, right before they heard Lance bark, "It's the landlord, open up."

"Oh shit," Caleb whispered, his eyes wide. "What are we going to do?"

Azrael looked toward the door, then back to Smellicious. She thrust out her arms. "Here, give me him. I'll pretend to shower. Just hold him off for a few minutes."

Caleb shoved the demon in her hands, and she ran to the bathroom, shutting and locking the door behind her. She tossed Smellicious down as she heard Caleb greet Lance. There was no way the landlord wouldn't notice the smell or see the mess Smellicious made, but they'd used this tactic many times before to avoid him. All she could do was pray it worked this time. She threw back the shower curtain and turned on the faucet.

Ripping her clothes off, she tossed them on the floor.

She heard Lance's voice. "I don't care that she's taking a shower *if* she really is. There is some kind of septic problem on this floor, and the smell has everyone complaining. I have to turn off the main to work on it, and it is located in that bathroom. Now step aside."

Oh shit. Azrael glanced at the sewer main. It was the reason they got the apartment cheaper than the other units. Now, it would be the end of them.

"You can't just barge in there! That's against our leasing rights."

"I can if it's an emergency situation."

She heard a key being slid into the lock. Azrael grabbed Smellicious and jumped into the shower, closing the curtain behind her. Cold water hit her naked body, and she broke into goosebumps. She struggled with the slippery demon before deciding to set him down, holding him between her ankles as he lapped up water from the bottom of the tub.

The door opened. She held her breath, squeezed her ankles tighter. Smellicious squirmed. *This can't be happening,* she thought. *That asshole actually has the nerve to come in here.* She clenched her fists as her heart pumped faster. She no longer felt the cold water piercing her skin because inside, her blood was boiling. Payback was a bitch, and she was going to deliver it to Lance on a silver platter.

She took a deep breath and shoved back the curtain, exposing her bare breasts. "Caleb, can you hand me...oh!"

Azrael pulled the curtain back around her, covering her chest. Heat set fire to her cheeks, a mixture of anger and embarrassment. Lance stood right inside the door, his turquoise eyes wide and fearful. Above the collar of his T-shirt, his skin took on a rosy tone. For the first time since she'd met him, the snarky confidence he always exuded was gone.

"What are you doing here?" she accused.

"I...um...." He reached up and rubbed the back of his neck, diverting his eyes. "I came to turn off the septic main. It'll just take a second if...."

He cut his eyes to her, but he looked away just as quickly. Not waiting for a response, Lance strolled over to the sewer main. Azrael didn't argue, didn't trust herself to speak. If it wasn't for the stink demon squirming between her ankles, she could almost find this situation amusing. For the second time that day, she felt in charge, a feeling she wasn't used to when it came to Lance.

He pulled a thin, cylindrical key out of his pocket and shoved it into the box beside the main. Azrael's drunken gaze slid from his muscular back down to his tight jeans.

If only he wasn't such a jerk, she mused.

The landlord placed the key back inside his pocket and stomped out, keeping his face turned the other way. Caleb, who had been standing at the door the whole time, gave her a wink before shutting it.

Azrael released the stink demon from between her ankles and leaned back against the shower wall, shutting her eyes. Vindication quickly became replaced by mortification.

I just exposed myself to a man who not only hates me but one I have to beg for a job. By tomorrow, he'll have regained enough confidence to laugh in my face.

Her eyes popped open. It wasn't tomorrow yet. When you have the upper hand, use it to your advantage. Wasn't that what Caleb always told her? She could still hear them talking, but the voices were further away, close to the front door. Jumping out of the shower, she grabbed a thin towel and wrapped it around herself as she raced out of the bathroom, slamming the door shut.

"Mr. Jacobs," she yelled, running through the hallway, water dripping down her body.

She turned, rounding the corner, and slammed into something hard. Her mind barely registered the solid wall she'd hit was Lance before her feet slipped, and she stumbled backward. He grabbed her around the waist, pulling her into him. Azrael found herself face to face with Lance, her wet body pressed against his warm one, his hand lying on the sensitive curve right above her buttocks. He looked down at her, eyes dark and hooded. Azrael's chest hitched.

"You okay?" he asked.

His voice was deeper than normal. Sexier. It rumbled through her, a gentle purr forcing its way beneath her skin. She nodded, tried to speak, but the only noise that came out was a sound similar to that of a cat in heat.

Lance let her go and stepped back.

"Then do you want to explain to me what the hell you want?" Although his words were brisk, his tone was soft. He crossed his arms over his chest, looking anywhere but at her.

I'd love to tell you what I want, she thought. The words nearly slipped past her lips before she stopped them.

Focus, Azrael.

"I need a job," she blurted out, her voice slurring slightly.

"What?" Lance stopped staring at the wall and looked at her. His eyes narrowed.

"I need a job, and you need a maid. Just for a few months." Azrael took a deep breath to calm herself. "You see, I got laid off work today —"

"You what?" he asked.

"Laid off, and there's no sense in asking me about the rent if you don't hire me because we won't have it. It would benefit us both if you hired me."

"No," he said, his tone that of a parent speaking to a disobedient child.

If there was one thing that sent her from angry to supreme bitch, it was being treated like she was beneath someone's notice. Especially by a man who managed a bunch of crummy, run-down apartments. She poked a finger at his chest. "Look here. I've put up with your crappy ass attitude since we've moved in. I don't know what your issue with witches is, and I don't care, but I need a damn job so I can pay our rent. You've had that sign up for months, so I know the position still needs to be filled. If you don't give me the job, you'll have to kick us out, and when you do, I will tell the apartment owners' board how you not only barged in on me naked, but you then refused to hire me when my credentials and background made me a qualified candidate.

Sexual harassment and discrimination typically don't go over well with them. Do you understand me?"

Lance held his fists clenched at his sides. Azrael crossed her arms over her chest and waited.

Through gritted teeth, he said, "Fine then. Meet me at six a.m. Don't be late, and you better as hell be sober."

He stormed out of the apartment, slamming the door behind him.

Azrael let out a long breath.

Caleb shook his head. "Baby girl, I don't know whether to be proud of you or scared for you. Either way, holy smokes, that was awesome. I wasn't sure if you were about to throw him on the floor and do him or rip his eyes out."

"Shut up," she said, walking off to fill her glass with moonshine.

Tomorrow would be living hell whether she was hung over or not.

Chapter 3

Her head hurt like hell, but she roused herself at five a.m., took a real shower, and got dressed. With a cup of coffee in hand, Azrael stared out the small living room window at the stained brick wall, which was their only view. Smellicious nipped on her ankles, and she wrinkled her nose. Tomorrow she would need to go by the butcher shop and buy him some scraps with what little money they had. Today the stink demon was just going to have to eat some moldy cheese. The saddest part was that the cheese smelled more appealing than her temporary pet.

Azrael rinsed her cup in the sink and put Smellicious in the bathroom with his food, barricading the door just in case he became impatient enough to try and hunt her down. With a sigh, she headed downstairs to Lance's office.

The door was open. Lance was hunkered over a thick ledger. She raised her hand, considered knocking, but then lowered it again. She didn't want to appear hesitant, not after last night's debacle.

"Good morning," she announced, stepping inside the sparsely decorated office.

He didn't say anything or look up, only pointed to a small

stack of paperwork on the desk. Stepping over, she picked it up.

Ugh…new hire paperwork.

Grabbing a pen, she looked around for a place to sit. The desk was scattered with loose folders and papers, and the only chair available seemed to be the one he was sitting in. The lobby was empty — only dents in the linoleum gave any indication it was furnished in the past. That left her two choices — either leave to fill it out, which was what she was sure he wanted her to do, or sit on the floor. Not wanting to give him the pleasure of her leaving, Azrael sat down on the floor, crossed her legs, and began to fill out the forms. Two minutes in, she heard him get up.

He stopped in front of her, his scuffed black loafers close enough to touch her shins. Figuring he'd ignored her when she came in, she did the same. After a moment, he cleared his throat.

"Here," he said, handing her a clipboard when she looked up. "You can sit at my desk. I'll be back in a few."

She took the clipboard, noting the tenseness of his shoulders and hawk-like gaze.

Guess he's still pissed, she thought irritably. *At least he's allowing me to sit in a chair now.*

He walked away, and she took a seat in his warm chair. Azrael rubbed her eyes, hoping he wouldn't have her work a full first day. She could use a nap.

The paperwork was the same as most other places. She filled out her work history, address, and phone number enough times to make her head throb. On the last page, her mouth dropped open. The pay rate was way more than she'd been expecting, considering it was supposed to be a minimum wage job. Suspicious, Azrael pulled out her phone and looked up the position online.

As of yesterday, the job was showing to pay $7.75 an hour.

Azrael's paperwork showed nearly twice that amount.

He's paying me more – but why?

Briefly, she thought it might have something to do with experience but then cast the idea down. Even if he paid by experience, she had none on record when it came to maid work. *Maybe he's just the asshole landlord with a heart of gold,* she thought with a snicker, but the longer she stared at the amount, the more she wondered. She finished the paperwork and waited for him to come back.

Lance took the clipboard from her and handed her a set of keys on an old ring. "Each key corresponds to the apartment number assigned to it. Cleaning will be done before noon. That includes straightening up, vacuuming, mopping, cleaning linens and bathrooms. They pay for this service, so you will do a good job. The code to the laundromat is nine-six-three. At noon will be lunch, and then you will work on cleaning the lobby and reorganizing the basement. Be sure to fill out a time sheet and leave it on my desk by three. Do you have any questions?"

Azrael grabbed the keys, trying not to show her irritation at him for speaking to her like a child. He kept a steady gaze on her, his eyes glinting.

He wants me to mouth off, to give him an excuse to fire me.

"No, sir," she said, forcing a smile. "You can call me Azrael, by the way, or Az, like Caleb does."

"I will do no such thing. Now get to work."

A smile tugged at the corner of her mouth, but she suppressed it. She made her way to the door and stopped, saying over her shoulder, "It'll be a lot more comfortable to work together if we call each other by our first names."

With two long strides, he met her at the door. "We don't work together, Miss Larken. You work *for* me. I'd suggest you don't do anything that makes me have to remind you of that again."

He placed his hand on her shoulder and pushed her out of the office. The door slammed behind her.

Chapter 4

I've died and gone to hell, Azrael thought as she picked up the last of the linens and tossed them in her cart. After the last week of running back and forth to check on Smellicious, cleaning, and dealing with Lance's snarky attitude, she was about ready to throw in the towel, no pun intended. Every day she went home to her smelly apartment, exhausted. Luckily, Caleb found tips in the Witch's Almanac to help with a stink demons' reek. They fed him three garlic bulbs a day, and it seemed to contain the putrid odor to their apartment. He also ground up some bulbs and made a garlic, lavender soap for them. It wasn't the best smelling, but at least they didn't carry around the demon's scent. Of course, that didn't stop Lance from giving her a weird look and wrinkling his nose slightly every morning when she checked in for duties.

The only thing she had to look forward to was sleep, but lately, her dreams were plagued by Lance. The more she saw him, the more he irritated her, the more she fantasized about him. Even in her dreams, her desire would be met with indifference. She would wake up aching with need. Those dreams stayed with her during the day. No matter how many times she told herself she didn't care if Lance found her attractive, her bruised ego said otherwise, and she ended up spending extra time on her hair and makeup.

Lost my damn mind, that's what I've done. I should hold a sign above my head, "Glutton for Punishment."

She pushed the cart to the next room on her list. Reaching for the door, it surprised her to see a "Do Not Disturb" sign hanging off the knob. Mr. and Mrs. Mayer were never home this time of day. One of the rambunctious kids across the hall must have put the sign there again. She raised her fist and knocked.

Through the door, she heard something slam into the wall before a male voice yelled, "Who's there?"

"It's maid service, Mr. Mayer."

The latch clicked, and the door swung open. Standing in it was a large man, mid-thirties, wearing a white T-shirt with sweat stains and a wild look on his face.

"What are you? Some kind of dim-wit? The sign says do not disturb," he said in a menacing tone.

"I'm…I'm sorry. I thought…," Azrael said, backing up, but stopped when she saw a woman's face peek around the corner. One of her eyes was swollen and bruised, blood crusting under her nose.

The man, following her gaze, looked behind him and yelled, "Get your ass back in there!" He put his robust form between her and Azrael, blocking the view. "Now, you mind your own damn business and get the hell out of here."

The door slammed in her face. Azrael stared at it for a moment, her hands shaking. She heard a loud crash inside, and then the woman screamed. Without thinking, Azrael ran down the steps to Lance's office.

When she burst through the door, he gave her a look that should have sent her running, but something must have shown on her face because he dropped his pen and slid his chair back, features softening. "What's wrong?"

"It's room number ninety-seven. I think...I think he's beating her to death." Her face felt hot, and she fought to blink back tears.

His eyes turned dark, menacing. His lips screwed into a grimace. "Stay here."

He strode past her and went through the lobby at a brisk jog, heading up the stairs. Azrael chased after him, catching up as he approached the apartment. Lance glanced at her as he placed the key in the lock but didn't tell her to leave. He shoved the door open, and she followed him inside.

They made it a few steps down the hallway before Mr. Meyer came around the corner, his face bright red, a huge throbbing vein on his forehead, and behind him, Mrs. Meyer. "Get the hell out of my —"

He stopped mid-sentence, realizing who was in his apartment. Lance took one look at the woman's face, and his eyes darkened. He raised his fist and slammed it into Mr. Meyer's face. Mr. Meyer stumbled backward, hands tented against his face, cursing Lance's name. Without a word, Lance locked his arms around the man's chest and carried him out of the room.

Mrs. Mayer, her eyes wide, started after her husband, but Azrael darted forward and grabbed her around the waist. "No, let him go. He can't hurt you now."

Several minutes passed, and neither man showed back up. Once the woman calmed down, Azrael took her to the bathroom to clean her up. As she wiped off her face with a warm rag, she asked, "What's your name?"

"Rosella," the woman whispered, tears seeping down her cheeks.

"It's going to be okay, Rosella."

Rosella grabbed some tissue and blew her nose. "He said he would stop, that he would get better. I've thought about leaving hundreds of times, but somehow he's always sensed it. He told me if I ever tried, he'd kill me. I wish you hadn't done this. It'll just make it worse."

"No, it won't." Azrael rinsed the rag in the sink. "We'll call the police, make a report. I'll help you."

"I've done that. It doesn't matter. He's a crooked lawyer. He's helped too many cops to get off the hook."

Azrael sighed. How many women had she seen in this same predicament? How many had come to Witches Corp, requesting her services, hands trembling as they paid a hefty fee for protection when it should be given freely?

I can do it, though. They won't ever know.

When she signed the contract for Witches Corporation, she signed away her rights to perform summoning outside of work. Caleb thought she was selling herself short, that she should go into business for herself. Azrael didn't believe enough in her powers to do that, and although they had no way to track magic use outside Witches Corp, she'd seen too many coworkers fired for attempting to get away with it.

She clenched her fists. It was ridiculous she couldn't help people without demanding a huge fee. This woman needed it, and she damn sure was going to give it to her. She would just have to trust Rosella to not to say anything.

"Come on." She grabbed Rosella's hand and led her to the edge of the bed. "Sit here and wait for me."

Azrael made her way to the kitchen. It seemed odd to see how normal their apartment was, given the situation. A picture sat on the mantel, a young couple smiling at each other. The puffiness and lines were gone from the man's face. Rosella was laughing, staring up at him. There was love in that picture, love and hope.

Maybe Caleb is right. Love often, but not long.

She had to give it to her best friend. Caleb spent his life playing matchmaker but refused to make his own matches. Azrael hadn't learned the hard way yet, but a part of her understood why Caleb refused the notion of love.

After digging through their kitchen cabinets, Azrael found what she needed. Carrying a box of salt, a piece of chalk, and a knife, she went back into Rosella's room. She sat the items on the floor. Rosella looked at her oddly.

"I'm a summoning witch," she said. "I'm going to summon you a protector demon."

"Isn't that against the law?" a powerful male voice asked from behind her.

Azrael turned to see Lance and let out a sigh of relief. "It is. I'm trusting Rosella to keep it a secret for me."

Rosella gave her a small smile and nodded. That was all the confirmation Azrael needed. On the hardwood floor, she drew shapes from memory, writing notes on the paper as needed. When she felt confident in her work, she reached for the bottle of salt to create a protective circle, but it was too far away.

"Mr. Jacobs, can you hand me that salt?"

He grabbed the salt and knelt beside her. Leaning in close, he whispered, "You can call me Lance. I think it would make her more comfortable."

"Oh...." Azrael couldn't think of a better response. The way his piercing eyes met hers, the closeness of his lips had her heart galloping. "Okay then."

Taking the salt, she finished setting up the protection. She asked Rosella to cut a small snippet of hair for the spell. Rosella lifted the scissors but stopped, her eyes drawn to a picture of her and her husband, which sat on the nightstand.

"Rosella," Azrael whispered, "the protection demon will only protect you from those who hurt you. Maybe your husband can get help, and you two can get back together then, but if you don't do this, one day he will go too far."

Nodding slightly, Rosella cut off a piece of her hair and handed it over. Azrael took it and added it to the center of the circle.

With her legs crossed Indian style, she said, "I will need complete silence."

She shut her eyes, closing her mind off as she sought the strands that connected all things to their purpose. In her vision, she was in a dark, immense room, stretching for an eternity. Above her head hung trillions of tiny silvery ropes. Azrael walked around the dark room, her palms grazing the silvery strands. Thinking of her purpose, she let instinct lead her. She felt like she was in the room for hours, although from experience, she knew it had only been minutes. Suddenly, she stopped, her hand holding a glowing thread.

"Perfect," she whispered.

Grasping the strand, she opened her eyes.

Chapter 5

Azrael placed her hands over the circle, and light swirled within, growing. She chanted under her breath. Somewhere in the back of her mind, she knew Lance and Rosella were watching. Light curled around the strand of hair, ebbing and waning. Azrael knew it was time. She pulled with her mind, and a loud explosion filled the room, followed by a huge plume of white smoke.

Probably should have warned them of that, Azrael thought as she heard the others coughing. The smoke thinned, revealing a tiny little creature standing in the middle. The protection demon, four inches tall, picked up Rosella's hair and clutched it in his tiny fist. Azrael held out her palm, and it climbed up, blinking its large, child-like eyes. Reaching down with her pinky, Azrael petted its short green fur. "Let's go meet your new momma."

Rosella's eyes widened as Azrael came over with the creature. As soon as she closed in, the protection demon jumped out of her palm and scrambled up Rosella's shoulder, nuzzling her neck. Rosella flinched, taken back, but after a moment, she giggled. Azrael's heart swelled at the sound.

Lance was staring at the creature, an odd look on his face. "I've heard of protection demons but have never seen one like that. It's just so small and...cute."

"Small, but feisty and very possessive. He'll do the job."

"Are you sure?" Lance asked, still looking uncertain.

Azrael smirked. "If you don't believe me, go over there and poke Rosella on the shoulder."

She could tell he was thinking about it. Rosella lifted her head, looking between Lance and the creature, an expression of curiosity on her face.

"Oh, what the hell," Lance said, strolling over to Rosella.

The protection demon kept his eyes on Lance as he approached. Lance paused in front of Rosella, staring at the demon who only looked back, head tilted. He lifted a finger and poked Rosella on the shoulder.

The demon blinked, and a small frown appeared on its face. It lifted its own finger and touched Lance's. Lance went flying backward, landing several feet away with an "oomph." The protection demon went back to nuzzling Rosella's neck.

Lance pulled himself off the floor and straightened his shirt. "I see your point, Azrael. Although a little more warning would have been nice."

"Would you have believed me?" she asked, smiling at him.

"Probably not," he said, matching her grin.

With Lance's help, Azrael cleaned up the floor and returned Rosella's stuff to where she'd found it. After leaving her number and instructions on how to take care of her demon, they left.

"How did you get rid of him?" she asked as they walked down the hall together.

"Quite simple. After showing him what it felt like to be beaten, I threatened to send out some videos I have of him forging documents in the lobby."

"You have cameras in the lobby?" she asked, surprised.

"Nope, but I've seen him out there doing it before he mails out his letters. It was enough to convince him. By the way, what you did in there, for her, that was pretty all right of you," Lance said in a soft tone.

"It wasn't a big deal. Caleb got beat up a lot in school, so I'm pretty used to cleaning up blood. Plus, I don't think it's fair to charge when someone has a great need. Saving someone's life is more important than worrying about your damn job."

Azrael made it a few steps before she realized Lance had stopped. She turned around to ask him why, but something in the way he was looking at her made her words stick in her throat.

"You're not as bad as I imagined you to be," he said, rubbing a hand over his stubble.

Azrael tried to still the rapid racing of her heart. "Oh, so you're admitting you've imagined me before?"

She expected him to laugh, but he didn't respond.

Why isn't he saying no?

Does that mean he thinks about me?

By the time he spoke again, her legs were trembling.

"You can take the rest of the day off, get yourself cleaned up. I'll finish the rooms." He brushed past Azrael, leaving her standing there, mouth hung open.

Chapter 6

"Well, what do you think that means?" Caleb asked, when she finished telling him about her day.

"I don't know." Azrael flung herself on the bed. "I can't do this anymore, Caleb. I've never hated someone so much and wanted them between my legs at the same time."

"Ew, Az. Please don't ever make references to your woman parts around me. Still, I can see why you're drawn to him. Not only is he sexy, but he's controlling. You've always sought out those characteristics in men. Daddy issues?"

"I am not one of your matchmaking subjects," she said, flipping over on her belly. "Speaking of which, how is that going?"

"I thought you'd never ask," he responded with a grin. "I made three matches today, two paid, one free."

"Fantastic! I'm so proud of you."

"I know, right!" Caleb sat down beside her. "I keep hoping I'll make it big someday, you know? Then we can get out of this crummy apartment, sue your ex, and live happily ever after."

"That would be nice," she admitted, reaching over to rub Smellicious's stomach. "Wait, you said two paid and one free.

Since when do you offer free services?"

"Well, the third was for me. A very lonely Calabreza warlock looking for a night of passion, no strings attached."

"Seriously? Have you sunk that low? Calabreza warlocks are complete douchebags without brains."

"Yeah, but he's a fricken hot douche bag. Full-on muscular build, purple eyes. Plus, he's game for whatever. Also, I kind of told him I was straight, and you were my girlfriend."

Azrael stopped petting Smellicious and sat up. "Why would you tell him something like that?"

Caleb fidgeted with the sleeve on his shirt. "Okay, you're not going to like this, but the guy was boasting about how he could turn anyone gay, and seeing an opportunity, I took his challenge. I told him you and I were an amazing couple, and I would never sleep with a man. To make a long story short, I might have told him to come over around eight tonight because you would be out for a few hours."

"You did not!" Azrael grabbed a pillow and smacked him in the face with it. "Did you not hear how bad my day has been? All I want to do is curl up into a ball and cry, and you're telling me I have to leave the apartment for *hours*?"

Caleb held his hands out in front of him. "I'm sorry, Az. I didn't know your day was going to be so sucky when I made the plans. I got some payments in already from today's matches, and I was going to give you my card, let you go do your hair or have some drinks or something. If you want me to cancel, I will."

Azrael shut her eyes and leaned against the bedframe. It wasn't Caleb's fault she was so pissy. It also wasn't fair to deny him a night in the sack. Heck, it had been so long since she'd been with someone, she probably would have done the same thing in his position.

"Az?"

She opened her eyes. "No, it's fine, Caleb. I'm just a little tired and moody. A night out might be exactly what I need."

"Are you sure?" he asked, concern coloring his tone.

"Yes," she said, hopping up. "But you've got to help me fix my hair and makeup. I'm going out sexy tonight. Also, you're in charge of making sure Smellicious doesn't leave. Two hours is the longest he's been without me."

"Crap, forgot about him," Caleb said, looking down at the snoring creature. "I'll figure it out. Now, let's go make you sexy."

~*~

Azrael slipped on her heels and stared at herself in the mirror. Caleb had fixed her hair so that the long red strands curled gently over her shoulders, a stark contrast to the tight black dress clinging to her curves. It had been a long time since she felt hot.

Caleb whistled from behind her, and she grinned. "Baby girl, I hope you're ready to get laid cause there is no way you're going to get turned down tonight."

She sighed. "I hope so. I'm in desperate need of something to take my mind off Lance."

"Or you could just march down there and show him what you look like tonight. Take what you want, Az. Life is too short not to."

"Not a chance in hell," she replied, leaning in to kiss him on the cheek. "You're the best. Thank you."

"Oh, I know," he replied, grinning. "Now, get out of here before you ruin my date."

Azrael raised her hands in the air. "I'm going, I'm going."

Grabbing her purse, she left the apartment and locked up behind her. Caleb, although he did it for somewhat selfish reasons, was right. She needed a night away, a night to feel sexy and carefree.

She took the steps carefully, not wanting to fall face first in the lobby. With the way her luck was going, she'd probably not only fall but land on the one man she was trying to avoid. Azrael reached the lobby, cutting her eyes toward his office. The door was shut, and it appeared as though the lights were out.

That's good, though. The whole point of tonight is to get him off my mind. Of course, I wouldn't have to get him off my mind if I could just get him in my bed.

Azrael sighed. Her hormones always had a way of steering her wrong.

"Two hours. Go out, get laid, get over him. You can do this," she mumbled under her breath as she stepped out onto the street.

~*~

The only bar within walking distance was the Blue Dolphin. For hook-ups, it wasn't as preferable as some of the downtown bars, but it would have to do. Azrael pushed open the door. Music came from the stage area, soft and eclectic. Hookah smoke filled the air. Making her way through the crowd, she casually glanced around. There was an odd mix tonight. Probably had something to do with the live band.

She picked a stool at the bar and sat down. From her vantage point, she could easily see and, most importantly, be seen. The bartender nodded, signaling he was ready for her order.

"Two Orion's, please," she yelled.

He flicked his tongue twice at her, a show of disgust, and she shrugged it off. Unless she was rich, she would never impress the creature behind the counter. Septoids, although fantastic at bartending, were a very snobby breed of demon. She watched as he made her drinks behind his back, flipping the bottle with one of his six tentacles. He slid the glasses to her, and she slipped him Caleb's card.

Azrael wrapped her hand around the first glass and let out a deep breath. She lifted it to her lips, swallowing the putrid liquid in one gulp. It tasted like cloves but smelled of spoiled garbage. She struggled not to gag. Azrael set the empty glass down and picked up the second one, downing it with much more ease than the first.

With a heavy buzz setting in, she swiveled in her chair, leaned back against the bar, and eyed the crowd. On her first pass, she caught the gaze of a fiery demon who smiled at her and thrust out his bulging red chest, but she decided to pass. She needed to keep to her own species if she was looking for a quickie. Interspecies sex could get complicated.

When her eyes scanned the crowd a second time, she saw a well-built man standing uncomfortably off to the corner, watching his other friends play pool.

Bingo. My age, handsome, and obviously bored.

Azrael slid off the stool and made her way in his direction. The music picked up, and the floors thrummed with a techno beat. The lights grew dim, lasers highlighting the smoke-filled air. Alcohol coursed through her system, and she straightened her shoulders. She passed the young man and smiled. He smiled back, his eyes roaming over her body.

Definitely interested.

Azrael picked up a pool stick and checked its weight. Finding one she felt comfortable with, she approached the man.

"So," she said with a smile, "is it your friends that bore you or just the game of pool?"

"Well, I would say both, but I think the game would be a lot more interesting if my partner looked like you," he said, uncrossing his arms and smiling back. "How about that table in the back corner?"

"Sure." Azrael followed him over to the table, her heart thrumming, palms sweaty. When he stepped away to grab a pool stick, a server passed by, and she waved him down, ordering another drink to calm her nerves.

Desperate times call for desperate measures.

"My name's Corbin," he said, returning to the table.

"Azrael," she responded, taking in his spikey blond hair and brown eyes. Although he wasn't as attractive as the man she'd been fantasizing about all week, he'd do.

The server came back with her drink, and they started playing pool. For the next twenty minutes, Azrael did her best to appear interested in his insistent chatter. From what Corbin told her, he was the best at any sport, knew everything about everything, and could lift more than all his friends.

Azrael ended up ordering another drink.

She beat Corbin at pool on the first round, but by the second, she was too drunk to focus. It was time they moved this party along to the point where sex would become involved. "Why don't we go check out the band?"

He took her hand, and she followed him to the other side of the bar. There were more people than when she arrived, most packed together on the dance floor, grinding under blue strobe lights. As they passed by a row of tables, she glanced to the left and stopped mid-stride.

Sitting at a table with a gorgeous blonde was Lance.

They were both leaned over, looking at a sheet of paper. Corbin tugged on her hand, and she realized she was standing in the middle of the bar, gaping at Lance. She walked away quickly, her heart racing. Out of the corner of her eye, she saw him raise his head and look in her direction. Whether or not he saw her, she didn't know.

Who cares if he saw me? Him or his damn date.

At least that explained why he wasn't interested in her. Not if his type was stunning, blonde, big bosomed models. She bit her cheek. So much for thinking he was a nice guy just pretending to be a petty ass.

Azrael walked faster, tugging her date to the dance floor. She pressed her body against Corbin and danced. A few groups around her were grinding against their dates. Corbin put his arm around her waist and steered her that way. A group let them in, and she bumped and grinded against half a dozen others.

Screw it. Why not?

Corbin ran one hand under her ass, pulling her close. Azrael no longer had to doubt his interest in her. It was obvious by the bulge in his pants. She closed her eyes and focused on the music, letting her body feel the rhythm. Someone touched her shoulder from behind, and she backed into them, grinding her hips against their torso.

"Azrael."

Her eyes popped open. She recognized that voice and that tone of barely controlled irritation. She spun around. "Lance?"

He was looking down at her, his eyes flashing. She shrank under that gaze but then gained her confidence when Corbin whispered in her ear. "Is he your boyfriend?"

"No. He's just my boss," she said, narrowing her eyes. "He's obviously confused about what the dance floor is for. Can I help you, Lance?"

He shut his eyes and breathed deeply through his nose. When he opened them, his expression was much softer. "Actually, yes. It's a work thing, and I hate to interrupt your...fun, but it came up suddenly and —"

The music changed into something faster, causing the crowd to move in. They shoved Corbin forward, knocking Azrael against Lance's chest.

She could feel the heat radiating from him, could feel him pressed against her belly button. Images of him flashed through her mind. Taut muscles. Sweaty skin. The length of him buried deep inside of her. Heat colored her face. Why did this keep happening?

Lance pinched his nose between his thumb and forefinger. "Can we please go talk somewhere else?"

She nodded. Azrael turned to Corbin and said, "Sorry, I've got to see what he wants."

Corbin brushed his lips against her neck and whispered, "Hurry back, sexy."

Azrael shivered, but she wasn't sure if it was from attraction or not. The instant she saw Lance, her desire for Corbin seemed to diminish. Lance was waiting for her at the edge of the dance floor, arms crossed over his chest. He nodded to the table he'd been sitting at with the blonde. Azrael followed him there and slid into a seat. "Where'd your date go?"

"Date?" he asked, mouth twitching into a grin.

"The blonde you were with," she said, brushing at her dress, keeping her eyes downcast. It wasn't a sin to notice someone else at a bar. It wasn't like she'd been stalking him.

Lance chuckled. "Her? Oh, she wasn't my date. More of a business associate, which brings me to the purpose of this conversation. I need to go out of town and won't be back for a few days. I know it's not your job, and it's the weekend, but I need someone to pick up the checks in my drop box and drop them off at the bank Monday. Also, feed my cat."

Not a date, she thought, biting her lip.

"Well?" he asked.

"Well, what?"

"Will you take care of the checks and my cat? Of course, I'd pay you double-time for this."

"Um, sure, that's fine. You have a cat?"

"Yes."

"You don't seem the type."

Lance smirked. "What animal do you think my 'type' would have?"

"I don't know," Azrael stammered. "A mean dog with big teeth."

"I'm a little offended by your impression of me," he said, cocking his head to the side. "Regardless, I would like to come back, and my cat still be alive. I can trust you with this, right?"

"Now I'm the one who's offended."

"Well, it's not like you make the best of judgements," he said, nodding his head toward the dance floor.

Azrael bristled. "What do you mean by that?"

Lance sighed. "Look, do we have to argue right now? I know we don't get along all the time, but I was hoping we could be cordial to each other."

"Well, it's a rude thing to say to someone. You act like you have some right to judge me. What's wrong with having fun? Do you even know what that is?"

"There's nothing wrong with having fun," he said, narrowing his eyes at her. "It's the company you're keeping. Most self-respecting women won't have anything to do with a shapeshifter."

"A shapeshifter? How the hell did you find out about that?" she asked, shaking her head. "Never mind, it doesn't matter. I was young and stupid back then. You can't judge me because of that."

Lance arched a sly brow. "I was talking about your date. Although now I'm thinking my statement was a correct assumption."

"Corbin? He's not a shapeshifter."

"Follow me." He stood and took long strides across the room, expecting her to follow. She sat at the table, balling up a straw wrapper between her thumb and finger as she debated blowing him off.

Damn him.

Azrael shoved her chair back and stomped over to Lance, who was slipping behind a curtained edge of the stage. "What are you doing?"

He didn't answer. She followed him up some steps, staying in the shadows. Several feet to the right, the band played on. Lance motioned her to a dark corner. He opened a small section of the curtain.

"Do you see your date?" he whispered in her ear.

Struggling to concentrate on something other than his warm breath against her earlobe, she searched the crowd until she saw Corbin dancing with a group. "Yeah, he's out there dancing. Nothing wrong with that."

"Look at the band now, Azrael."

She rolled her eyes but did as he instructed. The band looked like any other. A singer, guitarist, bass player….

Wait!

The bass player was the spitting image of Corbin. Same clothes and all. She turned and looked back out at the crowd. Her date was still there, dancing.

"Shit!"

Lance smirked at her. She pivoted on her heels and walked away.

Chapter 7

"I take it you didn't know?" Lance yelled.

She gave him a dirty look. He was lucky there wasn't even a hint of a smile on his face because she would have punched him. As far as she was concerned, this conversation was over.

Stupid ass thinks he knows everything. I'm over him, and I'm over Corbin. Hell, men in general.

Azrael walked up to the bar, balling her fist. The same bartender was there, so she held up two fingers. He slid her the drinks before Lance caught up. He grabbed one off the counter and downed it before she could stop him.

"What the hell are you doing?"

"Saving you from a hangover. You realize you have a drinking problem, right?"

She took her shot, too irritated to notice the unpleasant taste, and swiveled around in her chair. "What I know is that I am a grown-ass adult who can make her own decisions. Also, I don't remember offering to buy you a drink."

Lance waved down the bartender. "Put her drinks on my tab."

"In that case, two more, please," Azrael yelled.

Lance cut his eyes at her but didn't argue. To her surprise, he gave her a small smile and said, "I'd yell at you if that wasn't such a smooth move."

Azrael shrugged. "I never turn down a chance for free liquor."

The bartender slid their drinks over, and Lance signaled for the bill. Azrael looked at the shot glasses. Two became four as her vision doubled. "I think these are both for you. I may have had a touch too many."

"Finally, a good decision," he teased, leaning over and taking the shots.

On any normal day, she would have played along, would have enjoyed the fact Lance was being playful, but not right now. She slid off the stool, placing a hand on the bar to steady herself. Right now, she needed to get out of this place. She grabbed Caleb's check card. "Thanks for the drinks. Have fun on your trip."

"Where are you going?" He set his glass down.

"I need some air," she admitted.

He placed a hand on her lower back. "Let's go then."

The noise was suddenly too much for her. She let Lance lead her out. When they exited the bar, she closed her eyes and leaned against the brick wall outside, breathing in the cool night air. After a moment, when she felt steadier, she opened her eyes again. Lace was less than a foot away, staring at her.

"You okay?" he asked.

"Yeah. I'm sorry. It was just too stuffy and loud in there. Plus, I need to go home. Especially if I have to work tomorrow. Speaking of which, are you just going to slide the keys under my door or something?"

"How about we walk back, and I give you my spare set

when we get there?"

Azrael stared down the sidewalk. They were at least four blocks from home. On one hand, there was a part of her excited about being alone with him. On the other, it was a long walk, and she was dangerously close to puking, which would embarrass the both of them.

"You didn't drive, by any chance?" she asked.

"Yes, but neither one of us is sober enough to be behind the wheel."

"You're drunk?" she asked, squinting to get a closer look at his face. "You don't look drunk."

"Close enough that I shouldn't drive," Lance said as he began walking back to the apartment complex.

She pushed herself off the wall and followed. "So, that stern, grumpy expression is your permanent expression? I was thinking it was only meant for me."

"No, but it is more common when you are around," he said, grinning at her over his shoulder.

"Wow, I actually got a smile from you. You should drink more often." Azrael rubbed her arms. Although it was warm when she left, the night brought with it a chill, and there was a damp mist hanging in the air.

"I have a jacket in my car if you want to walk back," he said, nodding to her bare arms.

"No, I'll be fine. Thanks for the offer, though."

He nodded but scooted in several inches closer, his bare arms brushing hers. Heat radiated off his skin, giving her goosebumps, causing her to fantasize about him pressing her up against a building and sliding those arms around her. Thankfully, it was too dark for him to see the blush creeping up on her cheeks.

Stop thinking about it. Think about anything else.

"So, um, where are you from?"

"I've lived here for the last ten years or so," he replied, not making eye contact with her.

Something in his tone suggested he didn't want to further the conversation, which only made her more curious. "What about before that?"

"Um," he said, his eyes darting toward the street. "Well, I lived in Montana for a short time before that, but I'm originally from Demonium."

Azrael stopped short, her mouth popping open. She had the sense to close it before he turned around and saw her. "Demonium? You're a demon? I had no idea. What class of demon are you?"

"A warlock," he said, meeting her eyes. "But well removed. My family mixed with humans mostly, so I ended up with no power—hence, apartment manager."

At least we have something in common.

"Don't worry, having power comes with its own set of problems. I was born and raised here. My grandmother was a summoning witch, but it skipped a generation. I had to move to Demonium with her for a few years to learn how to control it because it was making things too hard on my family. You wouldn't believe the number of times I was in the principal's office because I accidentally summoned something. Sometimes I wonder what my life would be like if the portal to our world had never been discovered."

"Hard to say, although, can you imagine the look on the guy's face when he knocked down that wall in his basement? How do you handle that? Just go, 'Oh, honey, look, a swirling vortex to another world,'" he said with a chuckle. "What I would have given to be a fly on that wall."

Azrael giggled and quickened her pace to catch up. "According to some historians, he ran out screaming he'd found hell and his basement was full of demons. It's rather unfortunate that name stuck, though."

A loud group passed by them, and they had to split up to keep from being knocked down. For the next few minutes, they walked in silence. Azrael wondered why he always seemed so guarded. Her "screw me" outfit seemed to have no effect on him at all. Yet, there was something about the way he acted tonight that made her feel sexy.

"You said you summoned by accident? I thought summoning witches couldn't summon without using drawings and spells," he asked, cutting into her thoughts.

"For the most part, you're right. The spell helps us focus, but in extreme situations, we can do it without them. Think of it like an adrenaline rush. People can't normally lift cars, but with enough adrenaline, they might be able to. It's very rare, though, and usually turns out badly."

"Bad as in how?" he asked, his blue eyes focused on hers.

Azrael struggled to concentrate. "Um, it's hard to explain. You see, when I summon, I have to be focused on a purpose. Not just what I'm summoning, but the purpose of the summoning. Kind of like I did with Mrs. Mayer. Yes, I could have summoned a larger demon, but its purpose wouldn't be aligned to her, and I would have to do an attachment spell. When that spell wears off, the chances of the demon staying around to protect her are small. Now, if I can find a creature whose random purpose is a match to the client's, then it is much more successful. In some cases even, it's not a specific type of demon that is the best match sometimes it's just a demon whose purpose lies with the client. Still, a witch summoning blindly is like reaching into a box of sharp knives trying to find a fork."

"Huh, I guess I can see that. Still, how can you tell if the purpose is right?"

Azrael chuckled. "That is a lot harder to explain. Each summoning witch is different, but the strands are the same."

"Strands?"

"Yes. When I summon, I'm in a black void filled with silvery strands. If I clear my mind, it'll take me to the right strand, but I don't usually know why. I can just feel it. Sort of like I'm carrying a magnet with me and purposes that don't align repel, where those that do snap together, just like two magnets would," she said, slapping her hands together.

Lance didn't comment. They were less than half a block from the apartment, and soon he would be gone for who knew how long. She had the feeling that by the time he got back, Lance would be right back to his distant attitude.

Make a move then. What's the worst that could happen? Besides being fired or kicked out because he finds out about Smellicious.

Azrael sighed.

"Something wrong?"

"No. Yes. I don't know." She shook her head and took a deep breath. "Okay, you know what, screw it. I'm just going to say it, and for once, please don't be an ass."

He raked his hands through his hair and glanced sideways. "Azrael, maybe it's best if…."

The words trailed off. He seemed to struggle with how to finish the sentence. She got the sense he already knew what she was going to say, and it pissed her off.

"You know what? You're right. Let's not talk about it." She spun on her heels, preparing to put as much room as she could between the two of them for the rest of the walk, but her heel was stuck in a rut on the sidewalk and didn't move with the rest of her body. Azrael felt the heel snap off, but not before pain radiated up her calf.

"Dammit!" she yelled, tears pricking the corner of her eyes.

Putting all her pressure on the unhurt ankle, she tried to hop to the wall and nearly fell, but before she did, Lance grabbed her by the waist. "What happened?"

"My stupid heel broke, and I think I twisted my ankle."

"Here, I'm going to lean you against the wall," he said, carefully lifting her enough to keep the pressure off. When he sat her down, he bent to look at her ankle. "I'm going to take the heel off to see how bad it is."

He gently removed the straps, only causing her to flinch slightly in pain. His fingertips prodded the ankle, and she was surprised at how tender he could be. If it wasn't for the pain and embarrassment, she would enjoy his face mere inches away from her upper thigh. At the moment, though, she wanted to curl up in a ball and cry.

He set her foot down and stood up. "It doesn't look bad. If it's sprained, it's minor, but we still need to get some ice on it. Can you walk?"

Azrael tried to put pressure on it, but the pain was instant. She lifted the foot back up and shook her head. "I can't. If you could just help me, I'll take the other heel off and try to hop to the—"

Lance slipped an arm behind her back and one under her thighs, lifting her to his chest.

"What are you—? Oh, please, no. Dammit, just put me down," she argued, heat licking her neck and face.

"And watch you hop the rest of the way? That's ridiculous,

Azrael, and you know it. Plus, you'll probably just fall again and get seriously hurt, and my cat would die of starvation. Think of this as me being selfish."

There was no sense in arguing. Azrael squeezed her eyes shut and prayed this night would end soon.

Chapter 8

When they got to his apartment, he sat her down by leaning her against the door. With one hand around her, he used the other to unlock it. To her irritation, he picked her up again and carried her in.

It surprised Azrael to see his apartment was only marginally nicer than her own. She always assumed a landlord's apartment would be decked out with all the good stuff. It was also apparent Lance wasn't a fan of clutter because there were few furnishings. He carried her through the door into a bedroom, laying her down on the bed. His eyes darted to the right, and he bolted in that direction. For a moment, she thought he'd seen an intruder, but then she saw him pick up something that looked like a magazine off the bedside.

Lance knelt, seeming to straighten up the blankets, but when he stood back up, the magazine or whatever he was holding was gone. "I'll go get some ice for your ankle."

He left the room. Azrael considered scooting over to the other side of the bed to see what he'd hidden but decided against it. More than likely, it was porn, and the last thing she needed tonight was to get caught looking at his porn mags.

Well, at least I've made it into his bed, she thought, sighing.

Her ankle hurt like hell, and her head was throbbing. She leaned over and unclasped her other heel, throwing it to the floor. With the way things were going, she might have to scrape up the money to see a witch that dealt with hexes. She was beginning to suspect someone had put a curse on her.

Lance came back, carrying a bottle with two shot glasses stacked on top and a bag full of ice. "This should help with the swelling. Unfortunately, I have nothing for pain, so I brought this." He raised the bottle of whiskey. Azrael watched as he took the shot glasses off and filled them. Lance handed her both shots. She took one and handed the other back.

"You too," she said.

"Why, Azrael, I believe you are trying to get me drunk," he said, a glint of humor in his eyes.

"Pour us another, and I'll confess."

To her surprise, he did as she asked, taking his without question. Afterward, he sat his glass down and stared at her.

"What?" she asked.

"Nothing." He looked away and fidgeted with the collar of his shirt. "If you feel up to it, I thought I would give you some instructions for this weekend. Of course, if you don't think you'll be able to, with your ankle and all, I can ask someone else."

"No, I should be fine after icing it. Go ahead."

"I wrote some instructions down while I was in the kitchen." Lance pulled out a sheet of paper and handed her a set of keys. "This should about cover everything. Anyway, my cell is on there too, so if you don't feel up to it, just call me. Is there somewhere I can put these?"

"Actually, if you could just bring me my purse." She pointed to the small clasp she'd dropped on the floor before he laid her down.

Lance picked up the purse and handed it to her. She placed the note inside, along with the key. While she was doing that, he stood.

"Now's probably a good time to introduce you to Bumpkins."

She didn't have a chance to ask if Bumpkins was his cat before he left the room. Her cell vibrated, and she reached in her purse, pulling out the phone. It was a text from Caleb.

Hey, you coming home soon? My date's gone, and Smellicious is getting anxious.

I'll be up in a few minutes, she replied.

Lance came back to the room. In his arms was the ugliest cat she had ever seen. It had a squished nose and only one eye — the other was sewn shut. Its fur was a mottled mix of tabby cat and rabid squirrel.

Lance sat the cat down on her chest. "This is Bumpkins. He's really quite sweet when you get past his looks."

Bumpkins stared at her with his one orange eye, tail flicking back and forth. "Um, hi, Bumpkins."

The cat hissed and jumped down to the floor, exiting the room.

"Well, it takes time for him to get used to strangers. Anyway, I'm sure you two will get along just fine," Lance remarked.

"What happened to his eye?"

"He was an alley cat. Came with the building. After a while, I started feeding him. One day, when I stepped outside to give him his meal, he wasn't there. I found him a block away, bleeding and near death. I kind of nursed him back to health, and we've been together ever since."

The image of him carrying for an injured creature made her smile. "You know, you're not as big of a jerk as you appear."

"I don't know whether or not to take that as a compliment, but I will since it came from you."

"As you should," she said, taking the bag of ice off her ankle and setting it on the nightstand. "Anyway, I need to get home. Caleb says Smellicious is getting anxious."

"Smellicious?"

Oh, crap. He's the fricking landlord, you idiot.

"Um, yeah, I meant that *he* is getting anxious. Guess I'm drunker than I thought."

"Oh, okay then. Just grab your purse, and I'll carry you up there."

How am I going to get out of this? He'll want to carry me in, and then he will see the damn stink demon. FML.

She slid her legs off the side of the bed and tried to put pressure on her foot. It still hurt like hell, but she'd be able to hobble along. Azrael stood and took a few steps. As long as she hopped on one leg, she'd be okay. "I can make it to the apartment on my own. My ankle barely hurts anymore. Thanks for the offer, though."

"Quit being stubborn, Azrael. How the hell do you think you are going to go up two flights of stairs like that?"

"I'll be fine," she argued, stumbling out of the room. Azrael nearly made it all the way to the door before he stopped her.

"I'm not letting you go up there by yourself. If nothing else, I can at least help hold you up," he said, his arms crossed over his chest.

By the looks of the scowl on his face, she knew there was no getting rid of him. "Fine, just let me text Caleb real quick to let him know I'm coming. He doesn't like surprises."

Azrael pulled her phone out of her purse and, making sure Lance couldn't see the screen, she typed, *Be there in a few. Warning! Lance is with me. Meet us at the door when you hear us. Hide Smellicious!*

"Okay then, let's do this."

Lance wrapped an arm around her waist, and they made their way through the lobby. Deciding there was no use in fighting, she leaned against him. His cologne was something musky but subtle. His hand grazed the thin material of her dress, the sensation causing a slow burning in her core.

Lance cleared his throat. "So, how did you and Caleb meet?

"We met in grade school. I was an outcast, being a witch and all, and Caleb—well, he's just an oddball. We clicked instantly. When he came out and told his parents he was gay, they disowned him. My parents let him move in with us. He's kind of like my big brother and best friend wrapped in one."

"And the agoraphobia?"

"I think it's a mixture of things. Caleb was beat up a lot for being gay. Several years back, he dated a guy who was a proclaimed heterosexual. He fell in love, but the guy wouldn't be seen with him in public. He got suspicious one night and tracked him down at a bar. Caleb cornered him in front of his friends and told them they were lovers. The guy pretended not to know who Caleb was and let his friends beat him half to death. Ever since then, he's had agoraphobia."

Lance tightened his hold on her as they reached the steps. "I'll admit, the two of you are an odd combo, but I can see why it works."

Azrael didn't comment. She was trying to concentrate on how she was going to hobble up the stairs, even with his help.

Lance seemed to notice her hesitation because he leaned her against the wall, giving her a moment to rest. "Just let me carry you. What is your problem?"

She burst out laughing. "My problem? Seriously, have you seen my day? First the event with Mrs. Meyer. Then, I went out of my way to look sexy as possible just to be noticed because my self-esteem *needed* it. I end up with a shapeshifter and a twisted ankle, and the one man whose arms I have spent most of my night in doesn't give a damn whether I look good, thinks I'm a horrible judge of character, and a complete klutz. That's my problem."

Lance rubbed the back of his neck, avoiding eye contact. He opened his mouth to speak but then closed it.

I couldn't be more of an unappreciative bitch.

"Look, I'm sorry, it's just been a dreadful week. You didn't deserve that, and yes, you're right, I'll have to be carried up the stairs." Lance seemed hesitant, so she added, "Please."

He slipped his arms around her and started up the stairs. It wasn't until they reached the second floor that he spoke.

"First, I don't think you're a poor judge of character. I just think you're a little too open to others. That's not a bad thing, but it can be dangerous. Second, I don't think you're a klutz—I *know* it because I see you nearly trip and fall on your way out every day. I'd suggest you invest in some flats."

"Well, I guess that's better than—," she started.

"Wait. I'm not done," he said as they reached the apartment. "Lastly, how sexy you look did not slip by me unnoticed."

Azrael swore her heart skipped an entire beat before starting up again double time. Lance's gaze was intense as he lowered her to the ground. He kept one arm around her waist, leaving no distance between their bodies. She tilted her head, licked her lips. His blue eyes darkened as his pupils threatened to swallow the irises. Lance leaned in, his face mere inches from hers.

The apartment door swung open. "Az, I'm so glad you're—"

Caleb stopped mid-sentence, his mouth hanging open. Lance stepped back, putting distance between them.

"She's, uh, hurt her ankle. She'll need to have it iced. I'll just bring her in and put her on the couch," Lance said, stuffing his free hand in his pocket.

Both her and Caleb spoke at once.

"No, I can make it—"

"I've got her—"

Azrael hobbled forward as Caleb reached out, putting his arm around her waist and pulling her into the apartment. She turned to say goodnight, but Lance was already walking off, his back to her.

Chapter 9

"Okay, can we be done with the silent treatment, please?" Caleb asked, handing her a cup of coffee.

Azrael clasped it between her hands, closing her eyes against the morning sun streaming through the window. Last night, she'd slept on the couch with her ankle propped up and iced. Caleb had questioned her relentlessly about what happened, but with her mood and the fact he'd burst in on what she hoped would be a kiss, Azrael refused to talk about it. Now, having slept, she felt guilty about that.

"I'm sorry. I swear I'm becoming a hateful bitch lately. I don't know what is wrong with me," she admitted, grabbing Caleb's hand and squeezing it.

"Lack of sex, probably, unless someone scored last night," he responded, edging closer to her.

"Nope. No scoring. Just hurt both my pride and my ankle. Seriously though, thank you for icing my ankle and bringing me coffee. You're a lifesaver."

"And don't forget it." Caleb lifted her legs with care and slid under them, setting them across his lap. "Although I am practically foaming at the mouth to find out what events led to that lover's embrace you were in when I opened the door last night."

"Ugh," she replied, covering her face with her hands. "I don't even know what that was. Last night, I could have sworn Lance was going to kiss me, but this morning I'm doubting it."

"Looked like it to me. Why don't you just go down there and ask him?"

"Because he's out of town for a while. Speaking of which, I need to go feed his cat in a little bit."

"Feed his cat? He has a cat? Okay, wait, why don't you start from the beginning?"

For the next hour, she drank her coffee while relaying the events from the night to Caleb. With anyone else, the story would have only taken twenty minutes, but Caleb stopped her every few minutes to ask questions. When she finished, she set her cup of coffee down. "Anyway, that's when you burst out the door."

"He actually said he noticed how sexy you looked?" Caleb asked, his eyes wide.

"Yes."

"Az, he was totally going to kiss you. How can you doubt that? Look at the facts. He broke up your date, paid for your drinks, carried you when you were hurt, called you sexy, and that moment in the hallway—hell baby, the way he was looking at you made *my* knees weak."

"I don't know." Azrael shut her eyes. "He's just so freaking hot and cold."

"Not to mention he's your landlord and temporary boss. Sweetie, you sure can pick them. He's right about those judgement issues of yours."

"Shut up, Caleb."

~*~

It was around five o'clock before she felt stable enough on her ankle to go down to Lance's apartment. The list he'd left her was pretty easy. All she needed to do was take the checks out of the dropbox and put them in a deposit bag for Monday. That and feed the cat. Although she was positive he'd left already, she knocked and waited a second before sliding the key into the lock and opening the door.

The apartment was quiet. Azrael grabbed the checks from the box and sorted them. Minutes passed in eerie silence. Something felt wrong. Every few seconds, she would glance over her shoulder, sure something was behind her. Watching. Waiting. She checked to make sure the door was locked.

"Probably that damn cat," she mumbled.

Speaking of which….

Putting the checks away, she went in search of Bumpkins. "Here, kitty, kitty."

She shook the bag of food, but still no cat. "Come out, come out, wherever you are."

Stupid cat.

Azrael sat the bag of cat food down and searched the apartment. Both the living room and kitchen were empty, leaving her only the bedroom to check. From under the bed, she saw a grey and black striped tail.

"There you are, Bumpkins," she said, moving to the other side of the bed and leaning down. The cat was crouched beneath the railing, its body trembling. "Hey, I won't hurt you."

Bumpkins continued shaking. Azrael decided it was best if she left him alone. She was about to stand up when she saw a magazine under the bed.

Is that the one he was hiding from me?

Azrael glanced over her shoulder, even though she knew

she was alone. Curiosity got the better of her, and she slid her hands underneath the bed, pulling it out.

"You've got to be fricking kidding me."

Her face was on the cover. Underneath it, the caption read, *"Sexy Summoners."* She set the magazine down on the bed, her heart racing. Based on the condition, it wasn't new. Azrael picked it back up and flipped through to the centerfold. The corner was turned down to mark the page. She stared at her naked image, breasts bared, hair flowing about her shoulders, on her face a look of desire.

"How long has he had this?" she mumbled.

"Oh, that thing? About eight months or so."

Azrael dropped the magazine and spun around. A few feet behind her stood a man, his hands shoved in the pockets of his slacks, an expensive pair of sunglasses on his face. He strolled over to her.

Azrael took a few hesitant steps back. "Who are you?"

"Blais," he said, grinning at her. "By your lack of reaction, I'm guessing he hasn't mentioned me."

Although there was nothing to warrant it, a small voice in the back of Azrael's head warned her that Blais was a dangerous man. Not to mention the fact he was in an apartment that was locked from the inside. She thought it was unlikely Lance would have forgotten to mention a guest. "Well, um, he's not here, but I can tell him you stopped by."

"Oh, there's no need for that. I'll leave him my own personal message. I'm curious, though. What is your relationship with Lance?" he asked, moving closer.

It's the glasses, she thought. His features were no different than the average man's, and his tone was charming, but she sensed a darkness in him. A darkness hidden behind tinted lenses.

"I'm just the maid," she said, glancing around for the quickest way to escape, her mouth going dry.

Blais leaned down and picked up the magazine she'd dropped.

"Oh, I think you're a little more than that," he replied, flipping to the centerfold. "You know, I've been wondering what his obsession is with this thing. Not that you aren't sexy as hell, but it's unlike Lance to hold onto anything personal. Now I know why. Sexy and a summoning witch to boot? Tsk, tsk, tsk. Well, we can't have that now. So very unfortunate for you. I think I'll keep this, though." He rolled up the magazine and shoved it in his back pocket.

A bead of sweat ran down her forehead. Her eyes darted to the bedroom door. There was no way she could get past him quick enough, especially with her hurt ankle. She'd just have to stall until the opportunity arose.

"So," she said, leaning against the nightstand, hands feeling around for a weapon. "If you know Lance so well, what's the secret behind his guarded and grumpy attitude?"

"Well, that would be me." He curled his lips up in a toothy grin and reached for her. "By the way, you're discrediting my intelligence. Do you not think I'm aware of you stalling to plan some sort of escape? Lucky for you, I like to play with my toys before I break them."

Azrael darted to the side. The world seemed to slow. She saw Blais reach forward, watched as his hand slipped around her waist, and screamed as he tossed her into the nightstand. She slammed into the ceramic lamp, and it shattered against her lower back. Her knees hit the floor, the pain radiating through her thighs. She tried to crawl away.

His hand clamped over her mouth as he picked her up.

"Don't scream again, or I'll break your neck. There is a small chance I might let you live, for now at least, as long as you behave. Of course, I haven't decided yet. Do you understand?"

She nodded, eyes wide. He was going to kill her. She couldn't overpower him, couldn't fight. Couldn't summon without her spells. In that moment, she heard her grandmother's voice.

You don't need all that mumbo jumbo to cast a summoning spell. The power is inside you. Use it. Summon.

Gran could do it without a spell. Azrael, on the other hand, had never succeeded.

"Now, I'm going to let you go, and I want you to lie down on the bed and be a good girl," Blais said, removing his hand from her mouth.

She moved slowly, not because she didn't want to escape, but because she needed to concentrate.

Partition the mind, she thought, remembering her grandmother's teachings. *Think of it as two separate doors, one in the front, one in the back. Except the back one is hidden. Separate your magic from your mind.*

Azrael envisioned the back door, in it the room with all the strands of purpose. At the same time, she laid down on the bed like Blais instructed.

"Good girl," he said, sitting beside her. "Now, what to do with you? I sent Lance on that little goose chase so I could come here and kill that nasty looking cat of his, but you are a much better prize. If he'd just keep his nose out of my business, then I wouldn't have to leave him a little warning at all."

Azrael entered the room. *I need a protection demon. I need a protection demon. I need a protection demon.*

"So, now I have two choices. I could mess up that pretty

little face of yours as a constant reminder to him, or I could kill you and leave your body here for him to find," Blais said, smiling.

I need a protection demon. I need a protection demon. I need a protection demon.

Azrael spun around in the imaginary room, every strand repelling from her. If she didn't find one soon, she was just going to have to grab something random and hope it was distracting enough for her to escape.

"You know, now that I've given it some thought," Blais said, removing his glasses and wiping them on his shirt. "I'm going to need to kill you. Can't have a summoning witch on my tail. But first, I think I'll take those powers of yours."

Azrael's breath hitched. It wasn't his eyes that terrified her. They were a normal shade of medium blue. It was the tattoos on his eyelids. A taboo to all witches.

"You're a konsumo demon," she whispered.

"Oh, yes. A very successful one too. I've taken more powers from witches than any in history. But don't worry, it doesn't hurt. You won't feel a thing except when I remove your eyelids. That might hurt a bit. Since I need eye contact to withdraw your powers, I'm going to need to remove those. Can't have you blinking in the middle of the process. Hope you understand."

I need a protection demon. I need a protection demon. I need a protection demon.

Azrael watched as he pulled a knife out of his pocket and flicked out the blade. Its sharp edge glistened. Blais leaned in, his mouth pursed in concentration, knife hovering over her right eye.

I NEED PROTECTION!

Azrael felt a strong pull as her powers attached to a strand. She grabbed it and closed the partition, bringing herself fully back to the world. The tip of the knife brushed against her lids as she thrust her hand out, casting her power.

A cloud of smoke filled the room, and Blais jumped back. Azrael tried to roll off the bed in the opposite direction, but he grabbed her ankle. She screamed and kicked him in the face. He let go, and she fell to the floor. Blais started after her but froze when the smoke cleared. Lance was standing above her, looking down, a bewildered expression on his face.

"Azrael, what the hell are you—?" He stopped short, realizing they weren't alone. "Blais," he seethed, his eyes darkening as he looked at the other man.

Chapter 10

"Why is it you always show up and ruin all the fun, Lance?" Blais shook his head. "Never mind. I'm suddenly in a bit of a hurry, so we'll have to catch up next time. As for you, my sexy summoner, don't be remiss. I'll be coming for you again soon enough."

"You son of a bitch. I will kill you." Lance bolted across the bed.

Blais fled to the other side of the room and pulled something silver out of his pocket. Before Lance could get his hands on him, he disappeared into thin air. Lance made a loud growling noise and punched the wall. Pieces of sheetrock fell to the floor. He turned, white powder clinging to his clenched fists. His face softened when it landed on hers.

"Are you okay?" he asked, crossing the room to kneel at her side.

"I...I...no." To Azrael's surprise, she burst into tears.

Lance lifted her and carried her to the bed, where she curled into a fetal position.

"Shh...," he said, brushing the hair out of her eyes. "You're safe now. It's okay."

Azrael had no concept of how much time passed before she was calm enough to stop crying and sit up, but the sun streaming into the room seemed much lower on the horizon when she did. Lance was sitting beside her, his face screwed into a grimace.

"I'm so sorry, Azrael. I didn't mean for this to happen to you. I had no idea." He paused, shaking his head. "There is blood on the back of your shirt. Let me get you cleaned up, and we can talk about this."

"He was going to take my powers and kill me," she whispered.

"I know," Lance said, biting his lip. "Please, let me clean you up. I promise I'll explain everything."

He stood and walked out of the room. Azrael curled her knees under her chin, eyes darting around the room. Bumpkins jumped on the bed beside her, causing her to flinch. After a second, she picked the cat up and sat him on her lap. Anything to not be alone. Bumpkins seemed to understand because he curled up and started purring. Azrael felt calmer by the time Lance returned, carrying a bottle of rubbing alcohol and some towels.

"You can cover yourself with this," he said, handing her a towel and turning around.

She realized he meant for her to take off her shirt. For a second, she hesitated but then decided she was too hurt to care. Azrael slipped the shirt off and set it to the side, surprised by how much blood was covering the back of it. She covered her bra with the towel.

"I'm covered now," she said.

Lance turned around, taking care to keep his eyes on her face as he walked behind her. She heard him sigh as he opened the bottle of rubbing alcohol.

"It could have been much worse, as I suspect you know by

now," he said. "Blais is an evil man. Once I thought he was my friend. There was a time when I truly thought we believed in the same thing."

"He's a konsumu demon," she said, flinching as he cleaned the glass out of her wound.

"Yes, but a long time ago, he was a kid the same as I. A street rat begging for food. When we were sixteen, he came up with a plan to start our own business, to make our lives better. We each had our own skills and were very successful. I was content, but he wanted more. I knew he'd changed, felt his anger growing, but ignored it. Like I said, I was content."

He stopped cleaning her wound. She could feel the agony in his voice. "More money was coming in than should have been. Still, I turned my head. At some point, I could no longer ignore the reports of murder, of women whose eyelids were removed. The day I caught him...."

His voice trailed off, and Azrael shivered, the wounds in her back forgotten.

"Anyway," Lance said, putting the rag on her back again. "I confronted him. I wanted to kill him that day—still do. I've spent the last ten years trying to hunt him down. I watch the news, listening for stories of women whose eyelids have been removed. That's why I was gone this weekend. I hired someone to find him, to keep their ear to the ground. I had no idea he'd been watching me, Azrael, or I wouldn't have asked you to do this."

"Should we call the cops?" she asked.

Lance shook his head. "No, the cops can't stop him. They've been trying to catch him for years. He's too powerful. Blais has been taking witch's magic and storing it in amulets for a decade. Who knows what type of powers he controls? Okay, I've got you cleaned up. Just scratches for the most part. I'll get you a shirt to put on."

Azrael watched as Lance stepped around the bed and opened his closet. He pulled out a white button down and handed it to her. "Here."

She reached for the shirt. "Is he going to come back for me?"

"Put that on. I'll be back in a minute." Lance left the room, not answering.

Azrael stood and put on the shirt. She was rolling the sleeves up when he came back in.

"You didn't answer me," she accused.

Lance strolled over to her and sighed. He grabbed the other sleeve to help her roll it up. "Yes, he'll come back for you."

Azrael shuddered.

Lance slid his hand under her chin and lifted her eyes to meet his. "I will not let that happen. We're going to go upstairs and pack your things. I've got a safe place we can go until we can figure this out."

"You think he'll come after Caleb?"

"I don't know, but we can bring him too. Can I ask you something?"

She nodded.

"How did you summon me?"

"I don't really know. I was trying to summon a protector demon but somehow summoned you instead."

"Huh," he said, his eyes becoming distant. Finally, he dropped his hand. "In any means, we need to get going. Blais was caught by surprise, but that won't last long. Come on, Bumpkins."

Lance turned and stepped out of the room, leaving Azrael

and Bumpkins to follow.

~*~

On the way to her apartment, Azrael caught Lance up on everything Blais had said, leaving out the part about the magazine. When they got there, she stepped inside, followed by Lance. Caleb was pacing the living room, phone on his ear, his back to them. She held up a finger, cautioning Lance to wait in the hallway for a second. Caleb turned around as she sat her purse on the table.

"Where the hell have you been? I've been calling and texting. You should have been home hours ago," Caleb said, dropping the phone.

"I'm sorry, Caleb. I didn't mean to scare you. Lance and I will explain everything."

"Lance?"

Lance came around the corner and stood next to Azrael. Caleb's eyes darted back and forth between the two, then settled on the shirt Azrael was wearing. His eyes widened. "Oh, I see. Baby girl, please tell me you at least bartered to lower our rent payment before you —"

"Caleb," Azrael shouted, her cheeks flushed. "No, no... just stop. We don't have much time."

"Are you leaving or something?" Caleb asked.

"No," Lance said, joining the conversation. "Azrael was attacked by a konsumo demon. She's okay for now, but he will come back for her. I have somewhere safe to take the both of you, but we have to hurry. I need you both to pack and be ready in ten minutes."

Caleb's jaw dropped open, and he raced forward, pulling her to his chest. "Az, is it true? Are you okay? How did this happen?"

"I'm okay, I promise," she whispered in his ear. "I'll explain everything when we're safe, but we need to pack right now."

Caleb shook his head, "I can't. I want to be there for you, but I can't do this."

"He'll come after you too. You're going one way or another if I have to have Lance knock you out."

"Az—"

"No. Go get packed right now. I'll grab my stuff, and we'll give you a tranquilizer in five minutes. You won't even know you've left."

Caleb swallowed but nodded. He was walking off when Bumpkins darted into the living room. The cat ran up to Lance and tried to climb his pant leg.

"What the hell is up with you?" Lance asked, picking Bumpkins up.

Azrael had forgotten about Smellicious, but before she had time to warn Lance, the stink demon came barreling around the corner and slammed into him.

"What the bloody hell? A stink demon? This thing better not be yours, Azrael," he demanded through clenched jaws.

"It was a summoning gone wrong, and I accidentally attached him to me, and, well…." Azrael motioned toward Smellicious.

Lance put the cat on the counter and covered his face with his hands. "Azrael, you're going to be the death of me."

Chapter 11

They wheeled an unconscious Caleb into the diablo inter-dimensional portlines. His head lolled around the back of the wheelchair as if he were studying the limestone walls. The large dome ceiling was intersected by five white marble arches, between each a large screen televising views of other scenic cities and travel locations. Both humans and demons hustled about, some waiting on benches beneath the manmade gardens, others sleeping on the ground using their suitcases as pillows.

When Azrael found out Lance was taking them to Demonium, she was a little surprised. She figured that was the last place they needed to be with a konsumo demon hunting them down. Still, she had no other option but to trust him. After checking in at the front desk, they took their tickets to the security line.

"Registration papers and passports," called out one of the attendants, his feelers twitching impatiently when he looked at Caleb.

Azrael handed him her and Caleb's passports, along with the registration papers for Smellicious. He scanned each and handed them back. When Lance leaned in and gave him his papers, the attendant's eyes widened.

"Ah, Mr. Jenkins, welcome back. Would you like to take the scenic route?"

"Not this time," he said, angling his head toward Caleb. "We're in a bit of a hurry."

"Of course, of course." The attendant pointed them to the left. "Tunnel A7 is free to use."

"Thank you."

Azrael cut her eyes to Lance. She'd only fallen a handful of times, but her experiences included waiting hours, packed body to body, for a tunnel.

Lance shrugged. "I fall a lot and am on the preferred customer list."

She added that statement to the list of questions she was preparing to ask him when they got settled in. Although she had a feeling he wasn't going to be very talkative. Since they'd left the apartment, he'd been very close mouthed, going out of his way to avoid answering any of her questions directly.

They arrived outside the tunnel and scanned their tickets again. Two large steel doors, cut into the limestone, with the Diablo Inter-Dimensional Portlines logo painted on them, loomed ahead. A pretty blonde in a uniform approached them.

"Good afternoon. Thank you for falling with Diablo Inter-Dimensional Portlines. We will start boarding momentarily." The blonde, whose nametag read Debbie, typed several coordinates into her touch screen. "All right, stand back, please."

They took a step back and the doors opened with a loud whoosh. Inside was a circular room carved from limestone with a metal platform in the middle. On top of the platform was a large velvet cushion. The attendant ushered them forward.

"Please put all loose items, including shoes, belts, and

phones, in the bin located on the left side of the platform and the wheelchair in the allotted vehicle section. Pets go in the cages beside the vehicle section. When you are done, choose which scene you would like to see during your fall on the touchscreen to your right. If you need assistance with the unconscious passenger, let us know now."

"No, we'll be fine," Lance said, picking up Caleb and laying him on the cushion, not the least strained from carrying another grown man.

While he put away the pets, Azrael removed Caleb's belt and shoes and secured the strap across his waist. She did the same with her own items and placed them in the bins along with Caleb's.

"Do you want to come and pick a scene?" Lance asked.

"No, you do it. I plan on keeping my eyes closed in fear the whole time."

"Afraid of falling?"

"Yep."

"It's not so bad when you get used to it, you know."

"Let's just hope I never have to find out."

Lance grinned at her. While he went over to pick the scene, Azrael laid on the cushion and took several deep breaths.

Lance laid down beside her, and she had to scoot over closer to Caleb, her body squished between the two men. She was either going to have to cross her arms over her chest or lay them over the both of them. In the end, she decided to cross her arms.

The uniformed blonde stood at the front of the cavern. "This inter-dimensional trip is scheduled for arrival at 9:45 p.m. There will be a ten-minute fall, followed by a five-minute transition phase. When you land at your destination, please do not get up until the five-minute transition period has passed. If, at the slight chance, one of you becomes lost and stuck between dimensions, please do not panic. Our team will locate you and deliver you to your destination shortly. We will start the countdown to take off in just a moment. There is a stream advisory in effect today, so you will be experiencing above normal levels of turbulence."

Great, Azrael thought. The blonde attendant left, and she squeezed her eyes shut.

"You okay?" Lance asked as the doors shut.

"Trying to be."

"Do you want me to hold your hand or something?"

"No," she said between breaths. "I'll be fine."

The attendant's voice came over the loudspeaker. "Preparing for drop off."

The platform began to spin, and Azrael tensed. Unable to keep her eyes closed, she opened them and stared at the ceiling as the platform picked up speed.

I should have taken one of Caleb's tranquilizers.

The platform moved faster.

The attendant spoke over the intercom again. "Take off in ten, nine, eight, seven, six, five, four, three, two, one."

The floor slid open beneath them.

Azrael dropped her arms and grabbed onto Lance and Caleb as she felt them plummet. Above them, the empty room faded to darkness. Her whole body tingled. Others described the feeling of moving through dimensions as sensual. What a load of crap. The only thing sensual about this would be the relief she felt after landing. Everything became dark, and for a moment, it felt like they were floating in a vacuum. Then the screens came on. All around and above them was a moving scene of a room with a crackling fireplace.

"I thought this would be the most relaxing," Lance

whispered.

If I could just relax, it might be, she thought, watching the flames. It was almost like being there.

"Azrael," Lance said, putting his hand on hers. "You're about to break my thigh, and probably Caleb's too."

"Oh, sorry," she said, loosening her grasp.

"You need to focus on something else. What do you normally do to relax?"

"I drink."

He cut his eyes to the side. "Why am I not surprised?"

"Look, can you just talk about something, anything?"

"Okay then," he said. "It's a long shot, but I have a plan to destroy Blais."

"Really?" Azrael said, momentarily forgetting their fall. "What is it?"

"If you could summon him—"

"No." She squeezed her eyes shut.

"Azrael, just listen to me. This will work as lon—"

"No, you listen to me. There is no way in hell I'll summon that evil man. First of all, I'd have to be in the room. Secondly, you've already said that no one has any idea of what he is capable of. What would you do if I summoned him?"

"Killing him came to mind."

Azrael shook her head. "I won't, and I can't. Even if I could summon him, which the chances of that are slight, I wouldn't dare."

"I've tried other summoners. They won't touch the case because he's a criminal. You're my only chance."

"I'm sorry, Lance, but no. It's too dangerous."

He propped up on his elbow, looking down at her. "Is there nothing I can say to convince you?"

She shook her head. The fireplace blipped out momentarily, and their cushion rocked harshly, catching turbulence in the streams. Azrael squeezed Lance's hand and held her breath. After a moment, the cushion stilled.

"You know, I might be able to help you if you'll trust me."

Azrael threw up her hands. "Like I have any other choice at this point in my life?"

"Good point. In that case, close your eyes and don't move."

She gave him a sideways glance but did as he asked. He scooted closer to her, pressing against her side. The zipper from his pants brushed the back of her hand.

This is so not going to help me relax.

"Falling actually feels really good, Azrael, if you allow it to. I've known many women who've experienced complete bliss. You just have to teach yourself how to," he whispered in her ear.

Azrael's heart thudded against her chest. His voice sent electrical shocks down her entire body, causing her breathing to pick up pace.

"Take a few deep breaths," he whispered, putting a hand on her stomach. Her shirt had come up just enough for his thumb to brush her bare skin. "Now, I'm going to say some words to you. Don't focus on them, just my voice."

Lance put his face closer to hers. She could feel his five o'clock shadow brush her cheek. He began to whisper, his voice so low and soft. Azrael could not hear the words, but with every syllable, his lips caressed her earlobe. His thumb glided back and forth over her stomach while his soft voice pounded through her. Her core clenched, burned, then released with each octave. She'd never experienced such pleasure and pain from something as simple as being whispered to. Azrael let herself go, riding the myriad of sensations.

"We will be arriving at your destination in one minute. Please be sure to remain in position for five minutes upon landing, so you do not become disorientated. Once again, thank you for traveling with Diablo International."

"What the hell!" Azrael exclaimed, her eyes popping open. "Did I fall asleep? How did you do that?"

Lance was staring down at her, his eyes dark. "Just something I picked up once. I'm guessing it worked."

"I don't remember anything, just remember hearing your voice and feeling…." She let the words trail off.

"Feeling what?" he pressed, his voice shades softer.

Like I was having an hour-long orgasm.

She wasn't going to tell him that, though. Every time she suspected he desired her, he immediately turned around and acted like he didn't.

"Nothing. It just felt different," she said.

"Well, maybe we can try it again after you summon Blais."

Azrael grimaced. "I already told you I wouldn't summon him, so please drop it."

Lance gaped at her.

What did he think? I'd change my mind because he did… whatever the hell he just did?

The screen changed from the fireplace scene to a countdown for landing, and she tensed. "I wish it had worked long enough for me to forget about the landing. It's nearly as bad as taking off."

"Oh, I can help you forget that," he said, his eyes darkening.

Lance leaned down and pressed his lips against hers.

Chapter 12

He traced his tongue along her bottom lip, forcing it open. The initial surprise faded as she tasted him, felt his lips crushing hers, the five o'clock stubble rubbing her sensitive chin. She grabbed a handful of his hair and pulled him closer. Azrael pushed the kiss deeper, rolling her tongue against his, drinking him in. Lance groaned, and she felt the tremor slide down her throat. She clung to him, digging in with her nails, raw need consuming her.

Lance pulled away, and she moaned.

"Landing. Stay still," he said, his voice full of gravel.

A sense of weightlessness, of falling, washed over her. With a whoosh of air, the room stopped spinning, and Azrael found herself lying on a hard floor. Her vision blurred, white fog hanging around the edges. She blinked several times to clear it and tried to lift her head, but it was too heavy.

"Stay still. Give yourself time to adjust."

Lance's face came into view. He stood and walked out of sight, leaving her there while her body adjusted to the dimension. When she felt stable enough, Azrael sat up slowly. The room spun. "Ugh."

Lance came back into the room carrying Bumpkins, Smellicious at his side.

"How are you even standing right now?" she asked.

"Like I said, I fly a lot. You get used to it."

Azrael squinted, trying to see him better. There was an edge to his voice, and he was avoiding eye contact.

He just kissed me. Now he's acting all broody again. What the hell?

"So, um, where are we?" Azrael looked around. They appeared to be in a large library. Bookshelves covered the walls, and expensive-looking furniture surrounded them. She and Caleb were laying on a throw rug in the center of the room, the Inter-Dimensional cushion already gone.

"A safe house." He laid her shoes and phone beside her.

"Yeah, I figured that but whose safe house?"

"Mine," Lance said, seeming to become suddenly interested in the throw pillows on the couch.

"Yours? You mean this is your house?"

"Yes."

No fricking way, Azrael thought, barely stopping the words before they came out of her mouth. She stood, using the couch for support. With wide eyes, she walked the library, running her hands over stone carvings and marble tabletops. Glancing out the open doorway, she saw a large living room with a fireplace and winding staircase.

This is not a house. This is a mansion.

"If you own this, why do you stay at the apartment?"

"Because it wouldn't make any sense for me to fall every day of the week," he said, his arms crossed over his chest. "Anyway, I'm going to take Caleb to his room. Yours will be across the hall. I've got a few things to do, so go ahead and settle in."

"That's it?" Azrael spun around. "You're just going to throw us in our rooms and, and...?" She had no idea how to finish that sentence. Azrael gritted her teeth.

"What were you expecting?" Lance asked.

"I don't know. An explanation, maybe? I thought we would sit down and discuss everything when we got here."

Lance shook his head. "There is nothing to discuss. I brought you two here to keep you safe. That's it."

"Really? Really?" She thrust out her arms. "What about this place? How the hell do you own a mansion? What about Blais? What's the plan there? What's the story behind you two? Why do you think you can kill him? How do you think you can protect us? And...and...you fricking kissed me."

Azrael crossed her arms over her chest and glared at him.

He matched her stance. "I already told you. I used to be in business with Blais. We were very successful. That's why I own this home. As for how to kill him, I'm still working that out. This house has multiple protection spells. He won't find you here." He paused and took a deep breath before continuing. "The kiss was just a distraction from the landing, Azrael. Nothing more."

"A distraction?" Azrael could feel her nails biting into her palm.

"Yes," he said, holding her gaze.

"And you're going to stick with that story, huh?"

He didn't answer.

If the bastard didn't want to admit he enjoyed it, even though he kept a nude picture of her on his bedside, so be it. *Two can play that game.* "Fine then." She waved her hand at Caleb. "By all means, take him to his room."

"Azrael—"

She stomped off to explore the rest of the house, not giving him a chance to finish.

~*~

Azrael spent the next few hours walking around in awe. As far as she could tell, the house had nine bedrooms, five bathrooms, and three dens. There was a balcony on the second floor overlooking a courtyard. They appeared to be nested in a hill, surrounded by trees. Other than the long driveway leading out, she couldn't see a road. She had seen Lance get in his car over an hour ago and drive off, though.

A BMW. Of course, he drives a BMW.

Even though the house was fully furnished, she found it hard to put together anything telling her about his personality. So far, all the rooms looked like they were decorated based on a picture from a home improvement magazine. Azrael tried to open the last door at the end of the second-floor hallway, but it was locked.

"Is this where you hide your personality, Lance?" she mumbled.

For a brief second, she considered trying to break in but shrugged it off. With her luck, she'd get caught or killed by something in that room. She walked by the balcony and saw his car pulling in. Azrael decided to check on Caleb. When she got to the room, he was just starting to stir.

"Baby girl, you mind telling me where we are and what the hell is going on?"

She'd considered warming him up slowly, but the events of the day came spilling out of her mouth. When she was done, Caleb stared at her in silence.

"Well?" she asked.

"I don't know where to start," he said. "This is a lot to take in."

"I know." She covered her face with her hands. "I meant to tell you slowly, let you adjust, but I don't know, I couldn't stop once I started."

"Az, I'm not blaming you. I don't know how you've been so strong today. Come here."

She lifted her head to see Caleb holding out his arms. Azrael crawled over to him, and he pulled her into her lap, stroking her hair.

"Listen, this is a lot to take in, but first of all, I'm glad you're safe. I'm glad Lance is promising to protect you. That being said, I don't trust him."

"Caleb, we have no choice, he's—"

"Oh, I know we have nowhere else to go right now, but that doesn't mean we have to trust him. I think we should proceed with caution."

"Of course, we should. I never said we shouldn't."

Caleb put a hand under her chin and lifted her eyes to his. "Baby, I'm going to have to be honest with you. I don't think you are thinking about things clearly. Honestly, I've never seen you so blinded. Don't take me wrong, you're not the best judge of character, but this is different."

"You're acting like I'm some lovesick puppy who's just going along for the ride. I'm not an idiot. I don't trust him either. I know he's hiding things, being secretive."

Caleb frowned. "I don't want you to think I'm judging you. I just think this 'chemistry' between the two of you is clouding your thinking."

"Chemistry? There's no chemistry. He's an asshole who doesn't feel anything for me at all."

"Obviously. That's why he kept a nude picture of you on

his bedside and kissed you," Caleb said, frowning. "Even if you ignore all of that, look at this place. He's obviously rich, but he manages run-down apartments? Az, those have to be a front. This is his real life. Whatever business he ran with his demon friend had to be illegal. He could have lived here happily ever after if not. It's a cover up."

Azrael's heart sunk in her chest. "Oh, I didn't think about it like that."

"With what you've been through, both physically and emotionally, I wouldn't expect you to. That's what I'm here for."

"I don't know what I'd do without you," she whispered, snuggling in.

"You don't have to." Caleb leaned down to give her a peck on the lips.

"Dinner is ready if—"

Lance stopped mid-sentence. Caleb lifted his head. The two men met gazes, and she felt the air in the room grow thicker.

"Oh, you're awake. Good," Lance said, his face darkening several shades.

"Yes, I am, and thanks for the help," Caleb answered, smirking. He leaned over and kissed Azrael on the forehead. "We'll be down in just a minute."

Lance gave a slight nod, spun on his heels, and exited the room.

"What was that?" she asked.

"That, baby girl, was a jealous man."

Chapter 13

She led Caleb to the dining room. When she turned the corner, her eyes widened at the table full of food. Azrael's stomach rumbled. She couldn't remember the last time she'd eaten.

"I didn't know what you liked, so I just made a few different things. I hope that's okay." Lance fidgeted with the tablecloth.

"It looks great. With how hungry I am, the more food, the better. Thanks," she said, taking a seat. For the next fifteen minutes, they ate in awkward silence.

One more thing to add to the list, he can cook.

Azrael wolfed down the hamburger, had a helping of penne pasta and garlic toast, and even tried some of the chargue salad, a traditional dish of Demonium she hadn't tasted since she was a kid. She sat her water to the side, reached for one of the open bottles of wine sitting on the table, and read the label. *Three hundred years old, seriously? I bet he has a wine cellar. That'll be next on my list to find.*

She poured herself a glass and lifted it to her lips. As for taste, there didn't seem to be much difference between a five-year-old bottle of wine and a three-hundred-year-old one. She finished the glass in a few gulps and reached for the bottle again.

Lance crinkled his nose. "You do realize expensive wine should be sipped, not guzzled. Also, this brings me back to your alcoholism."

"Expensive wine? Heck, yeah. Hand me that bottle, Az," Caleb said, wiping his mouth on his napkin before holding out his hand.

She handed him the bottle and gave Lance a smirk. He shook his head, but she thought she saw the corner of his mouth twitch up.

Lance leaned back in his chair. "So, since Caleb is up, I think this might be a good time to come up with some options about what we are going to do about Blais's threat. I was thinking this solution will work temporarily, but since Azrael is not willing to summon him, we need to consider a permanent option to keep her hidden. I was thinking —"

"Whoa, wait just a minute," Caleb said, cutting in. "Can we just back up for a second? Admittedly, I've been a little out of the loop, but I think Az has caught me up for the most part. You can't just expect us to go along with any plan you make without you explaining what the hell is going on."

"I explained what was going on," Lance replied. "Blais and I used to be in business together. He's a killer. I'm going to kill him. I don't understand what part of that is hard for either of you to grasp."

"Well," Caleb tapped his fork on the plate, "where do I start? How about the part where our landlord, who owns a bunch of run-down apartments, lives like a king in Demonium? What type of business were the two of you in that you need a front to hide your riches?"

"We sold amulets, treasures of sort. I hunted them down, he sold them. No, it wasn't legal, but we were both young and successful enough we didn't care. I own the apartments to pay the taxes here. Since I'm no longer running an illegal business, I need to focus all my resources on trying to hunt down Blais. Satisfied?" Lance crossed his arms over his chest.

"So, you've contacted the police about these murders, you've got someone trying to track him down, and from what you've said, you've tried to hire people for magical assistance. Why the obsession? I understand he was your friend, but you've done all you can. Why not leave it in the hands of the authorities?"

Lance leaned forward and propped his arms on the table, studying his fingers. For a moment, he said nothing. Caleb shared a look with Azrael, and she shrugged.

"I'll admit, it is an obsession," Lance said, his voice low. He looked at both of them. "Blais was always there for me. He watched over me, fought for me. I looked up to him, practically worshipped the ground he walked on. It was always just the two of us." Lance paused and leaned over, grabbing the bottle of wine. He poured himself a glass and took several large gulps before continuing. "Then I met someone and fell in love. He killed her because of me."

The room rang silent. Although his face showed nothing of what he was feeling, the agony hanging in the air was gut-wrenching.

When Lance set his glass down, he narrowed his eyes at her and Caleb. "What, no more questions?"

"I'm sorry," Azrael whispered.

He flinched. "Don't be. It's my fault. My burden to carry. Not yours."

"I'm sorry, too, whether you want me to be or not," Caleb added.

"I don't deserve your sympathy, trust me. Now, can we

get back to the planning?"

They both nodded.

"Well, since you are refusing to summon Blais, and since I can't stomach the idea of having to permanently house the two of you for roommates, I think our best option is to find some people here in Demonium to cast a protection spell on the both of you. I'm willing to help you start up with new identities, but then you will be on your own."

"Wait. You're saying we need to go into hiding? Permanently?" Azrael asked.

"At least until Blais is dead. I see no other option. He will do everything he can to make good on his threat, Azrael. I know Blais."

"So, our choices are to summon him and maybe die or spend our lives in hiding? Gee, how gratuitous of you," Caleb said, sarcasm dripping from every word.

"I don't know what else to do. I really wish the two of you would stop trying to pin me out to be the bad guy. I'm trying to help."

"Could you summon him? Or maybe some protection demons for us?" Caleb asked, directing his question at Azrael.

"As for protection demons, very unlikely. The closer you are to a person, the harder it is to do a summoning spell. Your desires cloud the purpose. Even then, protection demons aren't infallible. I don't think I could summon Blais either. If he's that powerful, he's probably blocked himself from summoners. It would take an extremely strong witch to get past that."

"Which you are. Hell, Az, you summoned Lance from nothing."

Azrael could see the gleam in Lance's eyes. She didn't want to give him any hope she'd be willing to do it or could do it.

"Do I need to point out the stink demon incident?"

"She has a point there," Lance said, shifting in his chair.

"That's not fair. There were other circumstances involved there. She was distracted. She summoned you while your friend tried to kill her."

"Now he has a point," Lance remarked. "What kind of circumstance was it that led you to summon the stink demon?"

"Ugh, don't ask me that."

"It would be nice to know so I can get a better idea of what we are up against."

"It's stupid," she said, putting her face in her hands. "My ex came by and took a picture of me while I was trying to summon."

"That's it? An ex taking a picture?" Lance asked, disbelief coloring his tone.

"It was the same ex who took a nude picture of her and sold it to the Demonium Times as a centerfold," Caleb said, leaning in and folding his hands over the table. "You know the one I'm talking about."

Lance picked up his wine and took a drink. "Can't say that I do."

Really? I'm calling his bullshit.

She removed her face from her hands and locked her eyes on him. "It's the one you keep on your nightstand, Lance."

Lance choked on his wine and began to cough. She watched him from across the table, fighting to keep the smirk off her face. When he got control of himself, he glared at her.

She glared back.

Lance shoved his chair back and stood. "I'm going to bed."

"Why? Because you don't want to admit the truth?" Caleb challenged.

"No," Lance said over his shoulder as he walked out. "Because if I don't leave, I'm going to strangle the both of you myself."

~*~

Azrael kicked the covers off and flipped on the lamp with a sigh. Pillow top mattress, expensive sheets with a thread count she imagined cost more than a month's salary for her, and she still couldn't get her brain to shut down. The lamplight cast a relaxing glow, but it didn't reach the far dark corners of the room, didn't dispel her fear of being watched. It was quiet. Dead quiet. Azrael shivered.

Lance said it was safe here.

"Lance says a lot of things but doesn't bother to explain them," she mumbled, reaching down to pet Smellicious. The stink demon rolled over and snorted. Azrael stood and stretched. Closing her eyes, she recalled the image of Lance sitting at the table, his face pained.

"Ugh." She opened her eyes and kicked the nightstand, then winced at the pain shooting up her calf. Served her right. She should have listened to Lance when he told her she was a bad judge of character. Taken it as a warning, cut and run.

"Not a choice anymore," she mumbled. "I must be suicidal."

Smellicious groaned and lifted his tail. Whatever he'd digested for dinner seemed to amplify his already unbearable odor. Azrael ran to the window, eyes watering, choking back a gag. The panes were sealed from years of being shut, but after several hard pulls, she was finally able to push it open. She shoved her head out the window, breathing deeply.

"Like I needed another thing to keep me from sleeping."

It was either close the window and suffocate or leave it

open and worry about Blais getting in.

"Or...go bunk with Caleb." Azrael shut the window and tiptoed across the hallway.

She opened the door to Caleb's room. He was sprawled across the bed, his mouth slack. She pulled back the covers and slid in beside him.

Caleb opened his eyes. "What's going on?"

"I couldn't sleep. Mind if I bunk with you?" she asked.

"That's fine," he mumbled, his eyes slipping closed again.

Azrael scooted in and laid her head on his chest. The rhythmic beat of his heart lulled her to sleep.

~*~

The door swung open, slamming into the wall, waking them both.

"Have you seen—?" Lance stopped mid-sentence, eyes narrowing to slits. "Sorry. I couldn't find Azrael, and I thought something might have happened."

Azrael slid out from beneath Caleb's arms, dragging the blanket around her as she sat. Lance was standing in the doorway, hands on his hips. "I couldn't sleep, so I came in here."

"Yeah, well, the next time you two want to sleep together, maybe you could warn me. I woke up to find your room empty. I can't protect you when I don't know where you are."

Before she could comment, he pivoted and slammed the door shut behind him.

"Was that fear or jealousy?" Azrael asked, sagging against the headboard.

"Baby, it is way too early for me to psychoanalyze anyone, especially Lance," Caleb grumbled.

Azrael slipped out from beneath the covers with a sigh. "I guess I better go deal with that."

"Please do." Caleb covered his eyes with his arms. "Also, please let your boyfriend know seven in the morning is way too early for his pissy outbursts."

"Oh, trust me, I plan on it."

Azrael stormed out of the room and down the hallway. If Lance was concerned about her, he was sure going about showing it the wrong way. She'd had enough of his hot and cold bull crap. When she made it to his room, she threw open the door without bothering to knock.

"What the hell is your problem?" she asked, hands on her hips.

Lance was pacing the floor, running his hands through his hair. He stopped to stare at her. His sweats hung low on his hips, a white T-shirt clinging to his muscles. "I don't know," he said, running his tongue over his teeth. "I just…I couldn't find you. I thought you might be dead. I can't go through that again."

Softening her stance, Azrael studied his face. He looked different. *Vulnerable.* "I'm sorry. I didn't realize—"

"It's not your fault," he said, cutting her off and shaking his head. "I shouldn't have barged in like that."

She tugged on the hem of her shirt but kept her eyes on him. *He's afraid. Afraid and sad.* "Do you still love her?"

"Yeah, I don't have much of a choice," he answered, licking his lips.

"I'm sorry. I really am," she whispered. "I know this is going to sound shallow, but have you tried to move on, tried to forget this obsession with Blais and find happiness?"

"Of course I have. You think I like living this way? Even if I did try, what would happen? We barely know each other, and if you hadn't summoned me, you'd be dead."

Azrael shuddered. He was right. She couldn't imagine

living a life in which anyone you got close to was in danger of dying. *Maybe I have judged him unfairly.* What was he like before all of this? What type of man would the woman he loved see? The words slipped out of her mouth before she could stop them. "Did she love you, too?"

Lance's face fell. He stepped across the room and sat on the bed, leaning forward on his elbows. "I thought she would — that she could — but later, I wondered. I think she saw through me. A man she couldn't love. Didn't want to love. I never got the chance to find out, though."

"I'm sorry. I shouldn't have asked that."

"No, it's fine." Lance licked his lips. "You know since we're being honest with each other. You and Caleb. Are you two...?" He let the words trail off.

Azrael grinned and shook her head. "Together? No. Caleb's like super gay, and we're more like brother and sister anyway."

"Most brothers and sisters don't kiss and sleep together, Azrael."

"We're more comfortable with each other than I think most people are. Remember how I said I took care of him after he was hurt?"

Lance nodded.

"Well, that included changing his catheter and giving him sponge baths. You really find out what you're willing to do for those you love in those types of situations."

"Yeah, I guess I didn't think about that. I wasn't meaning to pry. I just didn't know if I should be expecting to walk in on the two of you, um, together."

"Oh, no, we've never had sex together." Azrael frowned. "I mean, we've had sex together, just not with each other." He gaped at her, and heat blossomed on her cheeks. "I, um, I mean, we haven't had intercourse with each other. There was this guy once who liked us both and —"

Lance shook his head. "I don't need the details, okay?"

"Okay," she said, biting her lip. "You know, since we're still being honest with each other, it's your turn again."

"What?"

"The magazine."

She'd expected a glare, maybe a brush-off, not the answer he gave her.

Lance stared directly into her eyes. "You look like her. The woman I loved. When I first saw you, I couldn't breathe. I thought you were a ghost come back to haunt me, but then you opened your mouth and ruined everything. She was refined, graceful. You're — well, honestly, you're kind of a mess and spastic, but you don't look that way in the photo. Sexy and sophisticated, but vulnerable. In that photo, you're more her to me than you. I know that sounds rude and horrible, but I'm trying to be honest. It's confusing."

"No," Azrael whispered, shaking her head, trying to ignore the knife twisting in her heart. "Actually, for the first time, something you said makes sense. Thank you for telling me."

It's not me he's attracted to. It's a dead woman.

"You're angry with me."

"No, not at all."

Lance stared at her for a long time. She struggled to keep the hurt expression off her face.

"Okay then. I wanted you to know that I plan to take the stink demon into town today to work with a demon whisperer about that smell. I've seen her train one before. While she's doing that, I'm going to see what I can find out about protection spells for the two of you."

"Can I go?" It had been ages since Azrael had visited Demonium, and she didn't relish the idea of being cooped in.

"I don't think that's a good idea. The house is safe, but not out there."

"Please. We'll be in public, and he won't attack us there. Look, I've had a really bad few weeks and need a break. It's been years since I've been to a Demonium market." Lance didn't say yes, but he sighed. She knew he wasn't going to argue further. "So, when are we leaving?"

"Around noon. First breakfast, then I have a few things to do."

"Sounds good. You want me to cook?"

"No. The last thing I want you near is an open flame or my food."

Chapter 14

"What are you staring at?" Azrael asked, setting her empty cup of coffee in the sink.

Caleb looked over his shoulder. "Lance working out without his shirt on."

Azrael bit her lip, suppressing a grin. Caleb winked at her, and she burst out laughing. "Fine then, scoot over."

They both stared through the small kitchen window at the man lifting weights under the morning sun. His jogging pants hung low on his hips. His chest gleamed with sweat, beads of it trailing down his muscular torso.

"Holy hell," Azrael whispered. "I think I'm in love."

"Me, too," Caleb said, smirking at her.

She punched him in the shoulder. "He's my fantasy. Stay back."

"Baby girl, that man would be the number one sought out ride on Fantasy Island if he wasn't such an ass. I just appreciate true beauty when I see it."

Lance turned around, and they both ducked beneath the windowsill. "Do you think he saw us?"

"Does it matter?" Caleb asked. "He admitted to obsessing

over a dead woman by looking at your picture. Do you really care what he thinks?"

"I guess not," she confessed. "It really feels unfair. I've made moves toward him, and he responded. I assumed it was because he was attracted to me, whether he wanted to admit it or not. Now that I know the real reason, I feel like a fool. I don't want to be the one chasing after him. It's embarrassing and humiliating. To make matters worse, I've ruined our lives. We are going to have to go into hiding forever."

"Is there really anything going on so great that we can't do that? Think about it, Az. Our lives aren't anything near perfect. A new start wouldn't be the worst thing to happen to us."

"What's sad is that you have a point. Now I'm even more depressed."

Caleb threw an arm around her and squeezed. "We always have each other. That's all that matters."

"I'm being broody. You sure you'll be okay by yourself today?"

"Positive. Lance loaned me his laptop, so I can get some work done. Plus, last night, I found the hot tub room. You guys stay gone as long as you want."

~*~

Azrael leaned against the leather seat and closed her eyes, feeling the rhythm of the road coasting beneath them. The air conditioner was going full blast, but the seat warmer was keeping her from freezing.

I've got to get me a BMW.

Lance hadn't said a word to her since they'd gotten in the car, but she was fine with the silence. After this morning's conversation, she wasn't sure she wanted to talk to him more anytime soon. There was no sense in dwelling on it anyway. He obviously had no interest in her, so what she needed to focus on was getting over her attraction to him and moving on. Of course, it didn't help that he looked sexy as hell right now.

Azrael opened her eyes a slit and checked him out. Lance was staring ahead, one arm holding the wheel steady, the other one propped on the console between them. Dark stubble grazed his jawline, and his hair was slicked back, small curls falling loose over his ears and forehead. Instead of the usual jeans and T-shirt she was used to, he was wearing a tailored white button down and slacks that hugged his muscular thighs. She had a feeling this was the Lance of Demonium.

In the backseat, Smellicious whined.

Azrael turned and reached through the cage to pat his head. "You'll be okay. It's just a car ride."

"I'm going to have to put my car in the shop for a week to get the smell of that creature out of it."

Azrael turned back to Lance, prepared to make a snappy comeback, but stopped when she saw him smirking. "Well then, you might as well just get rid of it. I guess I could be persuaded to take it off your hands if you really needed me to."

Lance cocked his head to the side and grinned. "I'll keep that in mind."

What, he's being amicable now? Friendly even? Dear God, please let me off this man's emotional rollercoaster.

"So, what did you like most about Demonium when you stayed here?"

"The lava pits were my favorite when I was a kid. I loved the way the water glowed red and orange and all the rock pets. Try explaining them to a kid back home, though. It's no wonder I was an outcast. What about you? What are some of your favorite things?"

"I like the like cinema here. Of course, I understand why they can't do that in our world, but it makes watching it much better."

"Could you imagine," Azrael chuckled, "telling actors they had to rip parts of their bodies off or really explode, then put themselves back together after the scene? Although, I hear the Actorium Demon cinema has been picking up popularity outside Demonium."

"Let's hope that continues then," he replied, his blue eyes catching hers, causing her heart to beat double.

Azrael nodded and let the conversation drop, turning toward the window, watching the twisted trees whip by, their gold leaves sparkling under the ruddy light of day. *Maybe I shouldn't have come. Maybe it's best if I avoid him altogether. Hell, maybe I should just summon Blais for him. I might die, but it's better than the heartbreak I'm going to have if I continue to be around him.*

"Azrael?" Lance said her name softly, and she glanced up to see him staring at her, a pained expression on his face. "I wanted to apologize for this morning. What I said was rude and cold."

"Even if it was rude and cold, it was honest. I'd rather have honesty from you than politeness," she replied.

Lance looked back out the front window, his voice low when he spoke. "I wasn't completely honest, either."

She waited for him to expound on his statement, but he didn't. Azrael clenched her jaws. *Damn him.* "You know what's worse than rude and cold? Making an odd statement like that but then not explaining."

Lance tightened his hand on the wheel. He opened his mouth to speak, but then closed it again. She waited.

"Here's the deal. It doesn't matter how either of us feels.

Our focus needs to be on Blais and your safety. Anything else would just get in the way."

Azrael turned back toward the window, her eyes stinging painfully. "You're right. Let's just get this over with and be out of each other's lives permanently."

They passed under a wooden bridge, and in the window's reflection, she saw him reach for her before pulling his hand away.

Chapter 15

"He likesss you," the old woman said as Azrael handed over Smellicious.

"No, I just put an attachment spell on him. He'll be over me in a few months."

The old woman cut her eyes to Lance, then back to Azrael. "Everything happens for a purpossse, child. Even the weakest witches know that."

Azrael bit her tongue. She knew there was no way to convince a witch who studied demonology that not everything fit into the *purpose*. "Well then, I'll just leave him in your hands."

"Yesssss," she muttered, staring down at the stink demon. "You do thhhhat."

She flicked her tongue out, and Azrael flinched. The old woman didn't notice. Lance grabbed her by the shoulder and pushed her out of the hut.

"Thanks, Eden," he yelled over his shoulder. "We'll be back in a few hours."

They stepped out into the busy marketplace. Dust and steam filled the air. Above them, a firestorm raged, clouds of pink and red swarming. Demons of all shapes and sizes wandered about, some shopping, some selling wares. Azrael stopped to watch a hodoo demon and his pet. When the demon moved the arms on the doll, the furry demon did the same thing, although he was facing the crowd instead of the doll. Lance stood and watched, his arms crossed over his chest. When the show finished, he dropped a few coins in the man's hat.

"What's next?" she asked, chasing after Lance as he made his way through the thick crowd.

"What's next is we find you some protection."

They walked a long way on the dusty streets. Several times Azrael stopped her attention on the events going on in the market. Each time Lance would grab her arm and pull her away. They ended up turning left into a dark alley. Lance entered a non-descript mud hut, and she followed. Inside, a lady sat at a table, in her hands a collection of glass baubles.

"I have already said I can do nothing more for you, Lance. Please do not press this issue."

The woman stared at the balls. Inside them, smoke swirled, small tendrils reaching out and caressing the woman's hands. From the side, Azrael could tell she was breathtaking, her features alluring, yet something about her tone screamed misery.

"Leolacent, I did not come for me, but for her."

The woman turned to face Azrael, who gasped, her face reddening. She tried to hide her reaction.

"Oh, you do not have to hide your pity from me. I know what my face looks like."

Azrael lifted her head. The worst thing she could do was ignore the honesty the woman in front of her was offering. "I'm sorry. I wasn't expecting it. You're just so beautiful."

"Half of me is," she said, chuckling. "The other half is the making of Blais."

Azrael stared at the left side of the woman's deformed face. One eyelid was missing, the skin withered and blistered as if she'd suffered a massive burn.

"Blais did this?"

"Yes. Luckily my fiancé came home before he finished the job. Now, what is it you are needing help with?"

"I need protection. Blais came after me and says he will come back for me. We were hoping you could help."

"We are very alike then, you and I." Leolacent grasped her hand and squeezed. "Come sit with me, and I will see what I can do."

Azrael took a seat across from the woman. Curious, she reached out to touch some of the glass bobbles but pulled her hand back at the last minute.

"No, go ahead, touch them, hold them. These are objects of purpose. They help me to read you, to see the best way to assist."

She picked up the pink ball. It warmed with her touch, and small tendrils of mist wrapped around her fingers. The other woman observed her. Azrael sat the ball down and picked up the next. Each one swirled in a different pattern. After examining all five balls, she handed them all to Leolacent. The witch took the balls in her hands, her eyes turning white. Her mouth hung agape, lips twitching as though she were mumbling. Azrael looked at Lance, who was leaning against the wall. He gave her an encouraging smile.

Several minutes passed before Leolacent's eyes cleared. She set the balls down, a frown on her face. "I can do nothing to protect you. Neither can any other witch."

"What?" Lance strolled forward, arms crossing his chest. "Why the hell not?"

"Because her purpose is cemented with yours. Since yours

is set, so is hers. I cannot hide her. Her only protection will be the protections I set on you. She'll see this to the end or die, the same as you."

"Is this because she summoned me? Because she used my purpose or whatever the hell you witches do?"

"The reason does not matter. The conclusion does. She cannot be protected from this," Leolacent said. "I need to speak to her alone. Please give us a moment."

Lance turned on his heels and stomped out.

"Always the temper of that one," Leolacent remarked, shaking her head. "Still, he has a big heart and means well."

"How long have you known Lance?"

"Since we were children," she said, her mouth tilting up in a grin. "I had a crush on him, but he didn't notice me from daylight. My family moved away, and that was the last I saw of him until he learned what Blais had done."

"I'm so sorry."

"Don't be. I lived, which is more than I can say of most of his victims. I sent Lance out alone because I wanted to explain to you why I cannot help you."

Azrael figured that was the reason. She'd heard nothing about purpose interfering with protection spells. Although Lance wouldn't know that. "I assumed there was a reason you were unwilling to do it, not that you couldn't."

Leolacent shook her head. "No, I did not lie. I cannot do anything for you."

"I don't understand," Azrael admitted.

Leaning in, Leolacent took Azrael's hands in both of hers. "What is the only thing more unbreakable than purpose?"

Nothing is more unbreakable than purpose. Except for....

"No," she whispered. "I don't—"

"Yes, you do love him, or you will, at least. I suspect the first."

Azrael closed her eyes and leaned back in the chair. "Not him. Anyone but him."

"I can only imagine your trepidation, especially with him being—"

Lance stepped into the room, cutting her off. "An impatient man is what I am becoming."

Her eyes popped open at the sound of his voice. He was staring at Leolacent, his jaw clenched, eyes intensely seeking hers. Leolacent shoved her chair backward and stood, her fists clenched. "She doesn't know?"

He grabbed Leolacent by the shoulder, pulling her out of the hut. Azrael followed, but Lance held up a hand. "You stay here."

The tone in his voice was dark enough to have her sitting without arguing. She watched them exit before slumping and laying her head on the table.

Did he hear us? Is that why he's acting so pissed off? And what is it I don't seem to know?

Does he think I'm in love with him?

Am I?

Azrael shook her head. "No, of course not."

Lance and Leolacent stepped back into the room. He looked calm, but she had a frown on her face.

"Come on. It's time to go."

Lance exited the tent. Azrael followed, but before she could leave, Leolacent grabbed her by the arm and whispered in her ear. "He doesn't know."

She nodded.

~*~

"You okay?" Lance asked.

She felt his eyes on her face, had felt them since they left the hut. "Yes, I'm fine."

Liar.

Although Lance had made no indication he suspected what her conversation with Leolacent was about, he'd been unusually sensitive to her feelings. She knew she should ask him about what it was Leolacent believed he was keeping from her, but she wasn't in the mood. Around them, the streets filled with crowds. A man to the left was haggling over the price of an expensive looking watch. His wife ogled Lance. At least that's what Azrael thought she was doing. Her eyestalks kept dancing around, making it hard to tell.

"I know you're worried, but we'll figure this out. We will find someone that can help, even if we have to search all of Demonium." He touched her shoulder, giving her a soft smile.

So that is what he thinks my problem is?

If she was being honest with herself, she'd have to admit she hadn't given it much thought. For some reason, deep down, she knew the protection route wasn't going to work. It was only the reason *why* which shocked her.

"Thanks," she said, forcing a smile.

"You know, we aren't supposed to pick up Smellicious for a few hours. Why don't we have some fun?"

Eyestalks was definitely ogling. This time Azrael was certain because when she glanced over, the woman retracted her eye.

"Like what? Do you even know how to have fun?"

"Touche," he said, grinning. "Come on."

He pulled her by the arm. A building stood off to the left, its marble exterior gleaming in the orange lighting.

Chapter 16

Lance slipped the host a large bill, which he grasped between his talons as he led them to a private room. Beneath the glow of chandlers and soft candlelight sat a table covered in white cloth. In the center was a small stand with a list of foods most Azrael didn't recognize.

"What is this place?" she whispered as the host walked away.

"It's the Cartisol, a place where culinary artists come to make themselves a name. It's also a demon-sum restaurant, except with a twist."

Azrael bit her lip. "What's the twist?"

"You taste everything blindfolded and try to describe it," Lance answered, smiling.

"I'm not an artistic person, Lance. They will hate me when I leave."

"Don't worry, I got us a private table. That way, the staff can't hear you. Plus, you don't have to be artistic. Just sensual. That's something I believe you have plenty of," he said, his eyes searching out hers.

Her palms started to sweat. "Um, so, how does it work?

Do we order food off the menu?"

"Nope." He nodded toward the two waiters rolling in carts.

One cart held multiple covered trays of what she assumed was food — the other, shot glasses filled with different colored liquids, smoke smoldering out of a few. The taller waiter handed them two black bandanas. The shorter one smiled and nodded, the thick tendrils hanging over his mouth bending in different directions.

He spoke, but his words were garbled to her.

Lance responded in the same language, and the waiter bowed before stepping out.

"Okay, so exactly how we are supposed to eat blindfolded?" Azrael commented, picking at the bandana.

"We're going to take turns feeding each other."

"Feeding each other?" she asked, struggling not to choke on her glass of water.

"Yep," Lance replied, picking up one of the blindfolds and standing. "I'll start."

He slipped behind her and placed the fabric over her eyes. They must have been magically treated because she was instantly plunged into darkness. He tied the ends together, his hands sliding down the base of her neck, causing her to shiver. She sensed him walking away. The room became silent, and the soft music playing in the background came to an abrupt halt.

"I hear it's easier to concentrate when there is no noise," he said. "On each tray is an appetizer, entrée, and dessert. Beside each plate is a list of the ingredients. You're supposed to guess as many ingredients as you can, then it's my turn."

"So, it's like a challenge. We see who guesses the most correct?"

"Exactly."

The wheels of the cart squealed, quieting as they stilled beside her. "I should warn you I'm very competitive."

"So am I," he leaned in to whisper in her ear. "Question is, how well can you concentrate?"

Her mouth popped open. She could swear Lance was flirting with her, but then again, it wouldn't be the first time she was wrong.

"Okay, appetizer first. You get two bites to guess." His thumb grazed her bottom lip. "Open up."

Azrael parted her lips, and he ran his thumb over them, tugging her mouth open wider. He slid a spoon across her lips, and warm, slick liquid touched her tongue. He slipped the spoon out of her mouth.

"Don't swallow yet. Taste it first," he said, his face close to hers.

Azrael let the broth settle in her mouth, trying to distinguish the taste, all the while struggling to ignore Lance being so close. When she couldn't detect any more flavors, she swallowed.

"Well?" he asked.

"Something floral, maybe grosnote? Lemongrass and basenuts?"

"Very intuitive. You're doing a lot better than I thought you would. There's only two more ingredients. Want to take another taste?"

She nodded.

Lance fed her another spoonful. Afterwards, he slid a small glass into her hand. "You don't have to guess the drink. It's a Siran Belaise. Each drink is supposed to pair well with the meal. You'll be happy to know they are all alcoholic."

"You know me so well," she said, grinning as she chugged

the shot.

Lance waited until she finished her drink before asking, "So, last two ingredients? Any guesses?"

"Feral root and something spicy, but I can't tell what."

"Correct on the feral root. The spicy note is a touch of blue chili." He untied her blindfold. "Four out of five isn't bad for a first time."

She smiled at him. "See, I can be refined. Your turn."

Lance smirked and took a seat in the chair across from her. She was a little unsteady at first when it came to feeding him, but it didn't take her long to get comfortable with it, especially after he only guessed three ingredients right.

He pulled the blindfold off. "Guess I will need to up my game."

"Guess so," she said, grinning as she tied her own blindfold.

She waited while Lance prepared whatever was next. This game was a good idea. A much needed break from her own mind. At some point, yes, she'd need to consider what Leolacent had told her, but Azrael decided it was best to not think about it for now. She'd have time to analyze her feelings later.

She felt Lance draw close. Like before, he ran a finger across her lips and tugged them open, but to her surprise, he slid between her thighs and knelt. The heat from his body was nothing compared to the fire coursing through her veins. Her stomach did a cartwheel when the rough pad of his thumb caressed the tender flesh of her bottom lip. The spoon slipped past her lips.

Something rich hit her taste buds along with it a small bit of al dente pasta. She didn't bother to try and unravel the flavors. The only thing she wanted to taste was him. Lance slid a hand behind her neck and leaned in. She could feel his warm breath on her neck.

"Concentrate," he whispered, a note of humor in his tone.

It was too late. Azrael swallowed the bite without thinking about it, barely keeping herself from wrapping her thighs around Lance to see if he could damn well concentrate.

Payback's hell, she thought, ready to take her turn.

"Did you swallow already?" he asked, pulling away from her.

"Yes." She tugged the blindfold down. "Pasta and some sort of sauce."

Lance grinned at her. "And that's all? Don't you want your second taste?"

"No, I'm pretty sure I can beat you."

Lance cocked his head to the side. "You're only two ahead."

Azrael didn't argue, just pointed to the other chair. Lance gave her a sheepish smile but sat down. She grabbed his blindfold, and he held his hand out to take it.

"I've got this."

He bit his lip, suppressing a grin as she walked behind him to tie his blindfold.

He knows I'm irritated with him, but I bet he won't be expecting my payback, Azrael thought, tying the blindfold a little too tight and causing him to flinch.

She loosened it and put her lips against his ear, whispering, "I'm sorry."

Azrael let her lips linger against his lobe longer than necessary before standing, making sure the back of her hand grazed his neck. She noticed chill bumps rise on the nape of his neck and smiled. Two could play at this game.

When Azrael lifted the silver lid on his tray, she smiled,

another idea forming in her mind. She pushed the cart right next to him and set a spoon in the bowl of greenish brown liquid.

"Hmmm...this might get a little messy. Guess I'm going to have to take special care. Don't want to ruin that nice shirt of yours."

Lance appeared amused by her playfulness but not concerned. Without giving time for doubt to set in, she slid into his lap, straddling him. Her skirt pooled up around her thighs, her silk panties rubbing against his warm slacks. He took a sharp intake of breath, then threw back his head, laughing.

She took the opportunity to settle herself deeper on his lap until his zipper rubbed the apex of her thighs. "Are you ready?"

He chuckled, "And I thought I played unfair."

"I warned you I was competitive," she said. "Now, stay still."

Azrael leaned over and put the spoon in the soupy dish, trying to ignore the sensation building between her legs. She brought the spoon to his mouth and ran her fingers over his lips. "Open up."

He did, and she slipped the spoon between them.

"Now, concentrate." She set the spoon down, making sure to shift across his lap before settling back in and running a hand over his hard chest. She watched him swallow, the Adam's apple in his throat bobbing. "Well?"

"One more taste," he said, his voice deeper than normal.

"As you wish," she teased, grabbing the spoon.

Azrael followed the same steps as before, but as she sat back down the second time, she wiggled her hips. She felt the bulge in his slacks. A moan slipped past her lips, and he slid one hand around her hips. With the other, he removed his mask.

"I think this game is over," he said, his voice thick and

needy.

He didn't seem irritated like she expected him to be. Instead, he looked conflicted. She waited, frozen in place, heart pounding, while he fought whatever internal battle he possessed.

There was a noise from the left, and they both turned to look. One of the waiters had stepped in. He glanced at them, and his eyes widened. He cut them to the floor and bowed, turning on his heel and exiting.

Azrael and Lance looked at each other. The situation, her in his lap, skirt damn near around her waist in a public restaurant, suddenly struck her as funny, and she burst out laughing. Lance joined her.

When the laughter died down, she wiped tears from the corners of her eyes. Lance picked her up off his lap and placed her in her own chair. "How about we eat the rest of the meal before it gets cold? I'll serve us since I don't foresee the waiter coming back any time soon."

The rest of the meal went well, both sticking to small talk, but occasionally, she would catch Lance looking at her like a man drowning in an immense ocean.

~*~

They grabbed a taxi outside the restaurant.

When the driver took them north, instead of back toward their car and Smellicious, Azrael stared out the window in confusion. When she opened her mouth to question it, Lance shook his head and said, "One more stop."

She settled back in the seat and shut her eyes, trying to clear her mind. Not only did she have to worry about a serial killer after her, but Lance was doing a serious number on her emotions. On one hand, there was this morning's revelation where he pretty much told her he only wanted her because she reminded him of the woman he used to love. Afterward, in the car, he admitted there was something between them. Then came the session in the restaurant. There was no denying the desire there. Hell, if the waiter had come any later, he might have honestly caught them in the act.

Don't forget the whole love thing. No, I take that back. Do forget it.

Azrael grimaced. Attraction she could deal with. Even if he was imagining his dead girlfriend. Hell, at this point, she didn't care what he was thinking about. All she knew was that her hormones were likely to spontaneously combust if she didn't do something about them, and soon. It wasn't like Lance was going to take care of the problem. She squirmed in her seat. God, what she'd do for someone to just rip her clothes off and make her scream.

"What are you thinking?"

"Hmmm?" she asked, opening her eyes.

"I was curious what you were thinking. You looked like you were about to punch someone. Since I am assuming that someone is me, I'd like to know what it is over," he said, his mouth turned up in a slight grin.

Her emotions were all over the place, and he didn't look like it bothered him the least bit. Him or his stupid ass sexy grin. "You really want to know what I was thinking about? Sex. I was thinking about sex. Hot, dirty, sweaty sex. The kind where you rip each other's clothes off on the beach and screw right there in public. That's what I was thinking about."

His mouth popped open, the grin successfully wiped off his face.

"Don't worry about commenting. It won't do either of us any good." The car slowed, and she straightened up. "Where are we going, anyway?"

"To the beach," he replied, casting his eyes to the floorboard.

"Well, we just hit the irony jackpot," Azrael muttered.

The car came to a stop, and she opened the door. Before she could exit, Lance put a hand on her shoulder, stopping her. "Azrael, I brought you here because you mentioned how much you enjoyed the lava pools. I don't want you to think...."

He let the sentence drop. Regardless, she knew what he was trying to say.

He doesn't want me to think he brought me here to seduce me.

"Oh, trust me, I know you didn't," she replied, sliding out of the car and slamming the door.

~*~

Azrael slipped off her shoes and dug her heels into the black sand. Cliffs of glass caught the orange sun, reflecting shades of pink and amber. She stared out at the water, watching as it took on the magenta hue of the sky, capping in shades of pink. In the distance, small feathered creatures dipped their heads into the lava pools which were left centuries after the last eruption. A breeze blew by, and Azrael took a deep breath, enjoying the dampness on her throat. The cool air seemed to calm her.

She knew she was treating Lance unfairly, at least with the comment she made in the car. Yes, he was being hot and cold, but he was trying to help her. It wasn't directly his fault she was in this situation. He didn't have to take her to eat or take her to the beach.

I'm being a bitch. Caleb was right. I do get pissy when I haven't had sex in a while.

Lance strolled up beside her, hands in his pockets. "I told the cab to meet us back here in thirty minutes. I hope that's okay with you."

"That's fine." She took a deep breath. "Look, I'm really sorry. There's no excuse for the way I've been acting. I appreciate all you are doing for me, including bringing me here. I promise to be on my best behavior from here on out."

"You have every excuse to act the way you do. I wouldn't blame you if you wanted me dead at this point. I'm glad you don't, but I won't say no to you behaving," he said, smiling at her. "How about we both agree to try to behave and be a little more understanding of one another's feelings?"

"Deal," she said, placing her arm through his. "Lead the way."

Arm in arm, they walked in silence, stopping at one of the lava pits the size of a car. Azrael crouched down until she lay on her stomach and peered inside. On the molten shelves sat crabs. She reached down to pet one, and it ducked its tiny head inside its shell made of volcanic rock. Azrael considered asking Lance if she could bring one back to show Caleb but thought better of it. Between Smellicious and Bumpkins, her rock pet wouldn't last a day. Inside the pool swam tiny translucent creatures that reminded her of cows. Bubbles rose from the center, popping with a hiss of steam.

She looked up at Lance. "I used to spend hours just watching the creatures in the pits. Those were some of my best memories as a kid."

"I'm glad I brought you then."

Azrael braced her hands under her and stood. Black sand coated her fingers, staining them slightly. She made her way to the shoreline to wash them off. Lance followed behind. When she reached the edge of the water, she grabbed her skirt and tied it up so it wouldn't get wet. The air warbled around her as strands of heat came from the water, and in some places, it bubbled with steam. The first time she'd visited a beach in Demonium, she'd been terrified to get into the water, even after her grandmother described them as hot springs. It took her father throwing her in to make her believe.

She put a toe in, testing the temperature as a wave rushed over her bare feet. Although hot, it wasn't hotter than a bath she would run at home. Azrael walked several more feet forward before turning to see Lance rolling up his pants.

"How's the water?" he asked, standing at the edge of the shoreline.

"Perfect." She walked in until the water reached mid-thigh. She closed her eyes and breathed deeply. The smell reminded her of ozone, the crackling of air right before a lightning strike.

She heard Lance come up beside her and opened her eyes.

"You don't want to go for a swim?" he teased.

"I don't think our cab driver would appreciate that."

Lance smirked at her right before scooping her up in his arms and taking off into deeper water. "Don't worry, I'll tip him well."

"Don't you dare," she threatened, her skin feverish from his touch.

Lance ignored her. When the water was up past his waist, he sat her down. Azrael glared at him, or at least, she hoped it was a glare. Inside she yearned for him, could still feel where his warm flesh had touched her bare skin.

"I hope you know this is not what I would call behaving," she accused.

"Couldn't say I took you to the beach and didn't let you swim. I could tell you wanted to. Plus, I want to show you something, and the only way to get there is to swim. Come on."

Lance ducked under the water and swam left. Azrael sighed and followed. After a few minutes, he swam around one of the glass cliffs and stood. She tentatively followed. When the water was shallow enough, they strolled up on shore, dripping wet. Lance grabbed her shoulder and led her to the cliff. She ran her hands across the thick weathered glass, its polished surface warm to the touch.

"It's right over there," he said, pointing to a spot a few feet away.

Azrael squinted. Lance tugged her forward, touching his hand to the cliff, feeling along the glass. That's when she saw it.

"A cave," she whispered.

Glass caves were hard to find since they were almost impossible to see unless you were right on one.

"A special one too. Not many people know about this, and those that do prefer to keep it to themselves."

Lance pulled her in between an arch of glass, the ground beneath them slick but warm. The cave swam with light, but as they walked further, it darkened.

"It feels like we're walking beneath the ocean," she said.

"We are. Now, for the best part." Lance crouched down. In front of him was a small opening. He put his legs out and slid through.

"Come on," he yelled from inside. "Just make sure not to stand."

Azrael shook her head. One day, her curiosity would get her killed. She lay down and slid into the gap.

As soon as she was on the other side, she gasped. Swirling light filled the cavern. It was only four feet high, the ceiling made of glass. Through the glass, she could see the ocean and all the creatures within.

"Oh my."

"Amazing, isn't it?" Lance said. "I discovered this when I was a kid. If you lay down, it feels like you're immersed in the ocean."

He took her hand and pulled her down. Above them, creatures swam by. Schools of draconian fish and lightning crawbugs went about their day, unaware of their observers. Lance propped himself up on his arm, staring at her.

"Well, what do you think?"

"It's amazing. Beautiful. Thank you for bringing me here," she said, her voice coated with wonderment. "I guess I forgive you for not behaving."

Lance ran his tongue across his bottom lip, eyes darkening. "I shouldn't have made that promise. I don't know if it's possible for me to behave around you."

The air in the room grew thick, her ability to focus dimmed. Lance shut his eyes and rubbed a hand over his face, giving an imperceptible shake of his head. Azrael knew he was trying to talk himself out of what they both wanted.

"Then don't behave," she whispered.

Before he had the chance to argue, she pressed her lips against his. He groaned, opening his mouth, and she rolled on top of him. His arms went around her as he deepened the kiss. She slid her hands across his chest, grabbed the bottom of his T-shirt, and tugged it up. Lance broke off the kiss long enough to help her remove it. His skin, warm and taut against her bare hands, had her trembling.

Lance ran a hand over her buttocks, holding tight, grinding against her. She became lost in a fog, emotions clouded by desire. The other hand skimmed her breasts before giving each one a gentle squeeze. She moaned as he gripped one of her nipples and rolled it between his thumb and finger. His breath hitched, and he slid his hand beneath her shirt and bra, grasping her exposed breasts. She ran her fingers underneath the waistline of his pants, the tip of her thumb caressing him. Lance growled in her ear and rolled, splaying his body over hers.

With his need pressed against her, he lightly bit her lip. He slid his hands between them, his deft fingers finding her sensitive nub through the satin panties. Slipping off to the side, he continued to rub himself against her upper leg as he plunged his hands between her thighs.

"You're so wet," he groaned against her lips.

His thumb swept across her delicate center. Pressure built deep within, extending down to her curled toes. She gripped his back tightly, her muscles tensing, begging for release. Her body stilled as an orgasm rolled through it. She arched her back and moaned, the pressure releasing in a wave of passion.

For a while, it felt like she was floating, then her vision cleared. Azrael's hazel eyes met his blue ones. His chest heaved, and he took several shallow breaths. She waited for him to take her.

Lance leaned down and lightly kissed her lips. "We need to get back before the cab leaves us."

She blinked. *What?*

Lance knelt and grabbed his shirt, sliding it over his muscular chest. He held out his hand and led a very confused Azrael out of the cave.

Chapter 17

They took the cab back to his car. Since they were still soaked, Lance was mindful enough to turn up the heat in the BMW. The warm air threatened to lull her to sleep, and she closed her eyes. Azrael must have drifted for a while because when she stirred again, they were nearly home.

"How was your nap?" Lance asked.

"I can't believe I fell asleep. I'm sorry. Don't know why I would feel so relaxed. You should try it sometime," she said, hoping her comment would elicit an explanation about why he stopped.

He bit his lip. "You look like a woman who just woke from a long hibernation."

"Considering it's been nearly a year since I've had a roll in the hay, that's pretty close to the truth," she admitted, leaning her head against the headrest.

"A year? That's all?" he asked, rolling his eyes.

"A year is a long time. I don't imagine you would understand."

He didn't answer, but she saw his knuckles whiten as he gripped the steering wheel.

"Has it been longer than a year for you?" she asked, concerned by the sudden change in his attitude.

"It's been a while," he said, quietly.

A sudden thought occurred to her, but she hesitated to ask. Lance was staring out the window, jaws clenched. She let the silence stretch, hoping he would elaborate before her curiosity got the best of her. For once, he didn't let her down.

"I haven't touched another woman since she died."

His words hung in the air like a death bag. Azrael didn't know what to say. She knew she should say something, should console him, but words failed her. Still, she had to try.

"Lance, I—"

"Please don't. Like I said, I don't want your sympathy. Today shouldn't have happened, but it did because I'm weak and selfish. I don't want that to tarnish what we did, but it's unfair to you to let you think otherwise. I'm not good for you, Azrael. Please keep that in mind."

His mood shifted so fast that it left her speechless. Before she gained control of herself, they pulled up to the house. Lance parked and slammed the car door as he stepped out. She stared in confusion as he marched inside.

~*~

By the time she got in, Lance was nowhere to be seen. She set a much less stinky Smellicious down and hunted for Caleb. He was in the kitchen, baking.

"Hey there. Hope you're hungry. Lance's pantry is stocked like a five-star restaurant, so I went crazy making food. We're going to have salad, baked potatoes, barbecue chicken, and lemon pie for dessert," Caleb said, as he pulled a pan out of the oven.

"Where's Lance?"

"I think he's taking a shower upstairs." Caleb turned and

looked at her, his face falling. "What the hell happened?"

She shook her head, then teared up, biting her lip. There was no way she was going to cry over this. She was emotionally exhausted and confused, but there was a part of her that didn't want to give into her emotions. "I don't want to talk about it right now. I think I want to take a hot bath, and afterward, I'll fill you in, I promise."

Caleb strolled over to her and pulled her into his arms. "When you're ready, I'll be here."

~*~

After her bath, Azrael felt much calmer. Once dried and clean, she stared at her reflection. Although she felt like a different woman, she didn't look like one.

She took a deep breath. Today had taken its toll on her. Hell, Lance had taken his toll on her. Still, it wasn't fair for her to judge him. He'd lost someone he'd loved, and she was the first woman he'd touched in a decade. Of course that would affect him. What she needed to do was to pull her ass together and be supportive.

You can do this, she thought, turning away from the mirror.

She stepped into the kitchen as Caleb was setting the last of the meal on the table. Lance was sitting at the table, pouring himself a large glass of scotch. Azrael mustered a smile on her face.

"Smells good, Caleb."

Caleb gave her a smile, but she saw masked concern behind his eyes. She and Caleb made their plates, but Lance finished his glass, pouring himself another one before he made his. Azrael struggled not to question him.

He's a grown man. If he needs to drown his sorrows, so be it.

She had to give Caleb credit. He did his best to keep an

upbeat conversation while they ate, even when Lance poured himself a third glass. During the conversation, Lance merely picked at his food, staring out the window. A few times, she caught him staring at her as if she were the first woman he'd ever seen. It was a major change from the playful man at the beach.

Before they finished, Lance stood, catching himself on the table as he swayed. "I'm going on to bed. Thank you for the meal, Caleb."

He walked away without another word. Caleb waited until he was out of sight before asking, "What the hell is wrong with him?"

"Me," she said, staring in the direction he went. "I'm what's wrong."

~*~

Caleb sat beside her on the bed, his head leaned back against the headboard, eyes closed.

"What are you thinking?" she asked.

"About everything you've told me. What else am I supposed to be thinking about?" He opened his eyes and stared at her. "Remember how obsessed I was over Jonathan when I thought he was cheating on me? Right before his friends nearly killed me?"

"How could I forget?"

"That's what this reminds me of, Az, and honestly, I'm a little scared. I've never seen you act like this. You've always been my rock. What I went through...I couldn't have done it without you. I just don't know if I can be that kind of rock for you."

"I don't need you to be me. I need you to be Caleb, my best friend who shrugs his shoulders when I do something stupid, the one who encourages me to take life by the balls. We balance each other out," she said, reaching over to squeeze his hand.

Caleb swallowed. After a moment, he shook his head. "Okay then, what do you need me to do?"

"Give me some advice. Tell me what you're thinking."

Her best friend curled his fingers around hers, bringing both their hands to his lap. "First, do you think the witch's prediction will come true? Do you think you are falling for him?"

She shook her head. "I don't know. My emotions are a complete mess."

"All right, we'll skip that then and move on to the sex part. It's obvious he wants you, and you want him. It's also obvious he's severely conflicted because of the woman he used to love. If I was making a match online, I'd find someone who had a determined personality, someone who wouldn't take no for an answer. But you're not just someone online. You're my best friend, and you're in danger. If I encourage you and something happens...."

"You can't control purpose, Caleb. If something is going to happen, it'll happen regardless."

"Then I say, go for it. You only live once. Go slip into his bed."

Azrael grinned. "You want me to go to his bed, knowing he's probably passed out drunk, and take advantage of him?"

"Take advantage of him? No, just give him the opportunity to take what he obviously wants. If nothing else, maybe I'll get a night of peace without you snoring and stealing the covers."

~*~

It was a little past ten when Azrael, clad only in a tank top and a pair of panties, tiptoed into Lance's room. Soft lamplight glowed from the bedside, illuminating his chiseled face. He was lying on his side, one arm tucked under his head. Her heart beat frantically.

She looked at the door, then back to the bed. She could walk away, and no one would know better — well, except for Caleb — or she could quit being a big baby and get into that bed. Taking a deep breath, she stepped over to the bed and slipped under the covers. Lance stirred, his eyes opening as she scooted close to him.

"Azrael?" he asked with a slight slur. "Everything okay?"

"Yes. I was just lonely," she whispered, running her hand over his bare chest.

That seemed to get his attention because he blinked several times, his eyes widening. She stared up at him from under her lashes, heart beating hard as she waited to see if he would throw her out of the bed or not. He ran his tongue across his lips. Azrael pushed the envelope. She pressed her mouth against his. At first, he didn't respond, but when she nibbled his bottom lip, he let out a groan and thrust his tongue into her mouth.

He wrapped his arm around her, slipping his hands under her and kneading her buttocks. Lance forced his tongue deeper, filling her mouth. Her whole body vibrated with need. Azrael tugged her tank top off, throwing it to the floor, exposing her full breasts. Lance dipped down, his lips grazing her nipples. She tugged his head up, pressing her mouth back against his while she rolled him over and straddled him. The length of him pressed against her. Azrael reached between them and shoved his sweats down.

She hovered over him.

"Don't," he argued gruffly, his mouth still against hers.

"I need you inside of me," she countered, tugging her panties to the side. "I want you so bad."

"No," he yelled, pushing her off him and standing up.

"What the hell?" she asked, falling against the headboard,

her naked breasts bouncing.

Lance tugged at his pants, covering himself. "I can't do this, Azrael. I'm sorry."

She stared at him, eyes narrowing. "Can't or won't? Because it damn sure seems to me that you want to."

He ran his hands through his hair, letting out a long breath. "I won't do this. Please understand. It's for your own good."

"Screw you, Lance. Like you know what's good for me? You come into my life and now I have a death threat over my head, and you expect me to just understand without explaining? If this is because you feel guilty sleeping with me because of her, I'd get it if you'd tell me that and quit acting so damn hot and cold." She grabbed her tank top and pulled it on, balling her fists.

"It's not that. Damn it, I'm just trying to protect you." Lance shut his eyes and rubbed his temples.

Azrael's gaze flickered down his exposed chest, following the hard lines running into his sweats. Even with how angry she was, she couldn't deny her desire for him. Her eyes caught something right above the waistband of his sweats. She edged forward to see it better and gasped. A wave of fear ran through her. It was a tattoo—a figure-eight tattoo. Lance opened his eyes. He followed her gaze and quickly pulled his sweats up to cover it up.

It was like an icy hand reached in and crushed her heart. Azrael backed off the bed, her lips trembling.

"I can explain," he said, reaching for her.

"You're a konsumo demon," she whispered, backing toward the door.

"I won't hurt you, I promise. Please just sit down, and I can explain." He came around the bed, approaching her, holding his hands out in front of his chest.

There was a noise from behind, and she turned in time to see Bumpkins and Smellicious smash into the back of her legs. She lost her balance but steadied when she saw Lance charge at her. Azrael turned and ran down the hallway, the pictures on the wall becoming a blur. She could hear his footsteps behind her.

Running into Caleb's room, she slammed the door and locked it. Caleb sat up, dropping his book on the bed.

"What—?"

"Lance is a konsumo demon. We have to get out of here right now." She ran to the window and tried to pull it up, but it was stuck.

"Dammit, Azrael, let me in. I'm not going to hurt you," Lance yelled from the door.

"Come and help me," she yelled to Caleb, who was still sitting there, eyes opened wide.

"We're on the second floor, Az. What the hell do you want to do? Jump? I can't go out there," he said, shaking his head.

Azrael realized he was right. The banging at the door stopped, and she saw Lance's shadow disappear from beneath.

"Look for a weapon, anything." Azrael dug around the room, looking for something sharp. Caleb jumped off the bed and grabbed a vase from the desk. She found a hammer in one of the drawers. It would have to do.

"What happened, Az? Did he try to steal your powers?"

"No," she said, shaking her head, her heart racing. "I saw his tattoo marking him. I freaked out and ran."

Azrael's phone buzzed on the nightstand, making both of them jump. Caleb reached over and picked it up.

"It's Lance. He sent you a text," he said, handing it to her, frowning.

With shaky hands, Azrael took the phone and opened the

long message.

I'm sorry I lied to you about what I was, but I figured you'd react the way you just did. Please come out so we can sit down and talk about this. No more secrets. I promise to tell you everything.

She handed the phone to Caleb, who read the message and handed it back.

"So, what do you think?" she asked.

"I've never heard of a demon wanting to steal your powers or kill you texting an apology. Did he try to hurt you?"

"No, but he lunged at me when I tried to run."

"You think it's because he wanted to hurt you or was trying to stop you from running?"

Azrael bit her lip. "Honestly, I don't know."

"Why don't you find out?" he asked, nodding to the phone.

With trembling hands, she texted him back.

How do I know I can trust you? You tried to grab me.

His response was almost instant.

I tried to keep you from falling over those damn animals.

"Well, what's he saying?" Caleb asked, coming to stand over her shoulder.

"He says he wasn't trying to grab me. He was just trying to keep me from falling over Smellicious and Bumpkins. They ran into the backs of my legs, and I lost my balance."

Her phone buzzed with another text from Lance.

I haven't hurt you this far, Azrael. If it helps persuade you, though, I want more than anything for you to summon Blais. At any point in time, I could have taken your powers and done it myself. Please meet me in the kitchen so we can talk about this.

"What do you think?" she whispered.

"I don't think we have much of a choice. As it is, even if we leave or escape, Blais is after you. I trust Lance a hell of a lot more than I do him. I think we just have to take our chances."

Azrael texted *okay*, allowing her finger to hover over the send button for a moment. Finally, she pressed it and nodded to Caleb. They headed down to the kitchen.

Chapter 18

When they walked into the kitchen, Lance was setting three coffee mugs on the table. In the center stood a carafe full of coffee and a bottle of Irish cream. He rolled his eyes when he saw the weapons she and Caleb were holding but didn't comment. Lance waved to the empty chairs at the table. They took their seats hesitantly, Azrael's eyes drifting down his bare torso to his sweats, which were currently covering the figure-eight tattoo.

"I didn't know if you'd want coffee or whiskey, so I decided we could have both," he said, not taking his eyes off Azrael's face.

"How do we know you're not trying to poison us?" Caleb asked.

"You don't. If you don't want what I've set out, there are Cokes and an unopened bottle of Fire and Brimstone in the fridge."

Caleb looked unsure, so Azrael leaned forward and poured herself a cup of coffee, adding a large quantity of Irish cream. At this point, if he was looking to kill her, he was going to do it, so why the hell not? Except when she looked up to find Lance staring at her as if she'd just thrown a lost puppy a bone, her hand shook, and she spilled some of the liquor. She stood to get some paper towels, but Lance beat her to it.

He pulled a couple off the roll, and when she reached for them, he took her hand, gently wiping off the liquid.

"Better?" he asked, his eyes soft.

Azrael nodded, her mouth gaping slightly from his sudden change in temperament.

He's a konsumo demon. He's a konsumo demon.

Caleb, apparently deciding the coffee wasn't poisoned, poured his own cup as Lance sat down, tenting his hands over his face.

After Azrael settled down in the chair with her steamy cup, Lance began to speak.

"I grew up in the slums, about five miles northwest of the markets we visited. My father was an abusive alcoholic, and my mother committed suicide before I was five. Having endured a childhood of hatred for what he was, my father insisted we never let anyone know of our heritage, that we tell everyone we were warlocks. He wasn't good for much, except refurbishing furniture, but he dwindled that money away with his drinking. The only other thing he was good at was beating the crap out of me. It was Blais that protected me from him, Blais that went out rummaging through dumpsters and begging for food. He isn't just my business partner and friend — Blais is my brother."

Lance paused, glancing up at Azrael, his face pale, a thick sheen on his eyes. Azrael felt her heart drop in her chest. Fear, along with heartbreak for the man who sat across from her, threatened to unhinge her emotions. She took a deep breath, trying to reel them in. "Please, continue."

Lance gave a slight nod and cleared his throat. "By the time Blais was fifteen, he and my dad were fighting constantly.

Blais believed my dad should embrace his powers and use them to make money. At the time, I was only twelve and didn't really understand what Blais was talking about, but I agreed with him, regardless. To me, Blais could do no wrong. It was during a very nasty fight that I stormed out, scared and angry. I walked to the beach, to the special place I took you today, and eventually fell asleep. My brother found me there the next morning. He was badly beaten, his left eye swollen, and his lip busted. Blais claimed that Dad beat him and then stumbled off through the woods on a drunken rampage. He never came back."

"Do you think Blais killed him?" Caleb asked.

"Not at first. Later I began to suspect, but honestly, if he did, that was the only killing I can forgive my brother for. If my father had lived much longer, he would have probably killed one of us."

Azrael stood and made her way to the fridge, grabbing the bottle of Fire and Brimstone and three Cokes. Pulling down glasses from the cabinet, she poured them each a drink. She could feel Lance's eyes on her the whole time, weighing her expression. Trying to control her shaking hands, she handed him a glass.

"I thought we could all use something stronger."

Lance reached for her glass, wrapping his warm fingers around hers, his eyes pleading before he released them and took the glass.

How long has he been alone? How long has he kept this to himself?

Although she had a feeling the story was going to get worse, much worse, she silently vowed to not leave him to suffer alone in this mess. "Tell us the rest, Lance."

He studied her face. Whatever he saw in her expression seemed to put him at ease because his voice sounded stronger when he spoke again.

"For years, we did whatever we could to work for food. Sometimes it was cleaning yards. Others, it was construction. When I was fifteen, Blais suggested we start our own business. I'd gather the powers. He'd put them in amulets and sell them. At first, the idea felt dirty to me. We'd done little things, like stealing, but that was only to keep us fed. Blais wanted profits. He had big dreams. He argued the facts. The witches would get back their power in a few weeks, and we'd be helping our clients. No one would be harmed, just inconvenienced. It took him a while, but one drunken night, he convinced me. A fertility witch walked into the bar we were in. Blais, who'd been keeping his ear to the ground, knew of several women who would pay dearly for a fertility witch's powers. I probably wouldn't have done it that first time, but before we'd finished arguing, she came over to the bar and asked me to dance. That night, I took her powers. I'd never done anything like that before. Harboring a witch's powers when you are not a witch is an incredible but terrifying feeling. Afterward, I practically ran out, searching for my brother. By the time I found him, I was shaking like a leaf. It took us three tries to get the spell from my dad's old book right before he was able to transfer the powers, but he did. We made a lot of money off that first sale. Enough that I didn't hesitate the next time he asked me to."

"Why didn't he steal the powers if you were so uncomfortable with it?" Azrael asked.

"As I'm sure you've noticed, Blais's powers come from his eyes. It's a bit hard to conceal. Plus, people naturally trusted me, women especially."

"Did you focus solely on witches? Why not warlocks? I thought your kind could steal any powers," Caleb asked.

"We focused on witches because of the means of power transfer. Konsumo demons typically have preferences based on how they take powers and whether or not they are in control of the means of stealing powers. Although Blais can pick and choose who he steals powers from, I have no control over mine."

"You can't control your powers?" Azrael asked, her mouth popping open. She felt inside herself for the core of her power, grateful when she sensed the pulsing of her magic.

"No," Lance said, diverting his eyes to the table.

"But, then how? How do you—?" She let the sentence hang in the air.

It was Caleb who answered. "Sex, Az. Our friend Lance here is a magic thieving whore."

Lance shut his eyes, breathing deeply. Azrael spun toward Caleb, who was looking at her, eyes full of pity. She darted her eyes between the two men. Then it sunk it. Caleb was telling the truth. Lance wasn't denying it.

Azrael burst out laughing. Lance's head popped up, his eyes wide, while Caleb stared at her like she was completely insane.

Probably am, she thought, laughing until tears ran down her cheeks.

"Your power," she choked out, "comes from your penis?"

"Azrael, he's telling the truth. It isn't a joke," Lance said, his jaw clenched.

"Oh, I believe it," she said, still laughing. "It fits perfectly with my very screwed up life."

Caleb reached over and grabbed her mixed drink, pushing it out of her reach. "Baby girl, I think you've had enough."

"Oh, no," she said, standing up to retrieve her drink. "I'm going to need this. Please continue your story, Lance."

He opened his mouth to speak, but closed it and glared at her when she chuckled.

"Sorry," she mumbled, biting her lip to rein in the laughter.

Lance waited to make sure she was going to behave before starting again. "Over the next several years, we became rich, richer than we should have been. I knew something was wrong, that something wasn't adding up, but I kept my mouth shut. I'd become fond of our lifestyle. It wasn't until rumors of the murders reached my ears that I started to doubt. There had been several times when Blais mentioned how he wished we could just kill the witches to keep their power, making our amulets worth more, but I thought he was just joking. One night, at a bar, I heard a fellow traveler mentioning a murder in a town we were at a few months before, where a witch was beheaded. I struck up a conversation. He told me the girl's name and when he thought she'd died. I could practically feel my heart beating out of my chest. The girl was one I stole powers from, her death occurring within days, maybe less.

"Over the next year, I kept hearing stories like this, but I refused to believe the truth, refused to believe my brother was killing them. Then one night, he came home drunk, and I noticed blood on his coat. I couldn't take anymore. I accused him. Of course, he acted like I was crazy, made me feel ashamed for even thinking that. Went as far as to show me the books, convincing me we'd come by the money honestly, or at least honestly for us. I apologized and hated myself, but the doubt was still there. That's when our relationship became strained. I was still working, but it wasn't the same. Blais sensed it, and we started fighting. He could tell I wanted out. I continued to work, and then one day, I met her, Sarah. It took me weeks to convince her to come to my bed. In that time, I fell in love. I slept with her, not to steal her powers, but because I couldn't turn her down. I loved her more than anything in the world, more than Blais.

"I woke the next morning feeling guilty, knowing she would soon discover I stole her powers. I ran out to the market and purchased the largest bouquet of flowers I could find and an expensive diamond ring, hoping she'd forgive me, that she'd understand. When I walked into the room, Blais was standing over Sarah's body, her decapitated head in his right hand."

Lance stopped speaking and turned, looking out the window. Azrael wiped at her eyes, noting Caleb did the same. For a while, they sat in silence, none of them wanting to fill it. Lance didn't need to tell the rest of the story. They both pretty much knew what happened from there. Lance was right about her. She didn't have good judgement, and more times than she could count, she'd put herself out there stupidly without knowing the consequences. This wasn't one of them.

"I'll do it," she whispered. "I'll summon him."

Chapter 19

After having tossed and turned all night, Azrael gave up on any more sleep and trudged to the kitchen, making her way to the coffee pot. She leaned against the counter, eyes closed as she waited for the coffee to brew, the sound of percolating liquid soothing her nerves. Last night, after agreeing to summon Blais, the fear of what she was going to do set in. But after the way Lance looked at her like she was an angel handing a dying man a second chance at life, she couldn't take it back. She'd told them they'd start today and headed off to bed so she could break down.

Heartbreak. Pain. Anger. The pain was because she wanted him, and she couldn't have him. The hurt was because she knew it would never work out. The anger was because she'd let her feelings for Lance grow stronger than just attraction.

I wouldn't have done that if he'd been honest with me in the first place, she thought.

Even knowing that she couldn't be angry with him. Not after the horrors he'd been through. No, her anger was directed at herself. She poured herself a cup of coffee and sat at the table. The first sip of warmth slipped down her throat, and she closed her eyes, cupping her hands around the cup. She wasn't aware of

Lance watching her from the doorway until he spoke.

"Did you get any rest last night?" he asked, hands shoved in the pockets of his jeans.

"Not really," she replied, opening her eyes, staring at him over the cup.

He looked disheveled. His hair was pushed back as if he'd been running his hands through it. There were dark circles under his eyes, and his face looked drawn, thin. The biggest change, though, was the way he looked at her. There was a softness to that gaze, a sweetness. She was used to the mask, the anger, even the desire, but this was something different. It was as if he was letting her see the real Lance. In that moment, she could see how easily any number of women would have fallen in love with him, how easy it would be for her too.

No, she thought, shutting her emotions down. *From here on out, it's business only.*

"Did you?"

He shook his head and strolled into the kitchen, grabbing a cup of coffee before sitting across from her. "I tried but failed. I couldn't shut off my mind."

"Did talking about it make it worse? I would think after all these years, it might feel nice to let it out, to know you have someone on your side," she said, blowing on her coffee.

"It was." He locked his eyes on hers. "Thinking about my past wasn't what kept me up."

The meaning behind his words was clear. Lance was insinuating that thoughts of her kept him awake.

Of course, now that I know we can't be together, he's going to start being sweet, showing his interest. That's just great.

She could tell he expected her to ask what he was thinking about, to open the door on his feelings about her. Although tempting, she knew it would only end up hurting both of them. "Well, I'm glad you're up because there are some supplies I will need for summoning Blais. Normally I'd make do with what was around, but I need to be extra cautious in case he's using something to block summoning spells. I'll make a list if you don't mind going to the market for them. I need to spend the day in meditation, preparing myself."

The business-like tone of her words seemed to catch him off guard. "Azrael—"

"Don't."

"You don't even know what I'm going to say."

"Is it about us? Does it have anything to do with feelings? With emotions?"

"Yes," he admitted, reaching across the table and putting his hand on hers. "But we need to talk about it."

She tugged her hand out from under his. "No. Not now, not ever. I've agreed to summon Blais for you, to risk my life. All I'm asking in return is for us to treat this like a business transaction. Not because of what you are, but because anything else is pointless. We both know it."

Lance covered his face with his hands, taking a deep breath before removing them. "If that's what you want—"

"It is."

"Then I won't bother you about it again. Go ahead and put together your list, and I'll head off to the market."

~*~

In retrospect, Azrael regretted what she'd said to Lance.

After spending several hours in meditation, clearing her mind to prepare her summoning spell, she'd been able to look at their relationship from a different point of view. But although her mind was clear, her heart was burdened.

She could spend all day weighing the pros and cons, but it would still come back to the same thing. Being with him meant she would lose her powers every time they were physically together — temporarily, at least. To her, that would be like losing a piece of her soul, of her being, of her *purpose*. Could she be with someone who took a part of her away?

Yet, as she sat in the library, feet curled up beneath her on the antique couch, she felt a sense of belonging. The way the pillows smelled, the way light streamed through the curtains, the way the ceiling fan lay shadows across the coffee table, all of it reminded her of him. She could smell his shampoo, hear his footsteps. He gave her a different sense of being, a different purpose. If she walked away, wouldn't she still be leaving a piece of herself behind? Either way, there was something at risk.

I can't choose, though, not until I know.

And there it was, the wrench she'd thrown, stopping the wheels from moving, stopping him from telling her how *he* felt. Was it just attraction or more? Could it be more if he was still attached to his dead lover, still obsessed with his murderous brother? So, yeah, she regretted her words.

She stopped tapping her fingers on the armrest and grabbed a handful of the velvet covering, clenching it in her fists. Caleb called her predictable, reliable, stable. It was true. She was all of those things. But now....

Now I have no control. Blais is after me. I might die today. I have no job, no certainty of a future, and no control of my own heart.

I don't know who I am anymore.

"Hey, you done meditating?"

Caleb startled her, and she jumped off the couch, steadying herself on the end table at the last second before she plunged to the ground.

"Whoa there." Caleb put his hands out in front of him. "Didn't mean to scare you."

"Not your fault. I was just lost in thought."

"I can imagine," he said, coming to stand in front of her. "You're going through a lot right now, which is why I wanted to check on you."

"I'm okay." Azrael plopped down in an armchair, placing her palms against her eyes.

"Yeah, seems it. Are you worried about the summoning? Or something else?"

"Both, but right now, I need to focus on the summoning."

"Az, you're a fantastic summoning witch. Witches Corp even admitted you were one of the strongest summoners they'd seen. You can do this. Get him here, and Lance will take care of the rest."

She pressed her hands harder against her eyes until she saw stars, and whispered, "I may not be able to summon him at all, Caleb. Not because of strength, but for the same reason, I can't summon something for myself, for you. I may be blinded because I'm too close to the situation because my purpose is too wrapped up with Lance's."

Dropping her hands, she leaned back in the chair, counting the ceiling tiles. *One, two, three, four, five....*

"You mean what that lady at the market said? That you were bound to his fate or something like that?"

"Yes."

Eighteen, nineteen, twenty....

"Yeah, but she said it was because you were going to fall in love with him."

Twenty-eight, twenty-nine....

"Az," Caleb said, his voice nearly a whisper. "You're not,

are you?"

Damn. Lost count. One, two, three, four, five....

"You are, aren't you? You're in love with him?"

Azrael squeezed her eyes shut, trying to block out the truth. She'd never lied to Caleb, not directly.

"Az—"

"No, I'm not in love with him, okay? All I want is to summon Blaise and piece our lives back together without Lance in them." She opened her eyes, intending to glare at her best friend, but stopped short.

Behind him, Lance was standing in the doorway, paper bag cradled in one arm, body stiff, a deadpan expression on his face. "Well then, by all means, let's get started."

Chapter 20

Twenty minutes later, after all the large furniture was removed and the only window blocked with a bookshelf, Azrael wiped a fine sheen of sweat off her forehead. So far, Lance had only spoken to her in clipped phrases, directing them on where to move things. She had no idea how long he'd been standing there, listening, how much he'd heard.

Well, he certainly heard that last part.

She considered apologizing. Hell, she should apologize, but what would she say? Sorry I said I'm not in love with you? That I wanted you out of my life? Well, that last one wouldn't be so bad, but considering she wasn't entirely sure how she felt, it would probably be better to leave it alone altogether.

"Okay, here's the plan." Lance stood by the doorway, hands crossed over his chest. "Azrael summons Blaise. As soon as you see the spell starting, Caleb, you grab her and pull her out of the circle. I will take him down the moment she's moved. If something goes wrong, run. Do not stay and help. You got that?"

Caleb nodded his head but tightened his hand around the metal bat Lance had found for him.

"Azrael?" Lance asked, his voice becoming stern. "Do you

understand?"

She tried to make eye contact with Caleb, but he avoided her gaze, eyes darting anywhere in the room but at her.

"Azrael?"

"I'm sorry, Lance, but that's not going to happen."

"The hell it—"

"Do you think I'm honestly going to run off while he kills you? Where would we go, anyway?" She turned to Caleb. "We both know you wouldn't be able to make it outside, to the car or anywhere else. I won't have you sacrificing yourself for me, and I'm damn sure I'm not leaving without the both of you. Our only chance is to stay here and fight if that's what it comes down to."

"Maybe we shouldn't do this, then," Lance mumbled, frustration crinkling his eyes.

"He's coming after us one way or another. Personally, I'd like it to be on my terms," Caleb said.

"Same here."

Azrael grabbed the supplies Lance had purchased at the market that day and set things out. She gave Caleb a bag of crystals to set around the perimeter of the room for protection. Grabbing the chalk, she began preparing her spell.

"Do you need me to do something?" Lance asked, squatting beside her.

"No. Just make sure you take him down."

"I plan to. Don't worry. I'll be out of your life soon enough." He rocked back on his heels, his eyes narrowed. "I hope you have your bag packed."

"Dammit." Azrael's hand slipped, causing her to mess up one of the symbols. She tossed the chalk down. "Are you really that dense, Lance?"

"What?"

"I told Caleb I wanted you out of my life. So what? First of all, you shouldn't have been listening to our conversation. Secondly, have you asked yourself why I don't want you in my life? What I'm so afraid of?"

"It's because I'm a konsumo demon, and you're scared to be around me."

"What?" This time it was Azrael's turn to be surprised. "No, of course not. You don't believe that, do you?"

She could see by his face that he did.

I'm such an idiot. I should have been honest with him. Of course he's going to come to his own conclusions.

Well, what better time to be honest, than when you're probably about to die?

"It doesn't matter to me what you are. You're a good person, whether you want to believe it or not. I just...." Azrael's bottom lip trembled. "It's how I feel about you that I'm scared of. I feel like I'm drowning, and the only thing I can anchor myself to is beyond my reach. Am I wrong, though? Is there any chance we can be more than...whatever we are?"

Lance slumped his shoulders. With his head hung low, he whispered, "No."

Azrael's throat constricted, making it hard to speak past the sorrow in her heart, even though the answer came as no surprise. "And that's why I have to go away."

"I understand," he said softly as he stood, moving out of the circle to give her room to work.

Azrael picked up the chalk and worked on the symbols, blinking rapidly to remove the moisture gathered in her eyes. How could such a simple word like *no* cause her so much pain? It was the same word she'd been telling herself over and over when she thought about the possibility of something working about between the two of them. So, why did it hurt so bad to hear it slip past his lips?

Focus, Azrael.

She closed her eyes, breathing through her mouth and exhaling out her nose. When she opened them, she shut everything out but the spell. For the next fifteen minutes, the room was silent except for the sound of chalk scratching against wood. Even Lance and Caleb became still, mesmerized in her work. When she drew out the last symbol, Azrael raised her head.

"It's ready."

Lance nodded, and he and Caleb took their places. Azrael crossed her legs, Indian style, and closed off her mind, seeking the room of purpose. She could smell the clove candles Caleb had lit, could feel small pulses of power coming from the crystals. When she could no longer feel the hard floor beneath her, Azrael opened her eyes. Eternal darkness surrounded her while billions of glowing strands floated above her head, stretching in every direction. She untangled her legs and stood.

The air was warm, like a summer breeze. Her ears could detect the faintest sounds of chimes. This was a place of peace. She released her fear, lulled by a sense of calm, of tranquility. Sometimes when she summoned, she wished she could stay there forever, but she knew from experience it was not allowed. The longer one stayed, the weaker the feeling of tranquility became, replaced by an eerie fear, a warning that one had overstayed their welcome.

Azrael walked, her steps making no noise. Beneath her feet, blackness. Although it felt solid, she knew nothing was there. It was rare, but some summoning witches got lost, never to return to their bodies, taken by the veil. The longer you stayed, the harder it was to find your way back. Azrael wasn't going to let that happen to her. It was time to focus on the task.

I need to find Blaise. I need to find Blaise. I need to find Blaise….

The mantra played in her head, over and over again. She walked around aimlessly, coming up blank. It usually didn't take this long for her to find a connection. Doubt set in. Along with it a sense of hopelessness.

I should give up. Get out of here. It's taking too long.

She shut her eyes, preparing to leave, but there was a strong tug to the right. Azrael followed her senses deeper into the abyss. Another tug. This time to the left. Several minutes later, another straight ahead. Her breathing picked up pace, and the hair on her arms stood up. She swiveled around, feeling as if she was no longer alone, as if something lurked in the darkness.

I'm so close. Just one more minute.

One minute stretched into five, then ten. The feeling of dread grew stronger, but she knew she what she needed was close. Azrael stopped. In front of her was a silver strand, the same as the billions around her, but she knew it was his.

Blais.

She closed her hand around the strand, feeling it pulse against her palm. Wrapping it in a tight fist, she pulled. Instead of coming loose like it should have, the strand wrapped around her wrist, squeezing tightly. Azrael screamed. Giving a vicious yank, she tugged with all her strength, but the strand only wound tighter.

It's a trap. Blaise set a trap.

The strand stopped moving. Still held in its grip, Azrael whipped her head around. There was movement in the dark. She wasn't alone. *They* were coming.

He trapped me here for the creatures of the veil.

She shrank down to her knees, her trapped arm hanging

above her head. He'd done it. He'd sent her on a wild goose hunt, keeping her there until she'd lost focus on how to get back. Now the creatures of the veil would take her away. Tears ran down her face. Her chest hurt. A shroud of hopelessness, of fear, sat on her heart. Azrael bowed her head, allowing it to swallow her. It was time to give up.

An eternity passed. An endless void of nothing. Then she heard the chimes.

Azrael lifted her head. Around her, the strands were swaying as if something large was moving through them. When the strands touched each other, they bellowed out a piercing chime. Whatever was out there was closing in.

"Who's there?"

No answer. The chimes grew louder. Azrael covered her ears.

"Please help me. I don't know where I am."

Silence met her plea. The strands highlighted a darkness, a large shadowy form crawling beneath them. It stopped a few feet in front of her.

Azrael gasped. It was too dark to see what was there, but she felt its essence. Whatever it was, there was something beyond human or demon comprehension, something belonging to the unknown. It moved closer, and she recoiled. She squeezed her eyes shut.

YOU DO NOT BELONG HERE.

A million voices came from everywhere. Beneath her, the ground vibrated. The chiming grew stronger, more fierce.

"I'm sorry. I'm sorry," she sobbed. "I...I'm st-stuck."

She felt the air move, felt a part of the creature hovering above her. The strand holding her wrist was released, and her arm dropped to her side, limp and numb.

THIS ONE STEALS PURPOSE, THE ONE WHO TRAPPED YOU.

"Y-y-yes." Shivers racked her body. She tensed her muscles, trying to stop the shaking, but that only caused them to cramp up.

YOU DO NOT BELONG HERE.

"I k-k-know."

GO THEN.

"Wh—"

Azrael's world became nothingness.

Chapter 21

"Is she doing any better?"

"Not really. She's still not talking, but at least she's out of the bed."

"She's been staring out that window for hours, Caleb. It's been days since she's had something to drink, something to eat."

"Don't you think I know that? What do you want me to do? I've tried everything. I-I don't know if she's...." He stopped mid-sentence, squeezing his eyes shut. "I can't lose her."

"Look, you need to rest. Take a break. I'll stay with her, I promise."

"And what about the lady from the market? Leola... something or other. What did she say?"

"Rest first, and then we will—"

"No. You tell me right now. What did she say?"

"She said there was nothing anyone could do. That it's up to Azrael to decide whether she wants to come back."

"Then let's make her want to."

~*~

She could hear them, hear how worried they were. Once or twice she'd tried to speak, but nothing came out. Azrael remembered being inside the veil, not knowing who she was, why she was there. When she'd come to, Lance and Caleb were standing over her. That's when it all came rushing back in.

In the veil, there was no pain. No expectations. No worries. Just her and darkness. Now she was back, in a world of fear, of uncertainty. She didn't want to let go of that small sense of peace she'd found before one of the creatures came, forcing her back. A strong set of arms slid around her waist, lifting her into the air before laying her on the bed. Lance lay down beside her. He lifted a finger, lightly tracing her jaw.

"Please come back to us, Azrael."

Blue eyes sought hers. Azrael stared, unblinking. She'd never noticed how many shades of blue his eyes held. There were flecks of turquoise and cornflower. His lashes were long, midnight black. She wanted to lift her hand, to run her fingers across the dark shadows under his eyes, but she was too tired.

"Caleb would be a mess without you. He needs you. Who will take care of him if you don't come back?" Lance cupped her hand in his. "It's not just him, though. I need you too. I know it's crazy, and I know you want to leave. I—I just…if nothing else, I need to know you are alive, that you're happy, even if I never see you again. Please, Azrael."

Something stirred inside of her. She flinched her hand in an attempt to squeeze his.

Lance took a sharp breath. "That's it. Come on back. Keep fighting." He ran his fingers through her hair, over her lips and face. "Come on, baby." His eyes were wild, frantic, hands all over her body, massaging warmth into her limbs.

She gasped.

"That's it," he whispered, trailing gentle kisses on her earlobe.

She turned her head, meeting his lips. The kiss was slow and sweet. A slow-moving heat filled her, starting in her lips and curling her toes. Lance's mouth lingered on hers for a moment longer before pulling away.

"Hey there."

"Hey," she whispered, her voice raspy.

"Welcome back," he said, a smile on his face, thumb still caressing her cheek.

"How…?" Azrael swallowed. "How long was I gone?"

"Summoning? Maybe an hour. Afterwards?" Lance bit his lip. "It's been two days. We were scared you would never come back. It was like you were comatose."

"I—I think I was in a way. I remember bits and pieces, but it's blurry. Like I was looking through a stained-glass window."

"What happened in there? Leolacent came by. She said you'd stayed in the veil too long, that your mind was lost."

Azrael closed her eyes and let out a shaky breath. She tried to speak, but her bottom lip trembled, and she bit it to stop the shaking.

"Hey, hey, it's okay. We don't need to talk about it right now. It's enough that you're back. Caleb's going to be ecstatic. How about we get some food down you? I bet you're starving."

His statement caused her stomach to growl, reminding her of human needs she'd been ignoring for days. Although hungry, she felt the need to wash first, to be clean. "Can I bathe first?"

Lance frowned. For a moment, he looked like he would deny her something as simple as a bath. Then he gave her a gentle smile. "Sure, but I'd rather you not be alone. To be honest, I'm a little worried you might slip away again."

"I won't."

"Humor me."

~*~

"Thanks, Caleb," she said, leaning back and closing her eyes as he blow dried her hair.

"I'm just glad you're okay. You scared the crap out of me." Caleb grabbed the round brush and ran it through her tangles. "You are never allowed to do that to me again, or I'll have to kill you."

"Threat duly noted."

Azrael pulled the cotton robe tighter around her. Not even the hot air blowing from the dryer could dispel the cold fingers of fear running through her veins. She shivered. Out of the corner of her eye, she saw Caleb glance in the mirror. She didn't have to look up to know Lance was standing in the doorway, that the two of them were passing concerned glances at each other. They'd been doing that since she'd come to. Neither asked her about what happened during the summoning, but she knew they were worried.

"Feeling better?" Lance asked, coming into the bathroom to stand beside her.

"Yeah, a bit."

"Good." He placed his hand on hers. "I made soup and sandwiches. I thought we could eat in the living room by the fireplace."

"That sounds good," she replied.

Lance turned and exited, leaving her confused. She didn't know what to think about his sudden change in attitude. Instead of hot and cold, he'd been treating her with an unexpected tenderness. And that kiss….

Azrael touched her lips.

Caleb stopped brushing her hair. "He was worried about you."

"That's nice for a change."

"I know you don't want to hear this, but maybe you should give him a chance, give the two of you a chance."

"You know that's not possible." She swiveled in her chair. "I thought you didn't like him anyway. What changed your mind?"

"I saw the look on his face when you flew out of that circle when we thought you were dead. I watched him fuss over you night and day. Maybe I gained a new perspective. He cares for you," Caleb said, turning on the dryer to finish her hair.

"He just needs me alive to summon Blaise."

"No, that's not it." Caleb shook his head. "He...I don't know. He seemed pretty torn up. We took turns watching over you. When he didn't know I was there, he'd whisper things I think he was too scared to tell you when you were awake."

"What kind of things?" Azrael asked.

"You'll have to ask him," Caleb said, turning off the dryer and leaving her to her thoughts.

~*~

"So he set a trap, or at least had someone else do it," Lance said, placing his half-eaten meal on the table.

"Yes. A very effective trap. It's dangerous to spend very long in the veil. You forget who you are, your purpose. I felt driven to find what I was looking for, but I stopped asking myself why long before I found it. By the time one of the creatures came, I barely knew who I was and had no idea of how to get back." Azrael shifted the blanket over her lap. Sitting between the two men, fireplace roaring, she was able to shake off the last remnants of what had happened.

"I'm sorry, Az. Maybe I'm just an idiot, but how can you get lost in a place that doesn't exist? You were here, not in there,"

Caleb said.

"I was here in body only. The veil exists. I was there in my mind, yet it's still as real to me as you are. Blais sent me on a wild goose chase, knowing I would stay too long. It's not a strong spell, but a smart one."

"So, what do we do now?" Caleb directed the question at Lance.

"There isn't much we can do. I'm looking into hiring a few other detectives, and Leolacent heard rumors of some witches in the northern region who are reputed to have untold powers. They might be worth a shot to get the both of you protected."

"I want to try summoning him again."

Azrael could have dropped a bomb in the room, and it would have been less explosive.

"No."

"Not a chance in hell, Az."

"If I have to tie you down—"

"I'll help him do it, baby girl."

She slammed her plate on the table. "Stop it!"

Both men clamped their mouths shut. Azrael stood and walked over to the fireplace, watching the flames lick the pieces of wood, slowly turning them into ash. "Blais is after me, not the two of you. He's using me, dangling my life in your face, Lance. I've been uprooted, nearly died twice, and trapped because of him. Before I did the spell, I was thinking about how I didn't know who I was anymore. I can't live like this. I want to take my life back. I'm not stupid. I know how dangerous this is, but I have a plan. The last thing I need is for the two of you to pound on your chests and think you can push me around."

Caleb sighed. "I'm sorry. I'm just worried about you."

"I know." Azrael returned to the couch and gave him a

light kiss on the cheek. "And I love you for that."

"What is this plan of yours?" Lance asked, arms crossed over his chest. "I'm not saying I agree, but I'm willing to hear you out."

"How about we discuss it tomorrow? I'm still working the details out and would like to rest first."

"Tomorrow then." Caleb stood and stretched. "I, for one, need to head to bed myself. Are you coming, Az?"

"I think I want to stay down here by the fireplace tonight. It's relaxing. I'll catch you in the morning, though."

"Sounds good. Night guys." Caleb patted Smellicious and Bumpkins on the head before walking out of the room.

Azrael nodded to the two pets curled up together in front of the fire. "They sure are getting comfortable with each other."

Lance grinned. "To my surprise, yes. Bumpkins hates other animals, especially after what happened to him. I should have known he'd befriend a stink demon."

"Smellicious isn't so bad now that he doesn't smell."

At the sound of his name, her pet lifted his head and sneezed, wiping the trail of snot on Lance's throw rug.

"I'm not sure I agree with you," Lance said. "Anyway, since you're staying down here, I'll get some blankets and something relaxing to drink."

Azrael stared at the fire, trying to sort out her thoughts. Lance was coming back with drinks, which gave her the opportunity to discuss what she and Caleb were talking about earlier.

He cares for you.

I care for him too, but that doesn't mean it'll work out.

Of course, Lance knew that too. They were in the same boat. Instead of fighting each other, maybe it was time to deal with this together.

Lance stepped back into the room with a blanket and carrying two mugs. He handed her a mug and sat down. "It's an old family recipe—one of the few things my father didn't suck at was mixing alcohol. Try it."

Azrael took a sip. The alcohol was barely detectable beneath the flavors of citrus and cinnamon, but it warmed her to the toes. "Mmmm."

"Don't be caught off guard, though. The alcohol content is strong."

"Even better," Azrael said, taking another sip. "I'm glad we have a moment to talk. There is something I want to discuss with you."

"What's that?"

Azrael set her cup down and turned to face him, pulling her legs up, so her knees touched his thigh. "I wanted to apologize for shutting you down the other day, for calling this a business transaction. It wasn't fair to you. It wasn't fair to either of us. If you'd allow it, I'd like us to be able to talk to each other about how we feel instead of ignoring it."

She couldn't read the expression on his face, wasn't sure if he was open to her suggestion. A second seemed to stretch into a minute. Then Lance set his cup down beside hers and scooted closer, bringing one hand up to brush a stray strand out of her face. He traced her lips with his thumb before leaning down and kissing her. His mouth was warm, inviting. *Consuming.* When he broke it off, she was breathless.

"That wasn't exactly what I meant by talking," she mumbled, his face inches from hers.

Lance chuckled. "I may have misunderstood."

"You know this won't work out, right?"

"I do." He leaned down and kissed her neck and ran his tongue under her jaw. "I'm finding it very hard for that to be a good enough reason to stay away from you."

"Does it bother you at all?" The words slipped past her lips before she could control them.

Lance stopped kissing her neck and pulled away. "Of course it does. I feel guilty every time I think about you, every time I touch you. I feel that way because I feel like I'm betraying the woman who died because of me, and all I'm doing is torturing us. But I can't stop. I'm just as scared as you are. Probably more so. Do you still...?"

"Still what?"

"Well, you know what I am now."

He wants to know if I still want him.

Azrael crawled onto his lap, straddling him. She took his face in her hands and kissed him deeply. His hands trailed down her back, giving her chills. She could feel him throb beneath her. He undid her robe, letting it slide to the floor, one hand reaching up and cupping her breast. A moan escaped her lips.

Lance broke off the kiss, laying his forehead against hers. "We may not have to worry about Blais. At this rate, I'm going to die from desire before he ever gets to us."

"There are other things we can do," Azrael said, trailing her lips down his neck.

Lance lifted her off him and stood, grabbing the blanket off the couch. "Not tonight."

"Why not?" she asked, poking out her bottom lip.

"Because I would like to take things slow. Maybe even convince you I'm not a complete ass."

"That's highly unlikely."

"Which brings us back to that bad judge of character you

have. Now scoot forward."

Azrael stuck her tongue out at him. Lance slid behind her on the couch, wrapping his arms around her waist and pulling them both down. "For tonight, we are going to sleep right here. After this last scare, I have no intentions of letting you out of my sight again any time soon."

She opened her mouth to argue, but Lance kissed her before she could say a word.

"Now sleep," he said, shoving a pillow underneath their heads.

To her surprise, she did.

Chapter 22

Azrael awoke warm and relaxed but alone. The fire had died down to a small flame, and sunlight streaked through the shimmering curtains. She sat up and stretched, reaching to the far end of the couch to grab her robe. Wrapping it around her, she made her way to the kitchen.

Caleb was licking icing off his fingers, and Lance was placing a large tray of cinnamon rolls on the table. Lance pulled off the oven mitts and smiled at her. She gave him a cautious smile back. It would take a while for her to get used to this nice version of him. He poured a cup of coffee and brought it to her.

"Good morning," he said, handing her the cup.

Azrael mumbled "Morning" as she wrapped her hands around it, bringing it to her lips. She leaned against the counter and closed her eyes, taking the first sip. "Mmmm."

"I would leave her alone until she's at least halfway done with that cup. Az isn't exactly the morning type," Caleb warned.

The sound of a chair screeching across the floor made Azrael flinch. She opened her eyes, narrowing them at Lance, who was pulling the chair out to sit in.

"I think I see what you mean," he said, carefully pulling

his chair out the rest of the way. Azrael closed her eyes again, listening to their conversation as she enjoyed her cup of coffee.

"So, what's on the agenda today?" Caleb asked.

"Training. With Blaise still on the loose, I think it's best I teach you two how to hold your own."

"Hey, don't knock it. I'm a beast with a bat."

"I'll take your word for it, but just in case there's no bat around, it wouldn't hurt to learn a few defensive moves. Anyway, a few hours of training a day wouldn't hurt either of you."

"Okay, then. Training. Anything else? What about looking into a way to destroy Blais?"

"I have a plan," Azrael said, looking over her cup of coffee at them.

Lance stood, took her cup of coffee, and set it on the counter. "Well, hey there. Glad you decided to join us." Cupping her face in his hand, he kissed her. He tasted of icing and hazelnut. Warm and inviting. When the kiss ended, Azrael had to grab the counter to keep herself from falling over. "Now, what was your idea?"

My idea? Oh, yeah.

Caleb was looking back and forth between the two, eyebrows arched over his glass of orange juice.

Azrael cleared her throat. "I couldn't summon Blais because I couldn't see the trap he'd set. Basically, he was using hexes to blind me. If I could use a clarity stone, I would be able to summon him, no problem."

"What's a clarity stone?"

"It's a crystal, about the size of an ostrich egg. To put it simply, it untangles hexes, allows the user to see through any traps or curses."

Caleb sat his glass down. "You're failing to mention that

there are only five clarity stones known to either this world or ours. Even with all his riches, on the slight chance we could find one, it would be priceless."

"That's true. Fortunately, I know where one is."

"Where's that?" Lance asked.

"Witches Corp."

~*~

After two days of training with Lance, Azrael was glad for the break. They packed their bags, leaving Caleb behind. She was worried about her best friend being alone, but Lance promised her he was safer than the both of them. They dropped Smellicious off at the demon whisperer to keep him calm while she was gone and headed out of Demonium. By the time they got to a hotel, it was late, and she was exhausted. Tomorrow she would visit Witches Corp, but for the night, they would bunk down in a hotel in case Blais was watching the apartments.

She heard the shower come on and removed her shoes, staring at the bed. Lance had been nothing short of a perfect gentlemen the last few days, except for training, where he was a relentless taskmaster. Other than a kiss here and there, he slid into bed with her every night, rolling over to face away from her. She might have argued, but after the grueling training every day, she'd been too tired. Not to mention confused as hell. Lance went from acting like he hated her to being....

To being what? Lover? Boyfriend?

She didn't have an answer for that. Frustrated, she'd complained to Caleb. Unfortunately, he was clueless too. His advice was less than satisfactory.

"Az, look, I want to help you out here, but this one's out of my league. What more are you wanting from him? You can't have sex. If you want some hot, unbridled make-out sessions, you need to let him know how you feel."

"What if he says no?"

"Who could say no to this?" Caleb asked, holding up a thin amount of black lace and shoving it into her bag.

"When the hell did you pack my negligee?"

"Well, you were pretty panicked the night we left. Figured one of us needed to be thinking of the future."

Azrael eyed her bag as she heard the shower turn off. Lance strolled into the room, towel drying his hair, sweats hanging low on his hips, beads of water on his chest and back. "There's still plenty of hot water if you want to shower."

She imagined him in the shower, her legs wrapped tightly around those hips. It must have shown on her face because Lance swallowed, Adam's apple bobbing hard.

"Thanks," she said, grabbing her bag and darting to the bathroom. She slammed the door and leaned against it, dropping her bag on the floor, black lace spilling out. Sex or no sex be damned, one way or another, she and Lance were about to become very acquainted with each other.

~*~

"Caleb, you are a lifesaver," she mumbled.

Along with the stuff she'd packed, she'd found a razor, some scented oils, and edible lotion in a Ziploc bag with a note that said, "Just in case." Freshly cleaned and shaved, she covered her body in lotion and added oil to her pulse points. She pulled out the negligée and slipped it on, checking herself out in the mirror. *I can't go out in this.*

Azrael's idea of a negligee was a sexy bra and panty set. This was one of Caleb's picks, one he ordered online for her last birthday. The top was sheer, allowing her nipples to press against the material, silhouetting her areolas. The front was open, her bare stomach exposed, and the panties were nothing more than a thin, see-through triangle in the front and back with a piece of ribbon connecting the two. It was sexy, seductive, but daring in a way she wasn't. She felt like a coward when she wrapped the robe around herself before walking out.

Lance was lying in bed, television remote in hand, flipping through channels. She studied his naked chest, the way his skin pulled taut around his hips and belly. He turned to look at her and switched off the television. "Nothing good on. Do you want to sit up and chat or just go to bed?"

"Um...bed sounds fine."

He slipped the covers down under his hips and patted her side of the bed. She took several slow steps, turning out the overhead light along the way. Lamplight cast the room in shadows. Lance gave her a small smile when she got to her side, only to let it slip off his face as she undid the robe and tossed it to the floor. Lifting the covers, she slipped beneath the sheets and rolled over to face him. "So, Caleb packed my pajamas."

Lance cleared his throat. "Well, Caleb certainly has good taste."

Azrael bit her lip and chuckled. At least he wasn't going to kick her out of the bed this time. He reached out and trailed his fingers down her bare arm. His eyes were dark, lustful, his fingers soft yet needy. Every inch of her responded to him. Her toes curled, and an ache spread from the center of her core, setting her skin afire.

"You know we can't do this, Azrael," he whispered, his voice full of gravel.

"I know we can't have sex if that's what you mean." She ran her hand over his bare chest, sliding it down to the top of his sweats and running a finger beneath. "I can think of plenty of other things we can do."

"Is that so?" he breathed out, shutting his eyes as she slid her hand down further, running her fingertip over his manhood. She grasped the length of him, squeezing gently, and he groaned. He opened his eyes a slit, his hungry gaze feasting on her chest.

"Patience, Lance," she teased, removing her hand.

With a swift movement, he lunged across the bed and hovered over her, his knees spreading her thighs, mouth latching on to the mesh covering her breasts. He gnawed at the thin material, nibbling and sucking. Azrael arched her back and thrust her hips against his.

"Patience, Azrael." He lifted his head, crushing his mouth against hers. Sliding a hand between them, he tugged on her panties, his thumb grazing her sensitive nub. She moaned.

"I see patience is not a virtue of yours," Lance mumbled against her lips. "Let's see what we can do about that."

He stood, his dark eyes drinking her in before placing his hands on her hips and sliding her panties down inch by inch. By the time he got them off, the ache between her thighs was insatiable. She pushed them together, writhing, muscles clenching in impatience.

"Spread your legs. I want to see you."

Azrael let her thighs fall to the sides, sheet gripped in her fist. Lance gave her a lazy smile, his fingertips brushing the tops of her feet. "So beautiful."

He crawled above her again, stopping between her knees. Bringing his head down, he nuzzled her stomach, tracing his tongue around her belly button as his hands explored her slick mound. When he plunged his fingers inside her, Azrael let go of the sheets and grasped his muscular shoulders, trying to pull him on top. She wanted to feel him inside her. *Needed to.*

Lance ignored her demanding hands and lowered his face between her thighs. With a light flick of his tongue, he spread her lips apart, exposing her center. His fingers plunged in and out of her as his tongue darted against her, consuming her need, devouring her abandon. She grabbed his hair, tugging, as he immersed himself in her core, stoking and licking until she thrashed around, her body quivering with release. Her thighs clenched around his head, her body begging him to stop, unable to handle it as yet another orgasm flooded through her. Lance increased his thrusts, his fingers pounding deep within. She clenched and throbbed around them as his tongue demanded more from her already swollen and spent sex.

As the orgasm subsided, she shuddered against the sweat-drenched sheets. Azrael was distantly aware of him removing his mouth, fingers slowly sliding out of her. He laid his head on her stomach, and she jerked, the nerves in her body responsive to every sensation. For a moment, she lay in silence, her mind unable to comprehend the magnitude of her body's pleasure. When she opened her eyes, Lance was lying on her stomach, dark hair spread across her pale skin, a self-satisfied grin on his face.

"Your turn," she said.

Chapter 23

"Thirty minutes and not a second more," Lance said, his arms crossed over his chest as he stood beside the rental, staring up at Witches Corp.

"What are you going to do if I'm late? Burst through security, pounding your fists against your chest and screaming out my name?"

Lance glanced down at her. "You are a very mouthy brat, you know that?"

"I didn't hear you complaining about my mouth one bit last night," she retorted, smirking at him.

He raised his hand and tweaked her nose. "Oh, your mouth is one of the most decadent and beautiful things I've ever experienced. It's when words come out of it that there's a problem."

"Lance!" Azrael punched him in the shoulder. "You ass!"

He leaned down and kissed the top of her head. "I never pretended I wasn't. Thirty minutes. I'm serious."

"Yes, Your Majesty."

Azrael turned and bowed before crossing the parking lot, purse slung over her shoulders. Her heels clicked on the sidewalk, and she slowed down, remembering the last time she'd worn them.

The night that started it all.

She tried to imagine the look on her face if she could go back and tell herself Lance was a phenomenal lover, that without even having sex, he'd given her pleasure in a way no one else had before. Hopefully, he felt the same. Azrael frowned at the thought. Last night was nothing short of wonderful for her. Lance, on the other hand....

"I'm sorry, Sarah."

He'd spoken those words repeatedly while he thrashed around in his sleep, caught in a nightmare she couldn't even begin to comprehend. Without having to ask, she knew the name of the woman he loved was Sarah. It was evident in the gentleness in his voice, the agony in his tone. Sarah, the woman he loved. The woman he still loved.

And I'm his lover.

At least she could give it a name now. There wasn't an inch of each other's bodies they left unexplored. Even spent and exhausted, she wanted more. She craved him, lusted for him. Her insatiable desire was only matched by his. It was a deadly game to play, not only with her heart but with her magic. There were so many times she came close to begging him to be inside her. It was on the tip of her tongue. Somehow she'd found the strength to ignore that desire. But for how long? She'd already tried to convince herself she'd only lose the power for a few weeks. No big deal, right? Except she knew when they broke that rule, they'd never stop.

Azrael paused her thoughts long enough to pull her keycard out of her purse. Right now, she needed to focus on the task at hand, not her sex life. The doorman opened one of the large glass doors.

"Welcome back, Azrael."

"Thanks, Otis. I'm just here for a visit, though." She leaned over to the small man and cupped her hands around her mouth. "Still grounded, you know."

Otis chuckled and whispered back, "Oh, I know. It's been rather boring without you around."

She smiled over her shoulder and stepped through the large glass door.

Witches Corp was nothing short of a maze bustling with throngs of humans and demons alike rushing in every direction. Fifty-nine stories high, it hosted some of the most powerful witches from both worlds. Navigating it, though, was another story. Nestled in San Jose, CA, the original designers made it into an homage of the Winchester House. This was partially due to the fact the home was accidentally destroyed when engineers stumbled upon an energy trail a few miles from the house. Wanting to find the source and thinking it might be an optimum spot for building, they dug deep into the earth, releasing a stream of energy that, to their surprise, was thousands of trapped spirits. Long story short, a portal opened, and the spirits left, taking the house with them. To this day, one engineer claimed several spirits turned around to flip him off as they took leave with it.

Still, homage is one thing, staircase mazes and moving portals are another. One wrong turn out of the breakroom, and you could find yourself eating a chocolate donut in the dressing room with a bunch of naked men. Azrael could vouch for that from experience.

That was a good day, she thought, a lazy smile on her face as she remembered the sexy, unabashedly naked cop who'd asked her to share her donut. Who knew eating a donut while having sex in a shower stall could be so damn hot? She'd signed the write-up form for her torn skirt, wrinkled shirt, and missing hose with a grin on her face.

Azrael headed left toward the visitor's desk but stopped short, her lucid recollection of the sexual encounter becoming a puff of smoke.

Behind the desk was an ozrath.

Bloody crap, they must be increasing security.

She tapped her fingers against her purse, glanced toward the entryway, feet planted in the direction of the counter. The door opened, light glinting off the panes of glass, then shut again. She could imagine Lance standing across the street, arms wrapped across his chest, checking the time on his Rolex every few minutes. Azrael glanced back at the ozrath, wearing the gentle expression of a child, a sweet smile plastered across its face as it stared dreamily at the ceiling. If she went out there and tried to explain why she couldn't do what she came here to do, Lance would laugh in her face and send her back. No one who hadn't experienced it could understand the utter torment dealing with an ozrath caused.

She tugged her purse higher on her shoulder and straightened her back. Inhaling deeply through her nose, she approached the counter in long strides. "Hi, I'd like a visitor's pass."

The childlike female lowered her gaze, chin tilting down until her head was perfectly aligned with her chest. "Hi?"

"Yes. Hi."

"Can I help you?"

"Yes. I would like a visitor's pass."

"Would you like a visitor's pass?" the ozrath asked, the ringlets in her hair bobbing with each fevered nod of her head.

"Yes."

"Would you like to know my name?"

Azrael shook her head. "No."

"Would I like you to know my name?"

"Probably."

The ozrath said nothing, only tilted its head to the side, touching its ear to its shoulder.

"I mean, yes, I would like to know your name," Azrael said.

"What is my name?"

Azrael sighed and read the name off the girl's tag. "Cherlisa."

"What is Cherlisa?"

"Your name. Now can I please have my visitor's pass?" Azrael gritted her teeth.

"Would you like a visitor's pass?"

"Yes. My name is Azrael Larken. I need a visitor's pass to the fifth floor. I should be on the visitor's list for Gracie and Logan Duncan."

The ozrath looked at her screen and pressed some buttons. Azrael glanced at the clock behind the desk, counting the seconds ticking by as she waited. She had to give them credit—when it came to security measures, Witches Corp was one of the safest places to work. A criminal would go crazy trying to break in, especially if they weren't used to an ozrath. As if it wasn't enough to have to deal with a creature who could only speak in questions, beneath their childish features, hid a deadly being.

"Is your name Azrael Larken?"

"Yes."

"Would you like a visitor's pass?"

"Yes."

"For the fifth floor?"

"Yes."

"Are you a guest of Gracie Duncan?"

"Yes."

"Are you a guest of Logan Duncan?"

"You know damn well I am. You're looking right at it on the screen." Azrael clenched a hand around her purse strap.

The ozrath continued to stare at her with an innocent smile.

"Yes, okay? Yes, I am a guest of Logan Duncan."

"Can you hold please while I print out your card?"

"Yes." *Finally.*

The clock continued to click by as she waited. She felt her phone vibrate and knew it was Lance asking her to check in. Tapping her nails on the counter, she watched as the card printed, each line taking an exorbitant amount of time. When it split out the laminated sheet, she reached for it, but Cherlisa was quicker.

"Would you like your pass now?"

"Yes," Azrael seethed.

"The pass for Azrael Larken?"

"Yes, dammit."

"To visit the fifth floor?"

"Ugh, yes."

"A guest of Gracie—"

"Oh my gosh. Here, just let me have it."

She grabbed for the pass, shrinking back in terror as the ozrath's mouth opened unnaturally, the skin on its cheeks stretching to accommodate six rows of razor-sharp teeth that snapped at her fingers. Azrael dropped her hand to her side as she stared into an endless chasm of grinding molars.

"Why don't you," she took a shaky breath, "go ahead and finish what you were asking?"

Cherlisa resumed her childlike form, plastering a sickly-sweet smile on her face. "Would you like me to finish my questions?"

"Yes, ma'am."

"A guest of Gracie Duncan?"

"Yes, ma'am."

"A guest of Logan Duncan."

"Yes, ma'am."

"Will you have a nice day, please?"

"Yes, ma'am."

Cherlisa held the pass out to her. Azrael reached up, pinching the end between her trembling fingers, waiting for the ozrath to let go before she took it. Beside the counter, the elevator doors opened, and Azrael stepped in, her eyes staying on the child-like creature until the doors slid shut.

~*~

She stepped out on the fifth floor, taking the familiar route to her cubical. Having originally been the wing for fertility witches, the carpet depicted a painting of an ancient god standing on a cloud — beneath him, hundreds were intertwined in a lover's embrace. Unfortunately for Azrael, her desk was placed on top of a male figure, his erect penis directly where she placed her feet. To amuse herself, sometimes she'd kick off her shoes and give him a little foot action, but she tried to keep it at a minimum.

Unlike some, she thought, glancing under the desk of her coworker three cubicles down, whose own male figure's penis was worn threadbare.

Gracie caught her eye and waved. Azrael made her way over to the small, slender woman with blue hair styled in a pixie cut. Beside her stood her twin brother Logan, his long blue hair tucked behind pointed ears. She grabbed the chair from her cubicle across from theirs and sat down at their desk.

"I've missed the crap out of you," Gracie said. "When the hell are you coming back? Ever since you've been gone, Regina's been trying to be all buddy-buddy with me and in full-on slut mode around Logan."

Logan gave a disgusted sneer. "She keeps coming to sit at your desk to talk to us, and every time Gracie's not looking, she uncrosses her legs, trying to get me to peek beneath her skirt."

"Oh, it can't be that bad, Logan. So, she's a little different. That doesn't make her gross," Azrael said, eyeing the orange-skinned girl with large freckles.

"First of all, she's dumb as dirt. Second, she's not wearing panties. Third," he leaned down and whispered in Azrael's ear, "she has tentacles coming out of her you know what."

"Really?" Azrael glanced at Regina with a little more interest. "Huh, I didn't know her species had that. Get me her number, and I'll give it to Caleb. He might be interested, female or not."

Gracie waved her hand at her twin brother. "Enough about Logan's problems. Get to the nitty-gritty and explain why you texted me you needed our help. Did someone hex you? Is that why you summoned a stink demon?"

"No, that was totally unrelated." Azrael looked up at the ceiling, trying to decide where to start. "So, there's this guy—"

"I told you it had to do with a guy," Logan said, cutting in.

"Shut up, Logan. I want to hear this. Go ahead, Azrael."

"Anyway, long story short, I have a konsumo demon after me."

"Are you freaking serious?" Gracie asked, her eyes

widening.

"Yes."

"Have you contacted the police?"

She shook her head. "They can't help because they can't track him down. I've got someone willing to help me, but I have to summon the konsumo demon before he can do that. Problem is, I tried, but he'd set up hexes. I got stuck in the veil."

Gracie covered her mouth.

"You're lucky to be alive, Azrael," Logan said, shaking his head.

"I know."

"Azrael." Gracie leaned over and squeezed her hand. "If you've come to us to help you break a hex, I want you to know beforehand that we can't break hexes inside the veil."

"Oh, I know. I wouldn't ask either of you to get involved that way. What I'm needing is—"

Azrael cut her sentence short as another one of their coworkers walked by. She recognized the big bosomed brunette from a few doors down and gave her a smile. The girl smiled back but gave a sneer when she saw Logan. He glanced up at her and turned around, pressing his nose against the cubical wall.

Azrael frowned. "What are you doing?"

"Is she gone?" Logan asked, his voice muffled.

"Um...yeah," she said slowly.

Logan turned around. "Now, what were you saying?"

"Okay, wait, what the hell was that about?"

Gracie rolled her eyes. "Logan got sent to magical banning for sexual harassment. Apparently, Loraine accused him of staring at her chest all the time. Now, whenever she walks by, he's not allowed to look that direction."

"Stupid binding spell," Lance commented.

"Well, you shouldn't have been staring at her boobs," Azrael said.

Logan grinned. "They are really nice boobs, though."

Her phone buzzed in her purse, and she pulled it out. There were three impatient texts from Lance letting her know her time was up. She texted back *five more minutes* and put the phone away. "Okay, I don't have much time, so I better get to it. Look, I know this is a huge favor to ask, but trust me when I say my life is on the line. I know you occasionally get to check the clarity crystal out overnight when you're working on breaking a particularly difficult hex. I need to borrow it."

Brother and sister exchanged a glance. Logan shook his head.

"Look, I swear I'll return it safely the next day. I'll even make it up to you. You know that good luck demon you guys have been begging me to summon, but I wouldn't because it's illegal? Well, I'll throw one in. Hell, two if it'll convince you guys. I really don't want to die."

Gracie looked at her and swallowed. "Azrael, it's not that. We want to help you. We do. It's just that the crystal isn't here."

"What do you mean?"

Logan stuck his hands into his pockets. "This week marks the fiftieth-anniversary Witches Corp has had the stone. They've loaned it out to have a special article written about it—there will be photographs, history, everything."

"Great. That's just great." Azrael covered her hands with her face.

"Well, you're not going to like this, but there might be a way for you to get your hands on it," Gracie said, biting her lip.

"And how's that?"

"Well, let's just say you're acquainted with the person

who's writing the article. Very well acquainted," Logan admitted.

She glanced between the two. Then it hit her. "You've got to be freaking kidding me."

Chapter 24

"So, let me get this straight," Lance said, slipping off his button down and throwing it on the back of the chair. "Your ex-boyfriend, the one who published nude pictures of you—"

"Just one picture."

"Who posted *a* nude picture of you, caused you to mess up your spell, and get laid off from work, is the one who has the stone, and you want to call him and ask him for a date?"

Azrael crossed her arms, trying not to be distracted by Lance's naked chest or the deftness of his hands as he undid his belt. "Um…yeah, I thought I might get him to invite me over. As soon as I find out where it is, I'll take it."

"There are several things wrong with your plan. First, what's to keep him from calling the police when you take it? Second, what if it's not at his house? What if he has it locked up? Kidnapping is the only option."

"I just think that's a little extreme. Why don't you give me a chance to convince him first before we run in guns blaring?"

Lance cocked his head to the side. "And how exactly do you plan on convincing him?"

Azrael grinned. She stepped forward, closing the distance

between them, and ran a finger down his bare chest to the top of his pants. "Oh, I have my ways."

Lance growled and grabbed her around the waist, slinging her over his shoulder. "We'll see about that."

She kicked her feet in the air, giggling, and pounded him on the back. "Put me down."

"As you wish," he said, tossing her on the bed and crawling on top of her. "Now, why don't you show me what you're not going to do to convince him?"

For the rest of the night, she did just that.

~*~

They got back home around three. Azrael opened the car door, letting Smellicious run around the courtyard before heading inside. Lance leaned against the car beside her, one foot crossed over the other, and ran a hand through his disheveled hair, staring off at the tree line. He'd been distant all day, making her edgy. During the night, he'd thrashed in his sleep again, and this morning she'd started to sneak into the shower with him but changed her mind when she saw him through the crack in the door. He'd was leaned over the sink, hands covering his face, body shuddering.

A part of her wished she could comfort him, to be the kind of person who could help him through this. Instead, she was jealous of the woman who held his heart, jealous of a woman who died for it. At some point, they needed to talk about things, about the future. She wanted sex—hell, nearly broke several times and begged him for it the last two nights. But even without penetration, Lance was far better than any lover she'd ever been with.

It's not just the physical, she thought, studying his face. Leolacent was right. She was in love with him, or at least halfway there. Did he feel the same about her? Could he move on from his past?

As if he could hear her thoughts, Lance said, "I need to tell you something, and I'm not sure how you will take it. Hell, I'm not even sure if you'll care."

Lance was staring at her now instead of the tree line. Purple clouds floated across the orange sky, casting his face in shadows. The wind picked up and the dark plume in the distance hinted of an impending storm.

"Okay," she answered hesitantly, "go ahead."

He reached up, rubbing the back of his neck. "Well, I, um—these past few days have been great, but I don't want to give you the wrong impression."

"The wrong impression," she mumbled, narrowing her eyes.

"No, that's not what I mean either. Crap, Azrael, just give me a second to explain." He uncrossed his legs and came to stand in front of her, taking her hands in his. "Look, I've asked a lot from you, I've put you through hell, and you've accepted me. The last few days have been the best I've had in a long time. I just don't know where this is going. You already know we can't have sex, no matter how much we both want it. I guess what I'm trying to say is that I care about you, and I think you care about me too. It's only fair if I'm completely honest with you."

"If this is about Sarah, it's okay. I understand, or at least I'm trying to. I don't expect you to just move on."

Lance flinched, his face darkening. "How do you know her name?"

"You yell it out in your sleep." Azrael lowered her head, studying the ground.

"I didn't realize," he mumbled.

"It's okay. I get it. You don't need to feel bad about it. You loved her. A part of you always will."

"That's the problem," he said. "My nights are full of dreams of her. I wake in agony every morning when I realize she's not there. My love for her is not something I'll ever get past. I told you I didn't think she loved me. That was I lie. I know she didn't."

She looked up at him, frowning. "How?"

Lance dropped her hands and paced. "It was a set-up. Blais knew I wanted out. He wanted me to stay. He hired Sarah to convince me to stay. Blais paid Sarah to make me fall in love with her. The night before I'd gone to Blais, swearing my love for Sarah, and told him I was leaving, taking her away from this life. Blais was livid. It wasn't until later I realized his anger was more toward Sarah than me. She'd failed to convince me to stay. In truth, she'd never asked. I believe she was playing both sides. Sarah hated Blais, tried to convince me my brother was evil, that we weren't safe when he was around. I was willing to turn in all my assets and take her far away from him. Apparently, Blais decided she was too much of a risk. He killed her to spite me. Now I'm stuck loving someone who never cared for me at all."

"I'm so sorry." Azrael reached out and touched his face. When she ran her fingers over his lips, they trembled.

"I wanted you to know this, to understand that no matter how much I wish I could give you more, there's a large part of me you can never have. I don't know if that matters, but it would be wrong not to tell you. I fought so hard to stay away from you, but I wasn't strong enough. So, if you want to stop doing what we're doing, I will understand. I don't want you to get hurt over my selfishness."

Azrael wiped a tear away. Lance lifted his hand as if to

touch her but then dropped it to his side.

"And if I don't want to stop, what then?"

"Then I will give you what I can."

She nodded. "I guess that will have to be enough."

His eyes widened. "Why? Why would you do that?"

"Because it's too late to do anything else."

"Don't say—"

Azrael cut him off. "Don't say what? How I feel? How about you let me feel what I feel and not try to judge me for it or ignore that it's there? Isn't that what you are asking me to do? Accept how you feel, or the lack thereof, for a better explanation?"

"Azrael, I didn't mean to upset you," Lance said, laying a hand on her shoulder.

"I know you didn't. I'm glad you told me. I am. Just give me some time to process."

"Okay," he whispered, his expression that of an abashed child. "Just please don't think this means I'm not trying. I'll do my best to make you happy."

"That's all I ask for then."

Azrael stood on her tippy toes to kiss him on the cheek. Lance turned his head, meeting her mouth. This kiss was different. There was a passion to it, but it was more caring, more *loving*.

He broke the kiss off and pulled her into his chest. "Come on, let's get inside before this storm blows in."

~*~

"So, let me get this straight," Caleb said, pouring them a drink. "You and demon boy are getting each other's rocks off, and you're calling this what, exactly?"

"Complicated is the first thing that comes to mind," Azrael replied, leaning back in the hot tub as Caleb handed her a glass. Lance had needed to go into town to drop off deposits and grocery shop, giving her and Caleb some much-needed alone time.

"People who are in complicated relationships rarely walk around with silly grins on their faces. The two of you have been acting like you're on cloud nine since you came back. The loving can't possibly be that good."

Azrael rolled her head toward him and grinned.

"Okay, that's it. Spill it. I bet he's huge. Plus, he's had so many lovers—he's got to be a pro with that tongue."

The grin slipped off Azrael's face. Somehow she'd managed to forget he was pretty much a whore in his past. She guzzled the last of her drink and set it down.

"Crap, baby girl. I'm sorry. I shouldn't have brought that up."

"It's fine. I'm getting used to all the crap that comes with being with Lance."

"I hate to ask this, but is he worth it? I mean, I'll take your word for it that the foreplay is fantastic, but his murdering brother is after you, you two can't have sex, and he's admitted that he can't get past his ex. You know me, Az, I'm all for relationships with no strings attached, but you're not that kind of girl."

"I can handle it," she said, filling up her glass. "The way things are going, I may not even survive the rest of this week. Right now, I'm just going to take what I get and enjoy it."

Caleb filled his own glass and raised it in the air. "To taking what you want."

Azrael smiled and tipped her own glass against his. For a while, they drank in silence, enjoying the heavy jets massaging their bodies. Tomorrow she would meet with her ex. To her surprise, Garrin not only answered her call but practically purred when she asked him if they could get together at his place. Of course, she didn't mention she'd be bringing an extra guest. According to Lance, there was no way in hell she was going alone.

For the first time since they'd broken up, she felt nothing but pity for Garrin. Although he was a shallow ass, he didn't deserve to be dragged into this situation. Maybe her lack of rage had to do with the fact Lance was keeping her very satisfied.

"I need to get laid," Caleb said, looking up at the ceiling. "Your boyfriend—"

"Lover."

"Your lover has a lot of rules about his home. One is no guests. If we continue staying here, Az, I might die from need."

"Well, maybe celibacy is the one thing that will work to help you get over your agoraphobia," she teased.

"Did I ever tell you you're kind of mean?"

"All the time."

Caleb threw his arm around her shoulders and gave her a squeeze. "Just try to keep yourself from getting hurt. If you can't, I'm always here to pick up the pieces."

"Thanks, Caleb," she said. "Keep a trash bag ready because I get the feeling this will end up in one hell of a mess."

Chapter 25

Azrael was thankful Garrin had given her the gate code, so she didn't have to explain her "chauffeur." Although she couldn't imagine anyone looking less chauffer-ish than Lance. The outfit he'd rented was too tight and looked ready to burst at the seams over his biceps. Between that and the way he held himself—jaws clenched, muscles tight—he seemed more like a mix between a male stripper and a cop.

They pulled into the driveway.

"So, you ready to do this?" she asked, chewing on her bottom lip. Lance was not happy about waiting in the car, but it was the best plan they'd come up with. Azrael would go in, talk a bit, try to get a tour, and find out where the stone was. When she found it, she'd text Lance, who would sneak in and steal it. Easy as that—she hoped.

"I don't like this, Azrael. Something feels wrong," he said, hands tight on the steering wheel.

"You're just being overprotective. It's going to go fine. I know Garrin. He's an egotistical jerk, but he's not a bad guy."

"You have the pepper spray I gave you?"

"Yes. In my purse." Azrael sighed. It was cute how jealous

he was, but also unnecessary.

"If he lays one finger on you—"

"I know, I know. Spray him. Now, can I please go in? It looks weird me sitting out here arguing with my chauffeur."

"Fine. But I'll be watching."

"I don't doubt that," Azrael mumbled, opening the door. Before she slipped out, Lance grabbed her arm.

"Hey...," he said, his eyes full of concern. "Please be careful. I don't want anything to happen to you."

"I promise."

Azrael shut the door and made her way up the stone steps.

~*~

Garrin opened the door, grinning at her with his perfect white teeth, sun-bleached hair pulled back in a low ponytail.

"Azrael," he said, gathering her in his arms. "How I've missed you."

"I've—uh, I've missed you too," she replied, giving him a loose hug, groaning when she heard the car door slam behind her.

"Who's that?" Garrin asked.

Azrael turned around. Lance was standing outside of the car, leaning against the passenger side, arms crossed over his chest, eyes hidden beneath dark glasses.

"That's just my chauffeur. You know, from the trip I won." Azrael gave Lance a dark look.

"Huh. Looks more like a bodyguard to me." Garrin put his hand on the small of her back, steering her toward the house. "Guess they thought of everything. How did you win the trip to Demonium?"

"I, um...an online thing."

"Well, regardless, I'll consider it a lucky break for me. I

thought I might never see you again." Garrin pushed the door shut and turned, gave her one of his one-hundred-watt smiles, and placed a hand on her shoulder. "I wanted to apologize for what I did. I never thought that photo would upset you. You're such a beautiful woman, Azrael. It seemed unfair to not share it with the world."

Yeah, unfair to the world, not me. What a pompous asshole.

"Why don't we just move past that?" she asked through gritted teeth. "We can't change the past."

"Exactly." He said, giving her shoulder a light squeeze. "And I promise it won't happen again."

That's because you won't ever get the chance to see me naked again.

"Thanks."

"Now, how about I give you a grand tour of my home?"

"That sounds great."

While Garrin showed her around, babbling on about his historic item collection, Azrael tried to figure out what had drawn her to him in the first place. Sure, he was sexy. Who wouldn't desire those lean muscles or that confident physique? Not to mention the charming smile and perfect ass. Azrael gazed at the back of his tailored jeans with a surge of guilt.

Okay, so what, he's hot, and I looked. He's not half the man Lance is, though.

She nodded her head, feigning interest. It wasn't until they got to the sitting room on the first floor that she no longer had to pretend.

"And I think you'll recognize this piece," he said, waving his hand toward the coffee table. On it sat a large purple stone with pearlescent facets on the side.

That stupid bastard. He's left the clarity stone sitting on his living room table, balcony door wide open. Azrael had to choke back a laugh. *You've got to be kidding me.*

"The clarity stone," she said, trying to sound nonchalant.

Garrin gave her a crooked grin. "Of course. I don't imagine this piece would be of much interest to you now, considering you see it so often."

"Well, it's still a nice piece."

"Aren't you a little curious why I have it, though?" he asked, angling his head to the side.

Crap! I'm horrible at this undercover thing. Should have acted surprised.

"Yes, I am very curious, but I'm a little tired and thirsty from the trip. Do you have anything to drink?"

"I'm sorry. I should have offered you one first. Why don't we go sit in the kitchen and enjoy a couple of glasses of wine?" He walked off without letting her answer, obviously expecting her to follow.

Don't look at his ass, don't look at his ass.

Azrael followed him. When they reached the kitchen, she set her purse down. "Do you have a restroom I can use?"

"Sure. It's down that hall. Last door on the left," he answered, pointing to the hallway across from them. "I'll pour us some drinks while waiting."

She nodded and stepped to the bathroom, closing and locking the door behind her. Azrael pulled out her phone and typed a text to Lance.

It's in the sitting room on the table. Balcony door is open. We will be in the kitchen. Text me when you have it.

Lance's response was swift. *That sounds easy, too easy. Something about this feels wrong. Please be careful.*

She stared at the phone, not understanding Lance's

apprehension. In all honesty, this was working out a lot better than planned. Maybe he was paranoid because he was so used to things being hard. Azrael tucked a loose strand of hair behind her ear and went to meet Garrin in the kitchen.

Garrin was sitting in a chair, leaned back, a glass of chardonnay in his hand. He was staring out the large window leading to the veranda, eyes glazed. She didn't think he even noticed her presence until she pulled out the chair beside him.

"Hey there," he said, handing her a glass. "Sorry, I was daydreaming."

"I'm no stranger to you zoning out." She immediately regretted bringing up something she remembered from when they dated.

"I'm surprised you haven't blocked those memories out completely."

Azrael swallowed. She'd tried to do just that but was apparently less successful than she thought. "No, not completely."

Garrin gave her a soft smile, his gaze drawn to the window again. She studied his profile, noting the crinkles around his eyes. Somehow, he appeared older than his thirty-two years. The silence grew, making her nervous. It was unusual for Garrin to not start a conversation, to act so serious.

Lance has made me paranoid.

"So, last I heard, you were dating Lindsey Barrett," she said, trying to start a conversation.

"I don't really date anyone, Azrael. Or at least there's no one I've wanted to date. You being the exception, of course, but that wouldn't have worked out." He took another swig out of his glass, eyes still glued to the window.

"What? Why would you think that?" Azrael set her drink down. The ice clinked against the glass, setting her nerves on edge. Maybe she shouldn't have been so quick to brush off Lance's concerns. Something seemed off.

But Garrin is as harmless as a bug.

They'd dated, slept together. He wasn't a stranger, wasn't a bad guy.

Then why does this feel wrong?

"Has anyone ever told you that you are a bad judge of character?"

Azrael froze, her heart skidding to an abrupt stop. He turned to look at her, his eyes cold and uncaring. Her heart rate picked up, beating double time. This wasn't the Garrin she knew. She edged closer to her purse and reached down. His eyes slid from her face to the hand dangling above the open handbag.

"Looking for something?" he asked, pulling the bottle of pepper spray out of his pocket. "This stuff can be painful, Azrael. It's best if I keep it safe."

Staring at the can, she swallowed. In a few minutes, Lance would have the stone and would worry when she didn't respond to his text. She just needed to stall until then. "Are you trying to tell me I've judged you wrong?"

"Oh, most definitely."

"I think I should go," she said, standing.

"I'm afraid that's not going to be an option." Garrin set his glass down. As he did, a shrill alarm started blaring. "Ah, our guest has arrived."

Lance, she thought, turning and running toward the sitting room. She heard Garrin's footsteps following her.

Chapter 26

Lance cowered on the floor, eyes burning with hatred as sparks of white light surrounded him. He jolted forward when he saw Azrael, his hand touching the electric web of power, and screamed. She ran to him. He must have seen the intent in her eyes, the panicked look of determination, because he yelled, "No! Stay away!"

"I can't leave you in there," she argued, looking around the room for anything to break the trapping spell.

"Just get out of here! Go!"

"Oh, I wouldn't recommend that," Garrin said as he strolled into the room, hands shoved into his pockets. "That's not the only trap I set today. Plus, I dare say I've been dying to meet the infamous Lance Jenkins. We wouldn't want her to miss what I have in store for you."

"Let him go, Garrin. He's done nothing to you. I asked him to get the stone for me."

He ran his tongue over his teeth. "Is that so? Well, by all means then, I'll set him free."

Garrin tugged what looked like a silver keychain out of his pocket and pointed it at Lance. One click later, the web of light surrounding him disappeared. Lance stood slowly, his eyes locked on Garrin, and moved to stand between him and Azrael.

"You don't have to do that," Garrin said, giving him a cocky grin. "I have no intention of hurting *her*."

Azrael licked her lips. "Look, Garrin. Can we please sit down and talk? I'll explain everything. We only needed the crystal because my life is in danger. We meant no harm to you."

"I know why you came. I know a lot more than either of you could possibly imagine."

"How do you know who I am? Are you working for Blais?" Lance asked, his eyes narrowed.

Flicking a piece of lint off his shirt, Garrin chuckled. Azrael cut her eyes to Lance. His face mirrored hers. If Garrin was working for Blais, they were in trouble. That meant Blais might be on his way, might be here right now. Lance mouthed the word, *"Run."*

Azrael turned, preparing to do just that, when Garrin looked back up, his face contorted into a menacing sneer. "No. Unlike you, I don't work for murderers."

Lance became stiff. "I've never hurt anyone."

"Oh, is that so?" Garrin waltzed across the floor, closing the distance between them. "Is that what you tell yourself at night? What you say when you visit Sarah's grave?"

A clock chimed somewhere in the house. Azrael watched as the two men stood eye to eye, Garrin with his fists clenched to his sides. Lance, face pale, eyes furious with pain. She didn't see it coming, but Garrin must have because when Lance charged at him, he sidestepped the attack. Lance stumbled forward, and Garrin moved with a swiftness she'd never imagined he had. Grabbing Lance by the collar with one hand, he rammed a fist into his back. The only thing louder than the thud of the impact was the whooshing sound Lance made as the air was knocked out of him.

Azrael rushed over to the two men, her heart galloping, mind racing. She had no plan, only knew she needed to stop Garrin, who had rolled Lance over, fists raised. She threw herself on his back, yanking with all her might, trying to pull him away. He was too strong. His fist slammed into Lance's face. Once. Twice. A third time. She began to scream.

Lance moaned. His eyes became slits, his mouth hung slack, and red welts dotted his cheeks and forehead. Garrin raised his fists again. She did the only thing she could think to do. Leaning in, she placed her mouth on his shoulder and bit him hard. He yelped and jumped up. She tightened her arms and wrapped her legs around him. Azrael bit down harder and tasted blood.

She didn't see his plan until it was too late. He lunged into the wall backward, pinning her against the hard stone, causing her to break her hold and cry out. Garrin flung her to the floor.

Hurt and breathless, she crawled toward Lance, hoping to get between the two. Lance was laying on the floor, barely conscious. Sweat rolled down her forehead and stung her eyes. She was prepared to fight if needed, but Garrin seemed to have lost interest in the two of them. Instead, he was pacing around the stone, shaking his head, jaws clenched.

"Wake up. Please wake up." Azrael shook Lance, and he moaned. If someone had told her Garrin was tough enough to take out Lance, she wouldn't have believed him. Garrin, at least the Garrin she knew, no longer existed. This man was a monster. "Lance, you have to wake up. He's crazy, and he'll kill us both."

Lanced moaned again, but this time his eyes opened a bit. "Azrael?"

"Yes. Please. We have to hurry," she whispered, slipping her arms around him to try to get him to sit. Garrin was still pacing and shaking his head.

"You have to get up. We have to get out of here before he attacks again."

Her words seemed to sink in because Lance pulled himself to a sitting position, wincing with every movement.

"Are you okay? Did he hurt you?" he asked.

"I'm okay. Let's just go." Her eyes darted toward Garrin. Lance followed her gaze.

Garrin stopped pacing and lifted a finger, pointing it at a blank wall. "Not a chance in hell. I won't do this. That was not a part of the plan."

"He's nuts," Azrael whispered.

Garrin continued, seemingly oblivious to their existence. "I wasn't going to kill him. I was just having a little fun. Bastard deserved it."

"Let's get the hell out of here," Lance whispered, rising to his feet.

She wrapped an arm around his waist to steady him. They backed away to the door. Azrael hoped they could escape before he regained his sanity, if there was any left.

With his eyes locked on the wall, Garrin didn't seem to notice their impending departure. "Blais will die. I don't need their help. I have the clarity stone, and I have a plan. I told you that. I don't care what those two are capable of, Sarah."

"Sarah," Lance said, his jaw dropping open.

Uh-oh.

That seemed to get Garrin's attention. He turned around, eyes locking on Lance. "Yes, Sarah. The woman your brother killed. Sarah here is insisting we work together to find and kill

Blais. Personally, you're the last person in the world I want to team up with."

"You're a soul-speaker," Lance whispered.

"Yes."

Lance crumpled to the floor, pulling Azrael down with him.

Chapter 27

Azrael pressed the damp cloth against Lance's head. Across from them sat Garrin, his nose crinkling in disgust every time she tried to coax Lance awake. At least he had helped her carry him to the couch. She'd been as reluctant to let him touch Lance as Garrin was to help, but in the end, she couldn't just leave him lying on the floor.

"Come on, Lance, wake up." The cloth didn't seem to be doing much good. As far as she could tell, the swelling seemed to be getting worse. He'd heal from the injuries, though. She wasn't sure he'd heal from what Garrin said. If it was true, if he was a soul-speaker, if he knew Sarah, then Lance's injuries would be the least of his concerns.

"I've got a bottle of acid if you want to use that. Came straight from the deoga snakes of Saratin. That stuff will eat through skin in seconds. Bet it would wake him up," Garrin said, a cocky grin on his face.

She chose to ignore his chiding. As it was, she wasn't certain about his sanity. That, and what his plans were for the both of them. With Lance unconscious, Garrin had the upper hand. Hell, she didn't want to admit it, but even with Lance conscious, Garrin still had the upper hand.

"What are you going to do with us?" she asked, dabbing at the drops of blood above Lance's brow.

Silence. She looked over her shoulder. Garrin was looking at her, his cocky attitude gone.

"I wasn't going to hurt you, Azrael. If you knew how hard it was for me to face him," he nodded to Lance, "and not kill him, you wouldn't be thinking the worst of me right now."

"Then why don't you tell me? What do you know? Why do you hate Lance?"

"Let's wait for him to wake up, and I will. It seems I'll be working with the two of you after all, and I'd rather not have to tell my story twice."

~*~

It took an hour for Lance to wake and another thirty minutes to calm him enough to agree to talk to Garrin. Both men were sitting in the kitchen, a cup of coffee in hand, eyes narrowed. Azrael decided it would be up to her to start the conversation.

"Tell us what you know, Garrin."

"I know everything," he responded, pointing a finger at Lance. "About him, his brother, the murders. I know so much it sickens me to have that asshole sitting at my table."

Lance shoved his chair back and stood, hands clenched around his cup. "I didn't murder anyone. I didn't know what Blais was doing."

"Maybe you did, maybe you didn't, but you had a part in it. Lying to women, stealing their powers, breaking their hearts." Garrin pounded his fist on the table. "People were killed because of you. You are a piece of filth! A dirty monster! Stand there and tell me you're not."

Lance shook his head and slumped down into the chair,

face drawn and pale. "No, I can't tell you I'm not."

Rubbing a hand over his stubble, Garrin eyed Lance, a thoughtful expression on his face. After a moment, he cut through the silence. "Well, at least we can agree on something. I think it would save us some time if we all just assume I knew everything, and I can start on *how* I know everything instead."

"Sarah," Azrael said, her heart aching when she saw Lance flinch at the mention of the name.

Garrin raised a finger. "I'll get to her in a moment. First, I want to explain what I am."

"I know what a soul-speaker is."

"No, you know what a normal soul-speaker is. Not what I am. I don't sit around and summon the dead. The dead come to me."

Azrael set her cup of coffee down and leaned forward. She'd heard of soul-speakers with exceptional powers like he spoke of. Soul-speakers had the power to contact the dead, either through crystal balls or summoning, but it was rumored there were those out there who didn't need those things. Even then, none had been recorded in centuries. "What do you mean by 'come to you'?"

"I mean, they seek me out. Lost souls come to me for help."

"Garrin, if that were true, you'd be the most famed soul-speaker in history. How does no one know? Your power would make you rich."

"First of all, I don't know if you've noticed," he waved his hand around the room, "but I'm already rich. Secondly, I'm already famous. I'm doing what I've always wanted to do — investigative journalism. Have you ever wondered how I've been able to break open so many cases to figure out what people are hiding? I help the dead, and in return, they find out information for me. Of course, they are never allowed to tell my secret. They get what they want, and I get my name in the history books as the best journalist that ever lived."

"Everything about you is a lie," Azrael breathed out.

"Some people would see it that way, which is why I prefer to keep my powers a secret."

Lance released a slow breath. "Sarah came to you."

"Yes. Many years back."

"Is she—is she here right now?" he asked, eyes darting around the room.

"She's over there in the corner." He pointed to the left side of the kitchen.

Azrael didn't know whether to laugh or cry. Sarah, the woman he loved, standing right there in the kitchen with the woman who loved him. What fucking bullshit. Even dead, she found new ways to ruin her life.

I'm going to hell. Not only am I having a pity party for myself, but I'm jealous of a woman who was murdered.

One glance at Lance's face and her anger drained away. He was staring at the corner, pale, hands trembling around his cup. The misery on his face was so deep, she felt it to her bones.

"Lance, it's going to be okay."

He glanced at her, but it was as if she were invisible as if her words didn't matter. If someone stabbed her in the chest, it would hurt less than the pain his apathy caused. Somewhere deep inside, she knew she had no right to be hurt, to be angry. He told her he would give her what he could. That he loved another. At the time, it seemed like enough. Now though….

"Can she hear me? Can I talk to her?" Lance asked.

Garrin chuckled. "Well, you could've if she hadn't just flipped you the bird and stormed out."

Lance sagged in the chair, eyes closed. As much as she wanted to reach out to him, Azrael had the feeling he wouldn't appreciate it. Instead, she asked, "What does Sarah want?"

"Same thing you two want. She wants Blais dead. She wants him to pay for what he's done."

"What about Lance? Does she want him dead, too?"

"No," he said, smiling. "She enjoys watching him suffer too much."

Out of the corner of her eye, she saw Lance give a lengthy exhale. "Why does she want us to work together?"

Grabbing a napkin, Garrin wiped off the rings left on the table from his coffee cup. "Because, as I'm sure you know, Blais is an impossible man to find, even for spirits. He has so much protection on him that neither I nor Sarah have even come close. The plan to summon Blais is the best plan we have. Of course, I had no intention of inviting murderous scum in on this, but she insists Lance has to be a part of it. In truth, I think she just hopes to see him killed by his brother, then me take out Blais."

With eyes zeroed on Garrin, Lance spoke through clenched teeth. "How did you know about our plan to have Azrael summon him?"

"Your plan?" Garrin huffed and turned to Azrael. "How did you find out about the apartment opening?"

"Um...an invite, I think. Yeah, that was it. Special discounted apartment. Wait...."

"Didn't you think it was odd how much Azrael looks like Sarah?"

Lance sat quietly, his eyes darting between Garrin and her. *At least he's noticing I exist.*

"Second cousins, once removed. They're related."

Azrael gasped.

"Sarah knew you'd see the resemblance and counted on you to be drawn to her, to convince her to summon Blais. She didn't expect you would need such a push, though. That's where I came in. I began dating Azrael, took that picture, and shoved the magazine under your door."

"You bastard!" Azrael shot out of her chair. "All of this was set up? You and your fucking dead girlfriend dragged my ass into this! You took a naked picture of me to set me up with someone you knew could care less about me and his murderous brother!"

Both men stood and began talking over one another.

"Azrael, I care—"

"I didn't intend—"

"...about you—"

"...for you to get hurt."

"You know what?" Azrael grabbed her purse and slung it over her shoulder. "I think it's time I take a leaf from Sarah's book. Screw you both."

She flipped them off and stormed out.

Chapter 28

"Should have grabbed the damn keys too," she mumbled under her breath as she passed by the car. She was too pissed off to go back in to demand them. She'd rather walk back than deal with any more of their bullshit. Between her half-broken heart and being set up, she was furious. Her life had been turned upside down. She'd fallen in love. All of it was planned. Well, maybe not the falling in love part, but at this point, Garrin and Lance could take the blame for that too.

Lance burst out the door of the mansion, and she picked up her pace. It was no use. He caught up with her in seconds.

"Can we please talk about this?" he asked, raking his fingers through his hair.

"Which part? The part where I was set up? Or maybe the part where the love of your life is hanging around?"

"Both." He grabbed her by the shoulder and pulled her to a stop. "I'm sorry you were set up. I'm sorry for everything you've been through. And I'm — I'm sorry about Sarah, too. More than anything, I don't want to hurt you. I've hurt enough people in my past. Please just talk to me."

Azrael sighed. What choice did she have? She already

loved him. Nothing could change that. "The way you love her, it's just not fair. When you found out she was in the room, it's like I didn't even exist. I was nothing to you."

"That's not true. I care about you very much."

Care, not love. She didn't have to say it out loud. Couldn't say it out loud. The crushing effect of his words must have shown because he started back peddling.

"Look, I didn't say there wasn't more there. I just...." He shook his head. "Look, right now is not a good time for me to sort out my feelings. I wasn't expecting her to be around, even spiritually." Sliding his hand under her chin, he lifted her face until their eyes met. In them, she saw a man exposed, a man torn apart. But in them, she also saw fear. "I know I don't deserve it, don't deserve you. I should push you away, tell you I don't care, but I can't. Garrin is right. I'm a monster. A selfish monster. I wouldn't blame you for leaving right now. You could stay with Garrin. I may hate him, but he can probably keep you safe."

"I want to stay with you," she whispered. He let out a deep breath and laid his forehead against hers. "So, what do we do now?"

"As much as I hate to admit it, we're going to need Garrin's help."

She pulled back. "What? Why? You don't think he'll let us use the clarity stone without him?"

With a shake of his head, Lance said, "That's not it. He caught me on the way out. That's why I took so long to catch up. He says that even with the clarity stone, going back into the veil might kill you. Those things you saw, apparently, they don't expect you to come back. You need someone to protect you while in there, and only the dead can walk freely in the veil."

"The dead? Who's going to—?" She shut her eyes. "You

mean Sarah."

~*~

Azrael stepped out of the car and turned to Garrin. "You better let me walk in first, so I can explain it to Caleb. He's still pissed at you."

Garrin shrugged his shoulders, but she noticed he stayed several feet behind. Glancing up, she saw some curtains upstairs move. She hoped it was Smellicious or Bumpkins who'd caused the curtains to sway. It would be hard enough to explain what was going on without Caleb knowing Garrin was there. She might have to barricade the door.

They stepped inside the foyer, and Azrael kicked off her shoes. Before she could take a step, Caleb came pummeling down the steps, baseball bat propped up on his shoulder, screaming like a banshee. "I've got you now, you SON OF A BITCH!"

Shit.

Sprinting, she ran between Garrin and Caleb, looking to Lance for help. There would be no help there, though. If anything, Lance looked quite amused by the situation. She flung her hands out. "No, Caleb. Stop!"

He came to a halt in front of her, eyes gleaming with hatred. "Not a chance, baby girl. I've been waiting for this moment forever. Move out of the way, Az."

"Listen to me. Garrin isn't who you think—"

"I don't want to hear it." He slipped the bat off his shoulder and held it out. "This bastard published a naked picture of you. He broke your heart. Don't you dare take this away from me."

"He's not who you think he is. Please put the bat down, and I can explain."

Caleb cut his eyes at her. "What do you mean? Like a shapeshifter?"

"Umm…yeah, something like that. And he's here to help. Come upstairs with me, and I'll tell you everything."

His eyes darted between her and Garrin. She couldn't tell if his resolve was wavering or not. If she didn't do something soon, there was a good chance he might use that bat regardless. "If he doesn't help us, I might die summoning Blais."

That got Caleb's attention. He lowered the bat and squeezed his eyes shut, breathing deeply through his nose. "Okay. We'll go upstairs and talk. You and me only, though."

~*~

By the time Azrael finished recanting the day's events, she was exhausted, both physically and emotionally. "Well?"

Caleb shifted on the bed. "Let me get this straight. Not only did that piece of crap take the picture of you, but he's the one who got you into all this in the first place? And you stopped me from beating his ass? I was only planning on putting him in the hospital. Now I'm going to kill him."

"Caleb—"

"Don't you Caleb me. He's got it coming." He leaned back and stared up at the ceiling. "But, I'll wait until after he helps us."

"Really?" she asked, grinning.

"Yes." Caleb nodded. "But you've got to promise me you won't stop me from beating the crap out of him if we survive this."

"Promise. He's all yours."

~*~

They sat around the fireplace. Azrael couldn't decide which was more uncomfortable, the walk of shame she did in college or this moment. Caleb and Lance were both staring at Garrin, eyes narrowed. Caleb's hand kept twitching in the direction of the baseball bat lying in the corner. Lance kept his arms crossed over his chest. Occasionally Caleb and Lance would look at each other, an odd comradery in their eyes.

Well, Azrael thought, *at least something good is coming out of this.*

Garrin appeared unaffected by their attitudes. He was leaned back on the couch, eyes closed, enjoying a glass of Lance's expensive scotch. She was pretty sure he hadn't asked permission to partake of the liquor cabinet, but it seemed like Lance was willing to let that slide.

"So, what's the plan? When do we start?" he asked.

Garrin had given them an abbreviated version before they left. He'd bring the stone and translate for Sarah. In truth, they weren't really asking Garrin. The question was up to Sarah to answer. Opening his eyes, Garrin stared at the far corner of the room. "She says we need to wait for the full moon when the clarity stone will be at its strongest."

"That's like two days away," Caleb argued, his eyes sliding back toward the bat.

"I agree. I don't think the full moon will make that much of a difference," Lance added.

Garrin leaned back. "Well, if you'd rather not wait to keep Azrael safer, then, by all means, we'll just do it now."

If looks could kill. Azrael could practically feel the heat intensifying in the room. It was like one of those old western stand-offs, each man staring the other down. No one budged. No one blinked.

"This is ridiculous. Everyone just stop being assholes to each other. Two days. That's all you have to deal with. Then we part ways *if* we live. So instead of making our last two days miserable, let's all at least try to get along."

Caleb sighed. "She has a point."

He seemed to be the only one willing to concede, though. She turned toward Lance. "Well?"

"Fine."

"Garrin?"

He glanced at Lance, his face set in a grimace, but nodded.

"It's settled then. Two days gives us more time to prepare anyway. I'd like to be as ready as possible."

As they were discussing plans on how to kill Blais once she summoned him, she leaned back and covered her eyes with her hand. A truce. It was better than nothing. Although, two days in the company of an ex, a boyfriend, the dead love of his life, and her best friend who was contemplating murder might leave her wishing for death.

Chapter 29

So far, they'd survived one day and one night. As for Azrael, she'd woken in a foul enough mood to send Smellicious and Bumpkins scuttling off and hiding in another room. Good riddance too. A cup of coffee without those pests running around her, mewling to be fed, was exactly what she needed. Last night she'd slept in bed with a man who refused to touch her. Not only that, but he'd spent most of the night tossing and turning, mumbling "Sarah" under his breath.

After he'd found out from Garrin that Sarah had been watching them for quite some time, he'd become distant. Apparently, the protection on his house only worked for the living.

Okay, she had to admit it. Yeah, it was a little weird loving on someone when you knew a dead ex could be watching. Even worse if it was someone you loved. But dammit, that didn't mean she had to handle it well.

"Whoa, you look like you slept in the devil's den last night."

Garrin came around the corner, hair perfectly styled, eyes clear as if he'd slept like an angel. She wanted to punch him.

Instead of giving into the urge, she grabbed her cup of coffee and stepped out on the veranda. The sun was rising, casting its reddish glow over the courtyard. An audible growl escaped her lips when she'd heard the door open behind her. Leave it to Garrin to not take her very unsubtle hint she didn't want company.

"Bad night?" he asked, sitting in the chair beside her, cradling his own cup of coffee.

"Personal boundaries, Garrin. Learn them." She pulled the hood of her sweater over her head. At least that blocked the view of him.

"Want to talk about what's bothering you?"

"What could be bothering me? Other than the fact that I'm hunted by one konsumo demon—not to mention I'm about to summon him—and dating another, absolutely nothing. Oh, and then, of course, I discover my ex set me up in this situation, bringing along with him my current boyfriend's dead ex."

"You know, I always liked your spunk. It was one of my favorite things about you."

"Bug off, Garrin."

"And go where? Inside surrounded by people who want me dead?"

"The one outside wants you dead too. I just have more tact."

She expected a snappy comeback, but all she got was silence. Azrael peeked around the hoodie. Garrin sat, hands stuffed in his pockets, an expression of deep regret on his face.

"Garrin, I didn't—"

"No." He shook his head, eyes lifting to meet hers. "You didn't mean it, but you should have. I don't blame you for hating me. The only consolation I have is to tell you how much it hurt me to hide the truth from you, to get you involved."

She opened her mouth, then snapped it shut again. A part of her wanted to scream at him, but what good would that do? It would change nothing. "I can't forgive you, but I can try to be civil, for now at least."

"I'll take it," he said, giving her a soft smile. "I actually followed you out here because I wanted to talk to you about something."

"And that something is?"

"Us."

"Yeah, that's not going to happen." Azrael rolled her eyes and set the cup of coffee down.

"Just hear me out. I know you're in love with Lance."

"I—"

"I talk to the dead, remember? There's no use lying to me." Garrin touched the tip of his finger to his forehead. "I also know you can't be with him in the conventional way. I don't want to see you hurt."

"Let me get this straight—you're trying to tell me you want to talk about us because things aren't going to work out between me and Lance? Because you care so much, right?"

An appalockatu landed on the balcony, stretching its rainbow feathers. Azrael leaned down, hoping to pet it. It'd been years since she'd been close to one, but it flew off before she could. *Darn it.*

"No, it's because I think we could be a comfort to each other." He shifted in his seat and looked around before adding, "I also know what it's like to love someone you can't have."

There was a moment, a hanging second, where her brain refused to process what Garrin said. Then it hit her. "Sarah. You're in love with Sarah."

"Shhh…," he said, looking around. "But yes."

"How…what?" She shook her head. "I don't even know what to say."

"You don't have to say anything. In fact, I'd rather you not. She doesn't know, and I'd like to keep it that way. The only reason Sarah has not moved on is because she wants revenge. If we succeed, she will be free. If we don't, there's a good chance we will all be dead. Regardless, it won't work out. I'm not asking you for a date, but it sure as hell would be nice to have a friend who understood, someone I didn't have to keep secrets from."

"I don't even know the real you," she whispered.

"Would it hurt to try?"

"At this point, we might be dead tomorrow, so why the hell not?"

Garrin grinned. "Why the hell not works for me."

~*~

"So, let me get this straight—you spent half the morning talking to Garrin, and Lance is being all distant, right?"

"Yep, pretty much." They were sitting on Caleb's bed, a carton of caramel swirl ice cream between them and a bottle of two-hundred-year-old scotch beside it. Lance would give them an earful about the scotch, but hell, they might die soon, and the only scotch she'd had was cheap. Unlike the wine, there was a big difference between it and aged scotch. She might have a new addiction.

Azrael ran her tongue over the spoon and stuck it back in the carton. "I don't know what to do. My only hope is that we live, ex-ghosty-girlfriend goes bye-bye, and we can move on."

Speaking around a mouthful of ice cream, Caleb said, "To your no sex relationship?"

"You're a real buzzkill, you know?"

"I do my best."

A loud ringing noise came from downstairs. Azrael froze. "Was that the doorbell?"

Caleb shook his head. "I don't know. Did Lance say anything about a visitor?"

"No. Not to me, at least."

"Do you think it could be Blais?" he asked, eyes wide. "I know it's silly to think he'd ring the doorbell, but he seems pretty cocky and confident the way you described him."

"I—I don't think so. Maybe we better go check it out." She set the carton of ice cream on the nightstand and tugged down her shirt. Maybe Caleb had a point. Yeah, it was unlikely Blais could find them, even more unlikely he'd use the bell. But hell, she'd never thought to ask Lance how the protection on his home worked. Maybe it was one of those things where you had to invite them in, like a vampire or something.

They took the stairs slowly, her behind Caleb since he insisted on bringing his bat. From the sound, whoever was visiting probably wasn't a threat. Voices drifted out of the den. She picked up Lance's voice and Garrin's, but the third one was female. Caleb pressed his ear against the door. After a moment, he straightened and said, "Sounds friendly enough. Guess I should leave this outside."

He leaned the bat against the wall and stepped into the den. Azrael followed.

Standing in front of the fireplace were Lance and a beautiful blonde who looked familiar. It took Azrael a few seconds to remember where she'd seen the woman. *At the bar. She was the one talking to Lance. Something about business….*

The woman glanced at her and Caleb, then back to Lance. "I was surprised to find you have even one guest, more so that you have three. If you're feeling a sudden urge to be social, my door is always open."

It was clear by the way she said it, her door wasn't the only open thing she was offering. Azrael gritted her teeth. Her irritation must have shown because Lance glanced at her, strolled over, and wrapped his arm around her waist.

"Maridale, this is Caleb and my girlfriend, Azrael."

He called me his girlfriend. Holy cripes.

Slightly mollified, Azrael gave the woman a small smile. "Hi."

"Girlfriend?" Maridale eyed her up and down.

Before she could say anything, Lance cut in. "Maridale has been working for me for years. She's a detective of sorts. Anytime she gets a lead on Blais, she reports back to me."

"Oh, um, does that mean you have a lead?" Azrael asked.

"Not much of one. There's just been rumors of someone fitting his description hunting a woman who fits your exact description. I guess I see why now."

Maridale strolled over to Azrael and grasped the ends of her hair, sliding her nails through it. Azrael slapped her hand away.

Maridale grinned. "A redhead, huh? After all these years of trying to figure out what type you found irresistible, I would have never thought a redhead. Well, two is better than one, you know."

For a second, the air around them seemed to warble, as though waves of steam rose from the ground. Azrael blinked, trying to clear her vision. When she opened her eyes again, she was staring at an exact replica of herself. "What the fu—?"

"Maridale is a siren. A particular one that can shapeshift into anyone you desire," Lance answered, shaking his head. "That's enough, Maridale."

"Fine." The air warbled again, and Maridale was back to her normal self. "But, keep in mind, two can be better than one. For the both of you."

She winked at Azrael and stepped back.

Beside her, she heard Caleb whisper, "Whoa."

"Wait a minute." Garrin looked at Lance. "Does she know what you are?"

"Yes. I've told her everything important to the case."

Garrin paced. "So, you're telling me there are two women in the room with three men, and both of them want to sleep with the konsumo demon who takes powers? This is absurd."

"Women love tortured men, and they love a challenge. Lance is both," Maridale said, smiling at Garrin.

"And the part where he takes your powers doesn't seem to bother you?"

"Oh, he takes *hours* to steal a woman's powers. A quickie wouldn't do a damn bit of harm."

Hours? Azrael's breath caught in her throat. "Is she telling the truth?"

He glanced at her and opened his mouth to speak, but Caleb interrupted before he could answer.

"Can you just shapeshift into humans?"

Maridale stepped closer to Caleb, taking in an eyeful, her lips twitching into a slight grin. "Well, aren't you an interesting specimen? And open-minded, too. Let's see what you might like."

She shifted forms so fast, Azrael could barely focus on one before she changed to another, several of them ranging from tentacle demons to males of various sizes. When she was done, Caleb, his eyes wide, said, "I think I'm in love."

Smiling, she turned to Lance. "Mind if I stay over for a bit?

It appears I've found my match."

Lance chuckled but then said, "No, but I should warn you, we plan on summoning Blais tomorrow. I'm sure Caleb here can tell you all about it."

Caleb put a hand on Lance's shoulder and squeezed. "Anything bad I've ever said about you, man, I take back. I'm officially joining the Lance fandom wagon."

"Glad to hear it."

Taking Maridale's hand, Caleb tugged her upstairs.

Garrin watched them and sighed. "And with that, I am officially surrounded by the craziest group of people I've ever met. Considering what I do, that's one hell of an accomplishment. I'm going for a walk or something."

"I'd like to go with you," Azrael said, ignoring the look of confusion on Lance's face. "Let me grab my shoes, and we'll meet at the door."

Chapter 30

"So, why did you really want to go for a walk with me?"

Azrael shoved her hands in her pockets. This was not a conversation she wanted to have with Garrin, but since he was the only one who could talk to the dead, there was no other option. "I wanted to talk to you about Sarah."

"What do you want to know?"

They paused in the shade beneath an ash tree. Azrael glanced up to make sure it was only partially bloomed. Getting stuck under one when its leaves caught fire was an incident she never wanted to repeat. Luckily, this one didn't look near ready to erupt.

"Is she here?"

"Yes."

"Can she hear me?"

Garrin frowned. "Yes. What is this about?"

"It's about privacy. I want time alone with *my* boyfriend, but I know he's not going to allow it if she's around. So, I'm wanting to ask Sarah, woman to woman, if she will grant us privacy, at least in the bedroom." She placed her cool hands against her face, hoping to stop the blush before it began.

"Azrael, if you're planning on doing what I think—" Garrin stopped mid-sentence and looked over his shoulder. After a moment, he turned back. "Sarah says she hasn't, and she won't intrude on your privacy. She's also a little offended that you think she would."

"I didn't mean to. I just had to know."

"Was that all you wanted to ask her?"

Azrael looked down, digging a small hole in the earth with the tip of her shoe. "I—I wanted to know if she still loved him."

Lifting her head, she waited for the answer, heart thrumming.

"She says," Garrin paused, seeming to listen, "that she never did love him. So, therefore, the answer is no. She also said for you to caution your heart."

"What does that mean?"

"I don't know. She left right after she said it." Garrin took her hands in his. "Look, ghosts tend to be melodramatic and vague, but I think you should heed her warning. If you're thinking about sleeping with Lance, please don't do this."

"That is none of your business, Garrin."

"You made it my business when you involved me in this 'woman to woman' talk. I care about you, Azrael. I really do. We're both in this screwy situation where our hearts are involved with people they shouldn't be. I just want you to be careful."

"We might all die tomorrow. Careful is not on my list of things to do right now."

"It should be now more so than ever," Garrin said, lips pursed. "Please tell me you'll give it some thought."

"Okay. I will."

Azrael hoped she wouldn't regret that lie.

~*~

She found Lance in the library, reading a thick volume about hexes. Although she knew he wanted to appear nonchalant, she'd seen him standing at the window, watching her and Garrin.

"Hey," he said, setting down the book. "How was your walk?"

"It was fine." She slipped off her shoes and sat down on the couch beside him, tucking her legs underneath her. "Can we talk?"

He bit his lip, the hesitation on his face clear, and said, "Sure. What do you want to talk about?"

"You know what I want to talk about. Maridale. What she said, is it true?"

Lance shifted on the couch. "In theory, yes."

"Why haven't you mentioned this?" She tried to hide her insecurities, but her lips trembled before she got the last of the sentence out. "Is it because you don't want to sleep with me?"

"No." He stiffened at the remark. "How could you even think that?"

"Well, it's not hard. First of all, you never mentioned it. Secondly, since the Sarah thing, you haven't touched me. What do you expect me to think?"

"Come here." Lance sighed and lifted her onto his lap, wrapping his arms around her. "Look, I wanted to mention it. I did. But every time I thought about it, I felt like the scum of the earth. What do I say? 'Hey, you want a quickie?' That's not only disrespectful, but you deserve much better." He leaned in and kissed her on the forehead. "As for the Sarah thing, I'm sorry. You're right. I haven't been fair to you. It's been hard. I won't lie. That doesn't mean I shouldn't be showing you how I feel about you. Can you forgive me?"

"Okay," she whispered.

"You're so beautiful," he whispered. Lance nibbled her bottom lip, trailing his fingers through her hair. "So, my turn to ask you something."

"Mmm...sure," she mumbled.

"Is there something going on between you and Garrin?"

"What?" Azrael jerked back. "Why would you even think that?"

"Well, for starters, he's your ex, and you've been spending a lot of time talking to him lately."

"No, there is nothing going on. Honestly, he's—" Azrael looked around before leaning in and whispering in Lance's ear. "He's in love with Sarah."

"What?"

She sat back and put her finger over her lips. "Shhh...."

"Are you serious?"

"Yes, and please don't say anymore."

"Fine then. Why the walk today? I saw him holding your hands out there."

"He's concerned about me...sleeping with you. I told him it was none of his business. I only wanted to talk to Sarah about giving us some privacy."

"You did *what?*"

"Look, I knew you'd never agree to be with me if she was watching, so I wanted to make sure she wasn't. She said she always respected our privacy just so you know."

Several emotions flickered across his features. Surprise, anger, regret.

"Are you upset, I asked?"

He sighed. "No, I guess not. I shouldn't be. I mean, this is really hard for you. If nothing else, it's nice to know she's not watching, at least."

"Which brings us back to the topic of this conversation." Azrael stood and held out her hand. "I think some privacy is exactly what we need right now."

Lance hesitated but placed his hand in hers. They made their way up to the bedroom together.

~*~

She'd expected hesitancy. Was prepared to have to convince him, perhaps even seduce him. What she hadn't expected was the brief flash of fire in his eyes before he crushed her against him, the lips seeking hers full of need. Azrael barely had time to kick the door shut before he lifted her hips, pressing his manhood against her. She wrapped her legs around him as he carried her to bed.

"You're so sexy," he whispered, laying gentle kisses on her neck.

Lance tossed her on the bed and stood, eyes grazing her body. She quivered when his eyes landed on her breasts, nipples growing taut beneath her thin sweater. The ache between her legs grew, a dark, needy cloud consuming every inch of her. Wanting. Waiting. Her pulse was thick, sluggish. Even it was filled with need. "Please, hurry."

"I don't think so," he whispered, leaning down until their eyes were mere inches apart. "Just because I can't be inside you too long doesn't mean I'm not going to enjoy every inch of your body. You'll be screaming for me long before I fill you."

"I'm ready to scream now," she moaned, arching her hips, desperate for contact.

Lance chuckled and bit her bottom lip. "Patience, beautiful."

He crushed his lips against hers, tongue thrusting into her mouth, scraping against her teeth. His knuckles played over her swollen nipples. She grabbed his taut shoulders, nails digging in. Beneath her hard grip, he shuddered. She felt the tremble of desire course through him. Thrusting her tongue deeper, she fought to break through his resolve, to push him into a world where patience and coherent thought were dissolved in a frenzied need.

Slipping her hands into his pants, she cupped her hands around him. He relinquished a fevered moan and pulled away, dark eyes filled to the brink with white-hot need. "Azrael...."

His voice was deep, husky, begging. It held a note of warning, but she wasn't going to listen. He wanted patience. She wanted to be destroyed by him. His eyes chided her while his hips pumped slightly, stroking himself between her cupped palm. She tightened her grasp, squeezing in rhythm.

"I want everything you are. No holding back. I need to know how badly you want me."

The dam broke.

Time became non-existent.

The room disappeared around them.

He tugged her sweater, pulling it off. Her nails scratched his tight abs as she returned the favor. Skin against skin. Her skin was hot, burning. Cool lips suckled her nipples, coaxing them until they became swollen, ridged. Lance's palm traveled the length of her stomach. Tucking his thumb under the waistband of her sweats, he shoved them down, panties and all. She had no idea how he got them all the way down — maybe she blacked out, maybe they dissolved — but the next thing she knew, he was standing, staring down at her hips, his eyes hungry.

"Open for me, Azrael," he demanded gruffly.

She did as he asked, exposing herself, trembling in anticipation. Reaching down, he slid the pad of his thumb over her delicate skin. Arching her hips, she pushed against his thumb, fingers digging into the sheets. He gave into her demand, slipping several fingers in at once.

An explosion of sensations rocked her body. He stepped back, fingers glistening with her need. "Not yet, baby. We're going to come together."

Lance slipped off his pants, swollen member alert against his belly. Laying above her, he stayed just out of reach. She ground against him, but he held her firm. "Look at me, Azrael."

She did, her eyes wanton.

"I...," he took a shaky breath, "I think I can stop. If you're not sure you want this. I...think I can...." Lance touched her face, hands shaking. "I've never wanted something so much, but I won't do anything to hurt you. I need to know you want this. Not because you're afraid of dying or because you're jealous."

"I want this. I want you," she whispered, swallowing against a raw throat. He may not want the truth, but she needed to give it to him. "I love you."

He groaned a feral sound and buried his face in her red hair. With a quick thrust, he plunged himself inside of her. "I love you, too."

Together they rode a wave of pleasure, both bodies and hearts colliding until it swept them away.

Chapter 31

"I'm in love." Caleb plopped down on the couch beside her, one hand pressed against his chest. "Maridale is perfect. He's the best thing that has ever happened to me."

"Wow, now I'm insulted." Azrael grinned at him. "Plus, I thought Maridale was a she."

Her best friend rolled his eyes. "You know that statement didn't include you. Anyway, sirens are all technically born male. That's why they can't breed. It's a genetic mutation. A beautiful, wonderful genetic mutation. I was so sore after we were done, I couldn't walk."

"You seem to be doing fine now," Azrael said, nodding to his splayed-out form on the couch.

Caleb grinned. "That's only because she can shift into a soother. They excrete this—"

Grabbing a throw pillow, she tossed it at his head. "Do not finish that sentence, Caleb. TMI."

In truth, she was ecstatic to see Caleb so happy. It'd been years since she'd seen him this excited over someone. Her happiness was quickly dampened, though. "Did you mean it when you said you were in love?"

"I don't know." He bit his lip. "I think—I think I might be. With Maridale, it's not just sex. We talked for hours. I haven't known anyone before who truly appreciated sexual liberation. Did you know he's got a degree in computer science and web design? He offered to help me with the website to get more leads. That, and he's into romantic comedies, double fudge ice cream, and understands my illness."

Uh, oh. Caleb was staring at the ceiling, mooned-eyed. The last thing Azrael wanted to do was burst his bubble, but the little voice in the back of her head wouldn't allow her to keep her mouth shut.

"Look, I'm happy for you, I really am, but he's a siren. That's not exactly the kind of demon you develop a relationship with."

"Neither is a konsumo demon," Caleb shot back.

Azrael bit her lip. He was right. She should be the last person to give judgement.

Caleb sighed and squeezed her hand. "Az, I'm sorry. That was harsh. I meant that we don't get to choose who we fall for. It's how we deal with it that matters. If I'm falling for Maridale, then I need to accept that he'll sleep with others. That's his nature. In return, I'd hope he'd understand my illness. It wouldn't be fair for me to ask him to shapeshift in bed because I want to experience everything, then not allow him to go out and do the same."

"Caleb," she whispered, "when the hell did you get so smart?"

"Oh, honey, I've just learned to listen to my heart. Speaking of which, where were you all afternoon?"

Azrael gave him a languid smile.

"No way! You two fricking did it? Holy crap! What was it like?"

"The simple, most amazing thing I've ever experienced." She knew she was grinning like an idiot but couldn't stop herself. "I can't even describe it. And—and he told me he loved me."

Caleb's eyes widened. "Seriously? Wow, Az, just wow. Did you tell him how you felt?"

"Yes, I told him first. I think he knew. I think he wanted to hear me say it. I didn't expect him to say it, though. I know he still loves Sarah, but when he said it, he was raw. Sincere. I don't doubt he means it."

Leaning over, Caleb kissed her on the forehead. "Well, congrats, baby girl. By the way, where is your boyfriend and our ghosty? I think Maridale wants to join this insane summoning, and he asked for me to call a meeting."

"He and Garrin are in the kitchen, discussing our impending death."

"You really need to work on your 'doom and gloom' attitude."

Azrael squeezed his arm and stood. "Think about it, Caleb. When has life ever let us be happy without bringing down the ax? Considering how happy I am right now, the only thing that's going to ruin it is death."

She ignored the concerned look on his face as she walked away.

~*~

Sleep eluded her. Even cradled tightly in Lance's arms, her mind kept going over the events of the next day. They'd planned until everyone was satisfied they'd taken every precaution possible. Yet she still did not feel confident. Maybe Caleb was right about her having a doom and gloom attitude. What he'd said earlier, about how it didn't depend on who you fell for, how you dealt with it mattered more, was stuck in her head.

She loved Lance. He loved her. What if they lived? Then what? She'd feel like this every day for the rest of her life? The intensity of it alone might kill her. Would she be willing to accept what he had to offer? She knew the answer to that question now. Hell yes, she would. That was the scariest part of all.

"Having trouble sleeping?" Lance whispered in her ear.

She lifted her head. "I thought you were asleep."

"Not asleep." He brushed a strand of hair out of her face. "Just enjoying having you in my arms. So, tell me, what's keeping you awake?"

Azrael ran her fingers over his five o'clock shadow, remembering how chaffed her face felt after their lovemaking. Their time entwined together was short, it had to be, but she thought of it as lovemaking, nonetheless. "I was thinking about you, about tomorrow—but mostly you."

"Good things, I hope?" The side of his mouth twitched up.

"Nothing I'd tell my mother about if that's what you mean."

Chuckling, he ran his fingers down her naked side, making her shiver. The room seemed to become a few degrees warmer.

"Are you ready to go again?" she asked.

He shook his head. "As much as I want to, and I really, really want to, twice needs to be enough for now. I worry that the more I become accustomed to you, the easier it'll be to access your powers."

Sitting up, she tugged the sheet over her chest and picked at a loose strand. "Is that why it takes so long? You're seeking their powers?"

"Not consciously, but yes, I believe so." He sat up and lifted her onto his lap. "Please don't overthink this, Azrael."

"Too late," she answered, enjoying the feel of his muscular

torso against her bottom. "Are you saying it may come to a point where we can never have sex because you'll immediately take my powers?"

She heard him sigh as he nuzzled her hair. "I'm holding onto hope that won't happen."

It's how you deal with it. Caleb's words came back to her once again.

She straddled him, felt him at the core of her. Ignoring the temptation to further things along, she locked gazes with Lance. "It doesn't matter. If that happens, we'll deal with it. I'll be happy as long as you're with me. I don't care if we have sex, and I don't care if Sarah has half your heart. I'll love you regardless."

Reaching up, Lance bunched a handful of her hair in his fist. "I don't deserve you. The very first time I saw you, I think I knew the impossible would happen. I gave you hell because I couldn't stay away from you, needed a reason to see you. I had no idea what an amazing creature you are. I'm scared about tomorrow. For a decade, I've chased my brother, knowing one day I would have to kill him. To me, that was the scariest thing I could ever imagine. Now, the thought of losing you is. We don't have to do this tomorrow. We could spend the rest of our lives in hiding. As long as we're together, I'd be happy."

For a moment, the idea tempted her, but then reality kicked in. Neither of them could live with themselves, knowing there was something they could do to stop a murderer. "Tomorrow we do this, we fight. I want a life where we don't have to constantly look over our shoulders."

Lance kissed her. It started out gentle, but she deepened it. He stiffened under her and whispered, "You ever hear the phrase, 'third times the charm'? We might have better luck tomorrow if we listen to wisdom."

"Is that so?" she mumbled as his hands grasped her hips.

"Mmm hmm."

"Well, I guess I can't deny the reasoning behind that."

Chapter 32

Lance and Garrin cooked breakfast. Maridale sat reading the paper, disguised as a Shillalan belly dancer, iridescent scales reflecting the light. Azrael and Caleb stared open-mouthed at the two men, who were giving an odd show of comradery as they prepared breakfast. While Lance flipped pancakes, Garrin told stories about different tribal traditions he'd experienced. When Garrin laid a plate of bacon and eggs on the table, Azrael broke. Joking around was one thing, but these two were pretending to be best buds.

"All right, are we going to die or something?" she asked as Lance set a stack of plates on the table.

He rolled his eyes, but a slight smile gave away his amusement. "Why would you think that?"

"You and Garrin. Last I checked, you two were enemies and could barely stand each other. The fact you two are being amenable terrifies me."

Garrin spoke before Lance could. "I have no plans of us dying today, Azrael. While you bums slept in, Lance and I talked. We realized that although we make formidable enemies, we'd be stronger as friends. Call it a short-term agreement. We both have the same goal, so why not work toward it?"

With narrowed eyes, she stared at both the men. Finally, she decided that today, of all days, she didn't have the time to dig deeper into the details. She filled her plate with breakfast, trying not to give either of them the stink eye as she ate. To her left, Caleb fed Maridale some of his eggs. Azrael struggled not to gag.

"When do we start?" she asked, her mouth full of bacon.

Garrin watched her closely. "Whenever you're ready. As long as it's the day of a full moon, the timing doesn't matter."

She knew everyone was staring at her, waiting for an answer, but she kept her eyes on the plate. What she wanted was more time. Time to enjoy Lance. Time to spend with her best friend. Hell, time to play with Smellicious. Even Bumpkins was wearing on her. Still, for the most part, she and Lance had said their goodbyes last night. Not in words but in the way they acted as if it was their last. As for the pets, she was sneaking large quantities of bacon to them under the table. It was the best she could do there. That only left Caleb.

"We can start in about an hour." She pushed her seat back. "Caleb, if you don't mind taking a break, I'd like to talk to you for a second."

~*~

"You're being all doom and gloom again, I can tell," Caleb said, shutting the door behind him.

Azrael threw herself into his arms and squeezed tight. "Maybe I just had the sudden urge to tell you how much I love you. Ever thought of that?"

He brushed a hand through her hair. "I love you, too, baby girl. It's going to be okay."

She leaned back and looked into his eyes. "Aren't you scared?"

"Absolutely terrified. I keep thinking about how I'm the only non-magical one in the room. I feel powerless to save any of you if something goes wrong. It would kill me if anything happened to you."

She squeezed him tighter. "If something happened to you, I'd just die. I love Lance, I do, but you're the best thing in my life. I don't want you to ever think you're not."

"I would never insult you by thinking that. I would hope you feel the same."

"I do," she said, taking a few steps back and giving him a grin. "Plus, you're not powerless. You have your bat."

"Yes, I do." He winked at her and grabbed the bat from beside the door. "Let's go kick some demon ass."

Chapter 33

Azrael finished drawing out her spell while the others went around, checking to make sure the windows and doors were securely boarded shut. No one wanted to give Blais the chance to escape, which also meant they were locked in. In front of her, central to the circle, was the clarity stone.

When she finished the last symbol, she looked up in time to see Lance showing what looked like an old photograph to Maridale. With a warble of air, Maridale changed into a middle-aged man, handsome in the face but unkempt.

Lance stepped back to examine Maridale, then nodded, an odd expression on his face. That's when Azrael saw the resemblance. Lance strolled over and knelt.

"Your father?" she asked.

"Yeah," he said, taking her hands in his. "He's the only thing I think Blais was ever afraid of. How are you holding up?"

"A bit scared, but I want to get this over with. I'm ready when everyone else is."

Lance nodded, then leaned down, kissing her gently on the lips. Before he pulled away, he whispered, "I love you. Come back to me." He stepped away, saying to everyone else, "We're ready."

Garrin took his spot on the far right side of the room. "Sarah will be waiting for you in the veil, Azrael. She'll help you find him safely. When you come back, Lance and myself will be ready to attack. Hopefully, the image of his father will distract him. Caleb will pull you to safety."

Caleb gave her a wink and patted the top of his bat.

"As you know, we've decided against guns since it would be too hard to shoot him without hitting someone else. But in case of emergency, there are daggers laced with poison in a bag beneath the couch."

"Are they for Blais or us in case we don't succeed?" Caleb asked.

"Either," Garrin answered with a straight face. "Are you ready, Azrael?"

"I suppose so," she said, taking a deep breath and reaching into the veil.

~*~

Warmth and darkness engulfed her. She opened her eyes and stood. Although the veil was quiet, she sensed she wasn't alone. Azrael turned around. The redheaded woman standing behind her gave a small smile. Her cousin. The woman both Lance and Garrin loved. Sarah.

The resemblance was undeniable. They both had flaming hair, high cheekbones, and green eyes, but where Azrael had a softer, more athletic build, Sarah was smaller, her features more delicate.

"Hello, cousin," she said.

"Um, hi."

Sarah sighed. "I'm guessing you're not my biggest fan."

"Why wouldn't I be? I mean, you only have the heart

of the man I love and dropped me into this crap hole mess of tracking down a serial killer before he kills me. Of course, I'm your biggest fan." Azrael rolled her eyes and turned away, trying to focus on Blais's purpose.

Sarah came and stood beside her, placing a hand on her shoulder. "I don't expect you to understand. I've done horrible things in the past, more than you know. But I've paid for my mistakes. I'm not asking for forgiveness, but I want you to understand that I brought you into this because I believe you're our only hope. I'm not the only one either."

She nodded to the left. Azrael followed her gaze. In the distance, she could see glowing shadows, hear murmuring. "What is that?"

"Other spirits. Women who can't move on because of what Blais did to them. They want to help. They all have faith now that you're here."

"No pressure there," Azrael whispered, eyes locked on the shadows.

"They're staying back because they don't want to get in your way, but they thought their presence might help you find Blais. They are all focusing on his purpose."

"That might help. It might magnify the purpose."

"We need to hurry, though. The veil feels...impatient. I sense the creatures here dislike the intrusion Blais has caused."

Azrael nodded. This was no to time for storytelling. She cleared her mind and began to walk. Sarah stayed quietly at her side. Twice she felt compelled to strands, only to notice a web of magic wrapped around them. The clarity stone was doing its job. On the third one, she knew she had Blais. That familiar click of success was only tarnished by the condition of the strand she was looking at.

"What — what is wrong with it?" she asked, eyes drawn to the black spots dotting the silver strand.

"I don't know for sure," Sarah muttered. "I've only seen a few like these before. I think the creatures of the veil have marked it somehow."

"Marked it for what?"

She shook her head.

Azrael stared at the strand. This was Blais's purpose, that much she knew for sure. What she didn't know was what would happen when she grabbed a marked strand. Would it trap her in the veil again? Would it kill her?

"Azrael, we need to do this soon. I can feel them coming."

So did she. A darkness was ascending upon them, one thicker, more ominous than the one she currently stood in. Her chest felt tight, throat dry. She knew what she needed to do, but fear held her in place.

"Azrael?"

"It's not fair," she mumbled.

"What's not fair? Azrael, we really need to hurry."

She took her eyes off the strand and focused them on Sarah. "It's not fair that he loves you. Even if I survive this, I'll still never have him."

"Really? Now is not the time to discuss this," Sarah argued.

"Maybe not for you, but I'm the one whose life might end the moment I grab this strand."

"Look." Sarah glanced over her shoulder. "Sometimes spirits can remove pain. I can't take away his love, but I might be able to make it not hurt him anymore."

"You can do that?"

"Yes. Get me Blais and consider it done. But hurry. They're coming," Sarah said, her eyes darting madly around the room.

Azrael nodded and reached for the strand. "If I die, tell Lance I love him."

Chapter 34

Smoke was everywhere.

Dark. Swirling. *Acrid.* It reeked of rot, of death. It clogged her nostrils, filled her lungs. Azrael clawed at her throat, whimpered, clawed again. *Can't breathe.* Tears threatened, then abated. The smoke, thick and dense, consumed her tears, shrouded her in its embrace. Held on.

Dear God, help me.

Something reached through the smoke and grasped her wrist. Hands, warm and slender, tugged, gripped harder, tugged again. She knew those hands. *Caleb.*

She allowed them to pull her out of the smoke, out of the darkness, to where the air was thinner. Her throat spasmed, then filled with acid. Turning her head to the side, she retched. A pool of ash-speckled bile clung to the floor. Strands of it hung from her lips. She wiped her mouth on her sleeve, looking up.

A dark cloud of smoke hung in the room's center, enveloping a figure whose form kept blinking in and out of existence.

Caleb cupped her face between his shaky hands. "Are you okay?"

"He's fighting the summoning spell," she croaked. "Or he's trying to."

He let go of her face, eyes darting between her and Blais. "What do we do?"

"Maridale," she said, rubbing a hand over her sore throat. "She needs to distract him. Help me up."

Caleb tugged her up. She stumbled a bit and held on to him for support. Across the room, Lance caught her eye. A brief flash of relief swept over his features before his focus returned to Blais.

The smoke still swirled around the center of the room, but it seemed to wane. Blais was winning.

"Maridale," Azrael yelled, catching the eye of the siren playing Lance's father. "Distract him!"

The siren approached the smoke storm. Azrael had to give Maridale credit. He didn't even flinch as he approached him. He reached into the smoke storm and grabbed Blais's shoulder before he could blink out of existence again, his face contorted into a mask of fury.

The smoke dissipated, and Blais stood before them all, fearful eyes focused on his imposter father. "Daddy?"

Maridale squeezed his shoulder tighter, eyes narrowing. Azrael wiped her sweaty palms on her pants. Out of the corner of her eye, she saw Lance slip into a crouch, a predator, his eyes on the prey.

Blais's eyes narrowed. "You're not my father."

Maridale remained silent.

Why doesn't he say something, dammit? Then again, how could he? Maridale had no idea what their father sounded like. To speak would give it away.

Lance tip-toed forward, a heavy blade in his left hand. His

attack would come from the side. From behind Blais, Garrin took several stealthy steps, a deadly looking baton clutched in his fist. They were planning an ambush.

Azrael grabbed Caleb's hand and squeezed. They exchanged a quick glance. He picked up his baseball bat and handed her a butcher knife. Tensed and focused, they could do nothing but wait and pray.

"My father is dead."

Blais lifted his fist. Azrael saw the glint of a blade before he drove it into Maridale's side.

"No," Caleb screamed, rushing forward.

With an evil grin on his face, Blais pulled the blade out of Maridale, and he collapsed to the floor, air warbling as he changed back into the blonde.

The fight had begun.

~*~

All three men converged on Blais.

Caleb got there first, bat raised high.

Blais ducked and rolled, planting a foot into Caleb's stomach. A low whistling noise came from Caleb as he hunched over, gasping. Azrael sprinted toward her best friend, a knife held in front of her. Pulling a small glass bobble out of his jacket pocket, Blais threw it on the ground between himself, Lance, and Garrin. It shattered, emitting a blinding white light. Azrael covered her eyes. When she opened them again, there was a solid glass wall between the two men and Blais. She, Caleb, and Maridale were trapped with him.

Lance screamed, pounded his fists against the glass. "Azrael, run!"

Maridale still lay on the floor, blood seeping from her wound. Caleb was hunched over his stomach but trying to stand up. She couldn't leave them. Blais turned to her and grinned.

"Why, my sexy summoner. It's been a while, hasn't it?"

"No," Caleb shouted between gasps. "Leave her alone."

It happened so fast, Azrael couldn't move to stop it. Couldn't think.

Blais reached out and grabbed Caleb by the throat.

Caleb's eyes widened, then narrowed, his feet dangling above the floor. "Screw you, Blais."

The world slowed. She saw Caleb flying, saw him hit the wall and crumple to the floor, body lying at an odd angle.

"No!"

She gripped the blade and lunged. The knife hit Blais in the thigh and sunk in. He wailed, arms cartwheeling. A hand caught her across the face. Pain erupted across her cheek, radiating behind her eyes. She stumbled, but Blais caught her arm, squeezing tight. Strands of hair stuck to her cheek, stuck to the wetness of the tears she'd spilled, tears she didn't remember crying. Distantly she heard Lance screaming, heard Garrin, but paid them no mind. Blais had killed her best friend. He was going to pay.

"What, you didn't like being stabbed? I thought a sadistic ass like yourself might take pleasure in the pain."

"Oh, I do take pleasure in pain." He reached around, grabbed a handful of her hair, and tugged hard. She screamed. "Other people's pain, that is."

Blais held tight, pulling until her skin felt taut. She still managed to grin. "What a lame-ass statement. You're nothing but a schoolyard bully."

The grin slipped off his face, and his nostrils flared. "You filthy bitch."

"My name is Azrael," she said, leaning back and kicking

with all her strength. Her feet landed on the end of the knife, plunging it in deeper. Blais let go, and she fell to the floor. On her hands and knees, she crawled away, looking for something to break the glass shield. Her eyes landed on the clarity stone. Blais was still crumpled on the floor, hands wrapped around the handle of the blade protruding from his thigh. Azrael got to her feet. Ran.

She picked up the clarity stone. Blais stopped struggling with the blade, his eyes glistening with hatred. "Do it, and they die."

"Doesn't seem like you've got the upper hand now, asshole." She lifted the clarity stone over her shoulder and threw it with all her might.

It hit the spell, and the glass wall shattered.

~*~

A blur of motion.

That's all Azrael saw. Three blurs, three men. She grabbed Maridale and pulled him away from the fight, leaving a trail of blood in her wake. Her heart thundered, hands shook. She laid Maridale by Caleb, then reached out and touched his face. Running her hands down the side of his neck, she prayed for a pulse. Fingers searching, she could find none. A quiet wail escaped her lips. Azrael pressed her ear against his chest, shut her eyes. Concentrated.

She gasped. There it was. The thud-thudding of his heart. It was weak, but it was there. Her eyes landed on the bat, and she picked it up, turned, and faced the fight.

"You were never as good at fighting as me, little brother," Blais said, his fist connecting with Lance's face.

Lance stumbled backward, caught himself, and looked at Blais, his eyes burning with hatred.

"That's why he brought help." Garrin slammed his open palm into Blais's nose. Blood spurted out. Lance charged, ramming into Blais's side. The two men fell to the floor, rolling around, throwing punches.

Azrael approached the scuffle, bat held high. Garrin came from the other side, baton in hand. They nodded at each other. It briefly occurred to her they were planning on being comrades in murder, and she was okay with that.

She should have foreseen it. Hell, they all should have expected it. Blais wasn't going to fight fair. A pocket watch slipped out of Blais's slacks. His eyes flickered toward it, hands reached out. Lance didn't see it—he was too busy, his hands wrapped around Blais's throat. Garrin saw it, though, and so did she. A dying man wouldn't reach for a pocket watch. Not unless that pocket watch could save his life.

They dove for it at the same time. Azrael grasped the chain, felt it slip through her hands, and saw Blais press the clicker. The watch opened.

~*~

She couldn't move, couldn't blink. But she could feel. Her heart still pumped, blood still raced through her system. She felt pain, could feel her shoulder aching from where she'd crashed into the floor. But she still couldn't move.

A shadow fell over her.

"Well, this will be fun." Blais reached down, cupped her chin, and twisted her head until it faced him. "I won't lie. I wasn't expecting such a battle. Give it to my little brother to up the stakes. But that's only going to make this a lot more enjoyable."

He grabbed her hair and drug her across the floor. The pain caused her eyes to water. She wanted to scream, wanted to pound her fists, but nothing happened. He dropped her to the floor. She heard a scraping noise, something heavy. Blais pulled up an armchair, lifted her off the floor, and tossed her in it. Her head thudded against the cushion and fell forward.

She heard his footsteps and sensed him walking away. For several more minutes, all she could hear was the sound of more furniture moving, an occasional grunt. *I'm going to die. We're all going to die.*

Azrael felt inside herself, reached for her power. If she could summon anything, anything at all, they might have a chance.

She found nothing but emptiness. Her power was gone. *No!*

Footsteps approached—he was coming back. Inside, she fought with all her strength, tried to move. No matter how much she tried, she only ended up exhausting herself. Not even a finger twitched. Blais tilted her head back and brushed a strand of hair out of her face. Smiled.

"So pretty and powerful. I was told I couldn't be summoned. Not with all the protection I have. Your powers will go great with my collection. Now, for the fun."

Blais stepped back. Behind him, Lance and Garrin were tied to chairs, facing her. Neither man moved. The dagger was missing from Blais's leg. In its place, he'd wrapped a long piece of cloth. Blood still seeped through. He wasn't wearing his glasses, and his eyes held the sheen of a madman.

"Welcome," he said, lifting his arms and spinning in a circle. "Welcome to my show. Today's guests will include a sexy summoner, a stranger, and my beloved brother, who has spent many years plotting my death. Oh, and the other two guests who," he paused, looked over to Caleb and Maridale, "well, let's just say they didn't make the final cut."

Blais pulled out the pocket watch, spinning it around in his hands. "This is an amazing little trinket. Took me many, many years to acquire its powers, but of course, I'll have to explain how it works later. Right now," he crossed the room and knelt in front of his brother, "I need you to hold out your hand. Oh, wait, you can't." Blais laughed and shook his head. "I guess I'll do it for you."

He placed the pocket watch in Lance's palm. "This will be no fun for me if I can't see the expressions of terror on your face, so I'm afraid I'm going to have to bring you back to the surface a bit." Blais lifted Lance's finger and pressed it on the latch release. The cover fell open. Blais grabbed the watch and took several steps back.

It was like he'd woken a dragon. Lance's face became a snarl, and a mess of curse words left his mouth. He rocked back and forth, struggling against the binds. "You son of a bitch!"

Blais narrowed his eyes. "Me? I'm not the one trying to kill you. All I've ever done is protected you, and you turned your back on me. You'd be dead now if I hadn't killed Dad, hadn't saved you. You were my brother, and I loved you!"

"Then let them go," Lance pleaded. "We'll talk, work things out."

Blais laughed. "You insult me, little brother. I know better. You'll never change, and I'm tired of having you on my heels like a feral dog. No, the chance for 'working things out' has come and gone. Don't worry, though. I plan on letting you live.

"You see, I've done my research too. A few questions here and there, paid a few people to watch you myself. It seems to me that you've gained a new love interest." He strode toward Azrael, cupping her face in his hands. She wanted to vomit. "Of course, I can see the appeal. She's quite a catch."

"Get your hands off her," Lance growled.

"Oh, I have plans to have my hands all over her. You can watch as I defile your girlfriend, make her suffer before I kill her. Then you get to watch me kill the rest of them."

"I'll kill you!"

"No, you won't," Blais said, shaking his head. "But you'll spend the rest of your life trying. You will be left to suffer, alone, for all eternity. Just like I have."

"You're a murderer. I didn't leave you to suffer. You chose your path."

"And you could have chosen it with me," Blais sneered. "What's a few lives? People die every day. Half of the world is dead inside already. They go about their day-to-day business like robots, wishing for something better. I have something better. I've chosen to live."

Lance's nostrils flared. "You're insane."

"Insane or not, I'm going to enjoy this." Blais placed a kiss on her head and began unbuttoning her blouse. His touch made her skin crawl. Disgust filled her stomach, coated her throat. *No! Please just kill me.*

"Azrael, wake up. Fight it! Summon something!" Lance fought harder against his restraints.

Blais stopped unbuttoning her shirt. "Did I forget to tell you? She can't use her magic. That's the best part of this little spell I've cast. You've always hated your magic, hated using it. The irony of that is this watch uses your magic to trap you, as it did all your magical friends. Now, I've finally given you a real reason to hate your magic.

"Keep your eyes open, Lance. You don't want to miss how much pain I'm going to cause her."

Blais pressed his cracked lips against hers, then tilted her head back, baring his teeth. A shadow fell over them, and Azrael felt her heart swell.

There, staring down at them, was Caleb, bat in hand. "Small oversight in your plans, Blais. One of us doesn't have magic."

Blais's head popped up, his eyes wide. Before he could move, Caleb swung, the bat connecting with a sickening crunch.

~*~

She heard the thump, saw his body fall to the floor, but couldn't look to see if he was still alive. Caleb raced around the chair, bat in hand. There was another sickening thud, then the resounding echo of the bat landing on hardwood. After a moment, Caleb stood in front of her, blood matted on his forehead. "I'm going to have you press on his stopwatch. I hope this works, baby girl."

She didn't feel the click, but she heard it. Within seconds she could move.

"Caleb!" She threw her arms around him, and he winced but held her tight.

"Hey, shh, it's okay," he whispered.

Azrael hadn't been aware of the tears spilling down her cheeks. Her chest hitched painfully, her throat tightening. Caleb stood, hands still on her shoulders. "We need to untie Lance and Garrin. I don't know if Blais is dead or not."

That brought her back to the present. She fought against the fear. Below their feet lay Blais, blood trickling from his ears. Although he didn't move, she thought she saw his chest move lightly. In a daze, she made her way to Lance. He sat still, his eyes locked on his brother. It wasn't until she cut his binds that he seemed to realize she was there. When he did, he jumped up, pulling her into his arms. His lips sought out hers, his hands caressed her face. "I'm so sorry, baby."

"He's not dead." With her attention focused on Lance, she hadn't seen Caleb release Garrin. He was standing over Blais, hand pressed to the vein on his neck. "The heartbeat is weak, but it's there."

Lance let go of her and took several steps forward until he stood over Blais. He and Garrin exchanged a long look. Lance shut his eyes briefly, then opened them again. "I'll do it."

"Do what?" Azrael asked, coming to stand by Lance.

He turned and grabbed her shoulder. "You should leave. Caleb too. Go to the den, call a healer for Maridale."

"But, I—"

What was going to come out of her mouth was that she didn't understand. Then it hit her. They had no intention of leaving Blais alive. He'd already bested them several times. To wait for authorities meant giving him another chance if he woke. That didn't seem to be a chance either one was willing to wait for. It wasn't a chance she wanted to take.

Azrael took his hands in hers and squeezed. "I love you."

"I love you, too." He leaned down and kissed her forehead. "Now go."

Caleb came to stand by her. In his arms, he carried Maridale. "Come on, baby girl. He's lost a lot of blood."

She turned, her heart heavy, but before they could make it more than a few steps, a darkness settled over the room.

~*~

"What was that?" Caleb asked.

Azrael looked to Lance. His eyes were wide, mouth open in shock. She followed his gaze. "Sarah?"

Sarah appeared fully formed. On her face was a look of terror. "Get away from Blais! Move now, or you'll die!"

Garrin moved first, heading straight toward Sarah, and behind him came Lance. He grabbed Azrael's arm, pulling her along with him. The room filled with the sound of chimes. A sound that was familiar to Azrael.

"The void," she mumbled.

Sarah nodded. In the center of the library, above Blais, appeared a hole, a tear through the fabric of the room. The hole grew larger. Inside she could see the strands of purpose. Her heart faltered. "What's going on?"

"They've come to take him," Sarah answered. "The creatures of the void are letting those he killed take their revenge."

A woman stepped out of the hole, her skin glistening in the darkness, her face in a mass of scars. Behind her, more women. They poured out, each marked with scars, their gazes locked on the murderer. The room filled. There had to be more than a hundred women packed in. With her back pressed against the wall, Azrael could do nothing but watch in awe. Lance locked his hands in hers, as did Caleb. The women stopped coming out. They circled Blais. One spoke.

"Wake up, Blais."

Azrael couldn't see, didn't want to see, but he must have done what the ghost commanded because a few moments later, she heard him scream, "No!"

The women shrieked in unison, their forms flickering as they tore at him. Blais continued screaming.

"What are they doing?" Lance whispered.

"They're tearing his soul apart. Blais will suffer for all of eternity." Sarah came to stand in front of Lance and raised her hands to cup his face. "You will not. It's time I take your pain. I have a promise to keep."

Placing a hand on his chest, over his heart, Sarah shut her

eyes. Behind them, the ghosts still swarmed around Blais, but the screaming had stopped. Lance gasped, his eyes widening, and Sarah removed her hand. "I can't take away the past, but I took away the pain. Take care of my cousin, and love her well."

She nodded to Azrael, then moved past her to Garrin. Sarah pressed her lips against his, letting them linger before pulling away. "I've always known how you felt. I feel the same way about you. Unfortunately, this can never be, and I must leave. I can take away your pain, too, if you'd like."

Garrin shook his head and touched her face. "No. I think I want to keep it. Something to remind me of you."

Sarah smiled. "As you wish."

Behind her, the women were re-entering the veil. There was no sign of Blais. Sarah squeezed Garrin's hand and followed them. When all the women were gone, the veil closed, and the room became light again.

Azrael sensed a part of that darkness would never go away, though, not for the five people left inside it.

Chapter 35

"Where's Lance?" Azrael asked, rubbing her eyes. It was the first time in weeks she felt truly at ease. The nightmares had finally abated, and after many late-night talks, it was decided she and Caleb would move in. Although marriage wasn't mentioned, she knew it wasn't too far on the distant horizon. She knew he was only holding back because he was a konsumo demon. He had a hard time believing she didn't care about that. If nothing else, she planned on proving in.

Then, there was Caleb. Having been close to death, he decided to tackle his agoraphobia. They went walking every day. At first, he hadn't made it over the threshold, but now he could make it several yards outside. Azrael was more than proud of her best friend. She also knew Maridale played a part in his desire to get better. He'd spent the first week here, healing under Caleb's close watch. During that time, she had a feeling her best friend had given his heart away.

As for Garrin, he left the day after they killed Blais, and she didn't try to stop him. She'd given him a kiss on the cheek and let him go mourn on his own. She called him every few days, reminding him he had a friend to talk to whenever he was ready.

"He's in the secret room in the hall. You know, the one he keeps locked," Caleb responded, grinning. "Seems to be in a good mood, though. Maybe we should go visit."

"You just want to snoop."

Caleb stretched, a childish grin on his face. "I've never been able to resist a locked door."

Azrael grabbed him by the hand, and they raced down the hallway. The door of the room was propped open with a large trash can. Lance stepped out, tossed a handful of papers in, and smiled at Azrael. "Good morning, beautiful."

"Morning." She took several steps forward and kissed him on the cheek, eyes scanning the room over his shoulder. It was about the size of a large closet, with handwritten notes and newspaper articles covering the walls. "What are you up to?"

Caleb peered around the door. "Oh, this is like one of those crime-solver set-ups. Like in the movies where they're trying to find a killer."

"That's exactly what it is," Lance said, waving his hand inside. "This is everything I've tracked on my brother in the last decade. I thought it was time to get rid of it, to move on."

Azrael grinned at him. "I think that's a great idea. Want some help?"

"Sure. I'm going to burn it in the fire pit out back. I'll get it started if you don't mind tossing this stuff in the can for me."

"Sounds good, but I'm going to require you to do it shirtless."

"I second that," Caleb said.

Lance shot Caleb a dirty look but laughed. "You're lucky I love you, Azrael. You are quite a package deal."

"A sexy package deal," she said, thrusting out her chin.

"Plus," Caleb chimed in, thumbs pointed at his chest,

"let's not forget who's the badass hero here."

"He's never going to let us live that down, is he?" Lance asked.

"I think we figured that out when he had the bat framed." Azrael rolled her eyes and punched Caleb lightly on the arm.

"Ouch," Caleb yelled, rubbing his arm.

"Some hero." Lance winked, then kissed her before walking away.

Caleb tapped her on the shoulder. "You're doing it again."

"Doing what?" she asked, watching the sway of Lance's hips as he left.

"Mooning over him like a love-sick puppy."

"Like you're not staring at his ass right now?"

"Of course I am. What kind of all-male-sexual would I be if I wasn't?"

Azrael punched him on the shoulder again. "Come on, let's get to work."

They stepped into the room. There were piles of paper lying on the floor and stacked on the desk. Sunlight streamed in through a small window. Beneath it lay Smellicious and Bumpkins, both curled into a ball on top of newspaper.

"All right then, you get the stuff in the drawers, and I'll start on the desk."

For the next five minutes, they worked in silence. Neither had to speak about what they were seeing. The magnitude of murders Blais committed, the women he'd killed. File after file, article after article. She kept having to remind herself that he was dead, that they'd done the world a favor.

"Hey, look at this." Caleb shoved a magazine in front of her face. "It's Sarah."

Azrael picked up the magazine, her eyes landing on

Sarah's picture. Caleb stood behind her and read the caption below. "Need a love spell? Visit my website at www.sarahspell. com. Top rated. Licensed and certified. Guaranteed or your money back."

"Sarah was a love caster," she mumbled.

"Are you thinking what I'm thinking?" Caleb asked.

She looked at the picture and read the inscription again. "Do you think she cast a spell on Lance?"

"I don't know," Caleb answered. "If so, why wouldn't he tell you? Plus, if she did, he could have just had it removed. *Derose igumante liosa corabon.*"

"What did you say?" Azrael asked, her eyes darting to Caleb, a weird feeling in her chest.

He pointed to a small line of text underneath the ad. "*Derose igumante liosa corabon.* That's her spell. She must have been a pretty strong love caster to have her spell copyrighted. Hey, are you all right, baby girl? You look pale."

"I've heard those words."

"Okay." Caleb stared at her. "And this is a big deal, how?"

"Because Lance said them to me." She held out the magazine, hands trembling. "On the flight here. I couldn't tell what he was saying at the time, but now that I hear them, it's as clear as day."

"Okay, just calm down. So what if Lance said them to you? He's not a love caster. If you're upset because of the Sarah thing, then...."

"Lance stole Sarah's powers, then Blais killed her. If Sarah cast a love spell on him and died, he wouldn't be able to have it removed, *and* unless he transferred those powers somehow, he is in possession of them."

Caleb's mouth dropped open. It wasn't until that moment

she fully grasped the truth behind what she said. Lance may have cast a love spell on her. He wouldn't have, though. Would he?

The more she thought about it, the more it seemed possible. They barely knew each other when he'd said those words to her. His only intention at the time was to get her to summon Blais. Then, she couldn't have a protection spell put on her because she was supposedly in love with him. "Holy crap, Caleb. Please tell me I'm wrong."

"I want to, I really do, but it's possible. I mean, you fell for him so fast." He shook his head, mouth pulled down in a frown. "Before either of us jumps to any conclusion, I think you should ask him. We were wrong about him before."

"Yeah. Of course. We'll ask him," she whispered, the words tumbling across her lips. "I'm sure I'm just being paranoid."

Caleb took her hand, and they went in search of Lance. Her chest was tight, face warm. *I'm just being silly. In a few minutes, this will all blow over.*

But that wasn't the way things ever worked out for her.

Lance was out back, shirtless as promised, leaning over the fire pit. He heard them approaching and glanced up, a smile on his face. Sunlight glinted off the sweat on his torso, and in his eyes was a look of complete adoration.

"Took you long enough," he said, coming over to kiss her on the cheek. "I'm shirtless, as promised."

Azrael swallowed and stepped back, her eyes meeting the depths of his. Against her chest, she cradled the magazine, trying to cover it.

The last few months had been hell. She'd finally found the one thing that made her happy. Fear of the truth, fear of what would happen between them if she was right, had her reeling backward. If Lance had put a love spell on her, she didn't want to know. She glanced at Caleb, conveying a silent message. *I can't do this. Not now.*

"What's wrong?" Lance asked, the smile slipping off his face.

"N-nothing."

He eyed them both. Then his gaze slipped to the magazine she held. "What's that?"

"Oh, I was just reading that." Caleb reached over and tugged the magazine away. Apparently, he'd caught her silent plea. "I'm going to run upstairs and grab the trash can. I'm not feeling ready to be outside today."

Before he could turn and leave, Lance grabbed the magazine and scanned the ad, turning pale. The three of them stood there in silence.

It was Azrael who broke it, but when she did, her voice was trembling. "She put a love spell on you. That's why you said you didn't want to love her, isn't it? You didn't have a choice."

Lance sucked on his bottom lip, inhaling deeply. "No, I didn't have a choice."

Throat dry, heart pounding, she reached for him. "Tell me you didn't cast a love spell on me."

He shut his eyes. After several long moments, he opened them again and met hers. "Please understand. At the time, I wanted nothing more than to stop Blais from killing. I meant no harm to you. When I did it, it wasn't without consequence. I made a promise to myself that I would take care of you forever, that I wouldn't let you suffer the way I have."

She took several steps away from him, her blood pounding in her ears. "So, this is why you're with me? Because you fucked my life over and want to stick around and what? Pretend to love me?"

"No!" He reached for her. "God, no, Azrael. I love you. That's not what I meant."

"Were you ever going to tell me? How could you do this?"

Warm tears cascaded down her cheeks. It was like someone had torn out her heart. She felt Caleb put his arm around her, but it did nothing to stop the budding pain.

"Azrael, please listen. I didn't think it worked. When Sarah cast one on me, I would have done anything for her, anything at all. But you—you resisted me every step of the way. Then I fell in love with you. I didn't see any reason to tell you because I truly believed the spell failed. I'd never tried to use her magic before, and I didn't want to take a chance of losing you by telling you I tried it on you." Lance placed a hand on the side of her face, his eyes dark, body tense. "Please forgive me. I'm so sorry. I can't do this without you."

"You've doomed me to a life where I don't know if what I feel is real or not," Azrael whispered. "And you want me to forgive you? Just pretend it didn't happen?"

"I told you I didn't think the spell worked," Lance said, throwing down the magazine. "I'm sorry. I'm not a good person. I never said I was. Not until you, at least."

Her legs trembled, and her chest hitched. Caleb pulled her to him, saying over her head, "It must have worked to some point. That's why Leolacent couldn't put a protection spell on her, why she was bound to your fate or whatever crap. She said it was because Azrael was already in love with you."

"No," Lance whispered, faltering backward. "It couldn't have. Azrael, please believe me."

"I can't," Azrael spoke through the pain in her heart. "I'm sorry, but I can't live this way."

"Please—"

"No." She held on to Caleb tightly, her legs feeling like rubber. "I want you to arrange a trip home for us. From there, we'll find a new apartment. I don't want to see you again after that. It's the least you can do for me."

Chapter 36

Azrael headed down the steps, heels clicking against each one. She tugged up her skirt, struggling to keep it from slipping down. Caleb had pinned it before she left, but one pin must have come loose because something sharp was poking her in the back. She didn't dare run up and ask him to fix it. The last thing she needed was to endure another episode of pity. Ever since she'd left Lance, Caleb had been a mother hen. She couldn't blame him. Most days, when she wasn't at work, she'd lay in her bed, crying until she fell asleep. If Caleb didn't force her to shower and eat, she might as well forfeit her life. In less than three weeks, she'd lost fifteen pounds.

Even though she'd gotten her job back, and they were living rent free since Lance refused to take their money, they still had to save up for their new place. There was no way in hell she'd accept the money Lance wanted to give them. That meant she wouldn't be buying any new clothes soon. Not that she cared. Azrael had sworn off relationships. It was just her and Caleb. Well, mostly. There was still Maridale to consider. Although she tried not to show her jealousy about sharing her best friend, she wasn't fooling Caleb. He went out of his way to make calls after she was asleep (or at least he thought she was) and restricted visits to when she was at work. These she only knew about because she could smell Maridale's perfume when she got home. It sickened her that her best friend was hiding his own happiness because she was so miserable.

She lumbered down the last of the steps to the lobby. Behind her, footsteps rang out. It was Caleb. Every time she saw him outside of the apartment, her heart swelled. He'd made so much progress. Even if she was destroyed inside, everything she went through was worth seeing him confident, unafraid of the world.

"Hey," he called out, phone pressed to his ear. "The movers say they can make it at five instead of six. Would that work for you? You might have to take off a bit early."

"I'm sure I can manage," she answered.

Caleb nodded, his eyes darting to the side. Without asking, she knew their conversation had been heard. Knew who was standing in the doorway of his office, looking like an abused puppy.

Her best friend gave her that look she'd begun to know so well. *Why are you fighting this?*

At first, Caleb had been on her side. Screw Lance. He'd ruined her life. Forced her to fall in love with him. He'd planned ways for revenge. Then, things had changed. She knew it was partially from listening to Lance beg at the door to talk. Afterward, she assumed Caleb had let him in when she was at work, begging her best friend to help. Then, after weeks of her crying and not eating, Caleb could no longer bear the animosity toward Lance.

"Azrael, all you're doing is torturing yourself. He loves you. I don't doubt that. You love him too, whether you want to or not. Why fight this? Why not be happy?"

She turned and looked at the man whose eyes were boring into her, bearing his broken soul.

"And what happens if I find my true mate? Do I suffer like he has, loving someone he was never meant to love?"

"Do you have a choice?"

She hated Caleb for his reasoning. He was right. It was inevitable. She'd be miserable forever without him, but would she grow to resent the man who'd done this to her? Maybe one day, she'd sort out her feelings. For now, though, she had every intention of fighting, of making him suffer for what he'd done. As long as she didn't have to see the suffering. Right now, Lance carried the look of a broken man, and her heart ached for him. It was one thing to imagine how miserable he was, another to see it.

"I've got to go if I'm going to take off early," she said.

Caleb shut his eyes and breathed out through his nose. "Okay."

She leaned forward, giving him a quick peck. Before she could pull away, he grabbed her upper arm, whispering in her ear, "At least say goodbye. End this so you can try to move on."

Pulling back, she saw the pain in her best friend's eyes. This was hurting him too. He didn't want her to say goodbye. He wanted her to fix this. To not suffer anymore. After all he'd done, she couldn't say no. She might not do it the way he wanted, but she'd at least show him respect. "Fine. I'll turn in the keys, say goodbye. Will that make you happy?"

"It's a start. I love you, Az."

"I love you, too."

She watched Caleb climb the steps before taking a deep breath and turning to face Lance. He was standing in the door, hands shoved in the pockets of his tailored jeans, sleeves of his white button down rolled up to his elbows. He stood there every day, watching as she left. Although she pretended to ignore him, she knew he was there. Caleb was right, though. It was time to quit ignoring the issue, to find closure.

Tugging the set of keys out of her purse, she made her way to Lance. This was the first time she'd looked at him directly in weeks. He stared at her, dark circles under his eyes, hair disheveled. His lips parted, a mixture of sadness and excitement.

"Here," she said, holding out her keys, the pitch of her voice a bit high because it felt like her chest was stuck in a vice grip.

He stared at the keys, then looked up at her. "Keep them. I won't tarnish the memory of you by renting out that room."

"Please don't do this."

"Do what?"

"Try to make me feel like the bad guy like, you're the one who's been hurt here."

Lance leaned against the doorframe. "It was never my intention to make you feel bad. I was just stating the truth."

Azrael stared down at her hands, swallowing back tears. She knew Caleb told the truth. Lance did love her. A part of her wanted to give in, to rush into his arms, but pride stood in the way. "I guess this is goodbye then."

"Azrael—"

"No," she said, her head popping up. "I don't want to hear it. I came to say goodbye because I knew that's what Caleb wanted. I've done that."

"I still love you. I always will."

His face mirrored her own misery. Before she said something she regretted, Azrael turned on her heels and marched to the door, breaking down into tears the moment she was out of sight.

~*~

"Well, aren't you all doom and gloom," Gracie said, plopping down on her desk, not bothering to push the papers she'd been working on out of the way. Azrael had been reading through some applications for summonings. She glanced at the clock on her desk. Several hours had passed, but she couldn't remember a single word she'd read.

"Are you okay?" Gracie asked, leaning in as she motioned Logan over. "You look like crap."

"Thanks," she mumbled, wiping the corners of her eyes. "Glad you noticed."

"Hey," Logan said, walking up, mouth full of pastry. "What's going on over in this corner of the world?"

Azrael had no idea how he stayed so thin.

He stopped chewing as his eyes set on her face. "Wow, you look awful. Upper management abusing you?"

She leaned back in her chair and shut her eyes. Great time for her friends to realize her suffering. As it was, she was about two minutes from a complete emotional breakdown.

"Can we do anything to help?" Gracie asked.

"Even if it's sexual in nature," Logan added.

She opened her eyes in time to see Gracie elbow him in the ribs. Logan grimaced. As for work friends, these two were as close as she got. A part of her felt bad for pushing them out of her life the past few months. She'd ignored their texts while with Lance, afraid that replying would somehow put them in danger. When she'd returned, they'd never questioned her cold shoulder, only accepted that she was back. She stared at her friends, stupidity and guilt settling on her chest. Out of all the people she could have asked for help with her current situation, why hadn't she considered her own friends?

"Actually, maybe you can help. Someone put a love spell on me, and I need it removed, but you have to promise to never speak a word of this to anyone else."

~*~

She told them everything, leaving no detail out. Gracie and Logan were hex breakers, some of the best, but they couldn't break a spell unless they understood every piece of the puzzle. In her case, that meant spilling the beans about Lance, Blais, Garrin, and Sarah. When she was done, neither twin moved. Until the words spilled out, she hadn't realized how powerful and traumatizing the last few months had been. She felt drained, exhausted.

"And that's why I need you two to help me. I want this love spell removed. If I still love Lance, then so be it. If not, I may hole up with Garrin, and we can be miserable together."

The twins glanced at each other, communicating in a way only twins can. It was Logan who spoke first. "What you went through, all of it is scarier than anything I could imagine. I wish we'd been there for you."

"Please don't. I don't want sympathy."

"Doesn't matter," Grace chimed in. "What matters is that you survived."

"I don't know if that's true," Azrael whispered. "I feel like I'm dying inside. I can't eat. Can't sleep. He consumes me. I need to move on."

Another glance back and forth, this one much more serious.

"What?" Azrael asked.

The twins merely stared at her.

"So, can you break the spell or what?"

"Azrael," Gracie said, slowly. "I don't know how to tell

you this. Logan and I have been feeling out your aura this whole time. There is no love spell on you."

"What?" She sat up straight.

Logan stood, pacing. "I can sense the spell on you, sense that he tried. It didn't work, though. Not because he was a novice. The spell is strong, one of the strongest I've sensed in that category."

"But it didn't work?" Azrael asked. Inside, her body was thrumming.

"No."

"I don't understand."

"Don't you?" Gracie asked, standing beside her brother. "A love spell will work on anyone—everyone except for one person. It's Witch History 101."

"A soulmate?" Azrael whispered.

Gracie nodded. "It's a strong spell. It didn't work because he's your soulmate. You love him regardless, and that love is stronger than any spell."

"No," Azrael said, standing. "It can't be."

"You were able to summon him blindly. That was *before* he cast the spell on you. If nothing else, that should tell you something. His purpose was already aligned with yours. It was meant to be," Logan added.

"I really do love him then?"

Both twins nodded.

Azrael plopped back down in her chair, hand pressed against her heart. There wasn't a spell. Lance was her *soulmate*. They could be together. Get married. Have children.

Children? No, that wasn't possible, was it?

"Okay, spill it," Gracie said, jumping off the counter. "You went from sad to happy to sad in less than a minute."

"I'm wondering if it's possible for us to be happy together. We can't have regular sex. I don't even know if we can have children."

"Is he worth—?" Logan stopped mid-sentence, turning around to face the wall. Loraine came around the corner, sneering at his back as she passed by.

When she was out of sight, Azrael asked, "How long did they put that binding spell on you for?"

Logan turned and grinned. "Until I stop thinking about her breasts every time she walks by. I think about them now on purpose just to piss her off. It's quite fun. You should try it sometime."

"If I could bind Lance from using his powers on me, I would."

Gracie patted her shoulder. "Unless you know someone high up on the board of witches council to plead your case, I think you should focus on accepting your situation as it is."

"High up on the board," Azrael mumbled, then lunged out of her chair, grabbing for her purse. "I need my phone. I have a phone call to make."

~*~

"They're ready," Garrin said, placing an arm around her waist. "You sure you want to do this?"

"I love him," Azrael responded, "but I need to know if he is willing to give up part of his powers for me."

"Normal people call that having trust issues." Garrin gave her a squeeze, the side of his mouth tilted into a grin. "Then again, no relationship comes without issues."

"I'm sorry, Garrin. I've been selfish. How are you holding up?" she asked, glancing up at him.

"I'm fine. I knew this day would come. In a way, it's kind

of a release. I'm free to pursue whatever I want for the first time in a very long time."

"And what is it you're wanting to pursue?"

Garrin shrugged, his eyes distant. "I'm not sure yet, but I feel something coming. Something big."

"In that case, I'll be sure to avoid you in the future. After all of this, I'm ready for a break."

Garrin held open the door to a huge chamber. "You'll get bored, trust me. Once you've had a taste of living on the edge, of saving people, you can't get enough."

"Let's hope you're wrong," Azrael replied, stepping into the dim room.

~*~

"Azrael Larson, you are here today to request a magical binding spell on Lance Jenkins. Is that correct?"

"Yes, ma'am." Her eyes flitted around the large, dark chamber. Only the stage was lit. Behind the podium stood a woman, her frumpy outfit and frown her only distinguishing features. There was a table behind her, several yards long but thin. Others sat at the table. She counted eight at most, but it was so dim, she couldn't be sure if she was right. From the look of mild disgust and confusion on the woman's face, Azrael knew she wouldn't be here if Garrin didn't hold such an important seat on the board.

"You do realize this is an uncharacteristic request for us to process?"

She cleared her throat. "How so?"

"You have requested a delegation of witches to bind a konsumo demon from stealing your powers in hopes to have sexual relations with him. The mere thought of a konsumo demon terrifies most witches. Yet, you want to be with one?"

"Yes," she whispered. "I love him. He's my soulmate."

The woman sighed, her shoulders slumping. "We cannot know that until he is here. If that is true, then we will grant this binding, but he must do so voluntarily. He has broken no rule, has harmed you not. The decision will be entirely up to him."

"I understand."

Someone stood at the back table and made his way to the woman. He looked frail, withered. He leaned in and whispered something in her ear. She nodded before he turned and took his seat.

"The magical squad has delivered the konsumo demon. They are bringing him in now."

For several minutes, silence permeated the room. Garrin squeezed her hand. When the doors burst open, she jumped. Two officers flanked Lance. He looked confused, angry. Then his eyes met hers, and his shoulders slumped. They dragged him to the front of the room.

"Lance Jenkins?" the woman asked.

"Yes." His eyes darted to Azrael. She saw the hurt and confusion in them.

"You have been called to the department of magical binding by Azrael Larson. Do you know why you are here?"

He glanced over his shoulder, brows furrowed. "No. I do not."

"Are you the Lance Jenkins who resides at Riverdale Estates, 143 East Demonium?"

"Yes."

"Are you the Lance Jenkins, Drifters Inn Motel Manager?"

"Yes."

"Are you a konsumo demon, brother of a suspected murderer, Blais Jenkins?"

Lance dropped his chin to his chest. This time his answer was a mere whisper. "Yes."

The woman at the podium watched him closely. After a minute, she cleared her throat. "There are rumors that the murders have stopped. Rumors that the suspect is no longer among the living. Rumors that there is a hero out there who did everything he could to bring justice."

Azrael glanced at Garrin, and he winked. She focused her attention back on Lance, who still hung his head low. The woman continued speaking.

"If that is true, we of the magical world are thankful to the man that ended this terror. But that is not what we are here for."

Lance lifted his head, looking at the woman.

"We are here because there are strong magics in the world, magics that even the best trained witches cannot touch. One of the strongest of those is the love of two soulmates. It is a rare phenomenon, but nonetheless, one to be taken seriously. Azrael, can you please come and stand beside Lance?"

"Yes," she said, her legs heavy as she trudged forward.

She stood beside Lance, felt his warmth, ached for the sadness she saw in his eyes.

"Azrael Larson, you have requested Lance be binded from taking your magic?"

"Yes."

"Why is this?"

"Because he's my soulmate, and I love him."

Lance inhaled deeply, his face registering shock.

"Lance Jenkins?"

"Y—Yes?"

"We cannot bind you by law. You must volunteer to submit to the binding. Do you volunteer?"

Azrael held her breath, eyes shut. This was it. He could say no. Hell, she wouldn't blame him. Unless he truly loved her, there was no reason.

"Mr. Jenkins?"

"Are you serious?"

Her heart slipped down to her stomach.

"About the binding, very much so."

"You can do that?"

"Yes."

"Really? Yes, of course, I volunteer."

Azrael opened her eyes and trained them on Lance. He was staring at her, a smile of wonderment on his face.

"When did you decide this?"

She shook her head. "The love spell didn't work because we're soulmates. When I realized that, I figured I might as well take care of that other little problem we had too."

Lance wrapped his arms around her and sought out her lips. She heard several people clear their throats but ignored them. After a moment, he pulled away. "I love you. I've never loved anyone this way. I'd give up anything for you."

"I know that now. I'm sorry I've been so stupid."

"No." He shook his head. "For once, you're showing you are a decent judge of character."

The woman at the podium interrupted. "The binding spell is done."

They both turned, asking at the same time, "Already?"

The woman shrugged, giving them what they imagined was a rare smile. "Honestly, the binding is easy. It's the politics around it that are annoying. Plus, I expect you two would like to get home quickly to take care of some personal things."

Azrael made a mental note to send the woman flowers. As

she and Lance raced out the door, she stopped to give Garrin a bear hug. When she was done, Lance did the same, whispering in his ear, "Anything you need, I'll be there."

Garrin nodded, staring off in the distance. "That's good because I feel I might have to take you up on that soon. For now, you two need to go enjoy yourselves. Life is too short to miss the fun."

They stepped out of Witches Corp, soulmates, their entire lives ahead of them.

For now, at least.

The End

With six titles accepted for publication in the last year, Heather's work has appeared in several anthologies and short story collections, including "Storyteller Magazine," "Zimbell House Publishing," and "Coffin Bell Journal."

Born and raised in North East Texas, Heather Harrison grew up with a family of misfits, leaving her with a wild imagination and a sharp sense of humor. After spending over a decade in management and marketing, she decided to pursue her life-long dream as a writer. With the very patient understanding of her family, friends, and some helpful strangers, her first book, *Franny's Fable*, was published in the winter of 2017. Heather lives in Dallas, Texas, with her family.